NEVER TRUST ME

MICHAEL RYDER

THOMAS PUBLISHING

CHAPTER 1

Let me start with my name. Callie Crawford. It's the one thing I know.

Which isn't the right thing to say, not at all. The words sound melodramatic, like I'm putting on airs or playing for sympathy or adopting a pose, and none of that has ever been me, at least I think. Two months have passed since I awoke from the accident. The haze is nearly gone. I know myself better now. I know more every day.

The mahogany cane in my hand, for example — I know its solid smoothness and heft, and I know that holding it makes me feel safe.

I know every bend, every dip, every twist of the trail of my daily walk along the bayou — the walk I'm on now, dripping with sweat as I push my way through the heat. I know the earthy aroma of this wild place, the pull of its moody beauty, the pulse of its oppressive humidity, the air sticking to my skin even as the midday sun burns away the morning mist.

I know the pain in my hip, never far from me but lessening by the day. I'm grateful for my progress, for my moments free of agony, but I'm an impatient sort — I know that about me, too. The fear and dread that came with the accident are fading, though too slowly. I was raised to accept what life delivers — to grit my teeth, to dig in, to endure — but God help me, acceptance has never been my strong suit.

Most of all I know this: With every fiber of my being, I love my daughter Ava. She's the light of my life, the keeper of my hopes, the reason I keep pushing forward, every single painful step, every single day. I see in her the girl I used to be and wish with all my heart that my parents were still here to watch their granddaughter grow up. They would love and cherish her as much as I do. I miss them terribly.

What else do you need to know about me, the broken bayou girl?

I cringe as I hear the words. Why do I call myself that? Since the accident, words leave my mouth without meaning to. It's one of my new "things," apparently.

I'm not from the bayou, or anywhere near here. I grew up in Connecticut, more than a thousand miles away.

Also, I'm no longer a girl but a grown woman, thirty years old, with shoulder-length brown hair, mostly straight, usually in a ponytail. My skin is smooth, pale, and lightly freckled. I burn easily in the Louisiana sun.

And I'm definitely not broken. I mean, I am right now, but I'm on the mend. I've always been active and will be again. I know the meaning of long hours and hard work. I was a waitress for years. I've always been athletic and fit. I did spin classes at the town gym. Josh and I went line dancing at Jeeter's on Saturday nights.

I see I just mentioned Josh. He's Ava's father. We used to be married. Ava adores him. Now that he's my ex-husband, I'm kind of back to adoring him, too — sort of. I mean, I do. But it's complicated. I'll tell you more about him in a bit.

Every morning, after seeing Ava off to school, I do my daily walk. The path takes me from the house into the heart of Boudreaux State Park. The park is a musky, pungent, unsettling place, a landscape of woods and swamps, filled with insects, deer, raccoons, and birds. Alligators, too, with their metallic eyes peering at me from the dark water. I wonder what they think as I hobble past. Do they see an injured creature? The perfect prey?

I know enough to be wary. I've been warned about straying from the path, about tripping or stumbling, about wandering or getting lost. I know the eyes of the bayou are on me, watching and waiting, even when I can't see them.

From the south comes a rumble of thunder. Storm clouds dot the horizon, heading in from the Gulf. There's an old oak tree I've heard about, deep in the park, that I've never seen. I've made it my goal to find it. Every day I get closer. But with rain coming, the old tree will have to wait. Around here, only a fool ignores Mother Nature.

Finally, a half hour after turning back, I reach the edge of the park. My hip is holding up, but I pushed my pace today and I'll pay a price later. The storm's nearly upon me, the wind kicking up in gusts, the first drops of rain splattering as I emerge from the trees and limp across the parish road into the gated community I now call home.

Everything on this side of the road is manicured and perfect

— crisp green lawns, freshly stuccoed houses, beautifully paved driveways — but I don't have time to think about that as I hurry toward the house I live in at the end of Sycamore Lane.

I'm climbing the front porch steps when the storm really hits.

And that's when, as I shake off the raindrops, I see a note taped to the front door. A single sheet of paper, folded in half. Curious, I open it and see:

5309

Four numbers, handwritten in blue ink. Nothing else.

How *odd*.

I look around. The rain's really coming down now. Who put the note there? And why?

A strange thought hits, jolting me with sudden unease:

Am I being watched?

CHAPTER 2

eart beating faster, senses on alert, I gaze around anxiously, my eyes darting across the front yard to the houses and woods beyond.

Don't be foolish, I tell myself sternly. *You're not being watched.*

No one ever comes to Sycamore Lane. Our house is at the far edge of the neighborhood, on a quiet road that dead-ends at a cul-de-sac with four houses. All of them are brand-new. Ours is the only one occupied. The place is as peaceful and tranquil as it gets. A thicket of trees — oak and poplar, I'm told — surround the four houses like a protective blanket.

No one's here but you, I tell myself. *Get real.*

A gust of warm air rips across the porch. I take a deep breath and force myself to calm down, my fingers insistently rubbing the note, the paper now wet to the touch. Even though no one's watching — I accept that now — I'm not wrong to be a little freaked out. The note is *weird*.

Maybe the note isn't for me, I realize. *Maybe it's for Beth.*

Relief rushes through me at the thought. Her car isn't in the driveway, which means she went to do the shopping before picking up Ava at school. Perhaps someone came by — a friend, she must have friends — and left the note for her?

I haven't mentioned Beth yet. She's the young woman who's been helping me and Ava for the past month. She comes every morning and stays through the afternoon. I'm tempted to call her Ava's nanny, but the truth is, she's more like a nanny for *me*.

Josh insisted on hiring her. He wanted someone to help me out.

"You're on the mend," he said. "Come on, you need this. Knowing you'll have someone around to give you a hand — it'll make me feel better."

He seemed so earnest when he said it. So sincere. He's always been good with people.

I shook my head. I wasn't keen. I can be stubborn. "I don't need the help."

"You know you do. Just until you're better. Consider it a trial run."

"No, I'm good."

"You will be good," he said gently. "You're getting better every day. But right now, a little bit of help will go a long way. Please?"

Still reluctant, still not convinced I needed help, still not ready to admit how much the accident affected me, I allowed myself to give in. "A trial run. Ava and I will decide. She gets a vote, too."

"Of course," he said, his eyes filling with emotion. Josh has many faults, but he loves his daughter. "Whatever you say."

The woman who showed up the next morning was Beth. Twenty-four, slim, pretty, white, with brown shoulder-length hair and watchful brown eyes. She seemed shy and nervous, eager to win my approval.

She needn't have worried. Josh was right — I needed the help and Beth was a godsend. She cleaned, she cooked, she did grocery runs, she did the laundry. Always with a smile.

"Why are you here?" I asked her one morning as she was unloading the dishwasher, a week after she arrived.

She looked up, startled. "What do you mean?"

"I mean, you're so smart. You could be anywhere, doing anything you want."

She shrugged. "I have goals. I'm saving up for nursing school. Your ex-husband's paying me really well." Her voice went soft. "Plus, I like being here. You're like.... I'm hoping we can be friends."

"Of course," I said with a rush of warmth. "We should get to know each other better."

"I'd like that," she said with a shy smile.

And so our friendship began, tentatively at first. I was self-conscious about having someone help me — I've never been in this position before — and Beth by nature is more of a listener than a talker.

But talk we did. She's from the next parish over and moved to Boudreaux to care for an ailing great-aunt. After her aunt passed, she found work as a waitress at the diner on the edge of town.

"I worked as a waitress, too," I told her. "In New Orleans for five years."

"Mr. Dupre told me. He said that's how you met."

And just like that, I'm back to Josh. Eight years have passed since we met in New Orleans — eight years that seem a lifetime ago, my memories of our years there infused with a hazy blend of nostalgia, regret, and gratitude. So much happened because we met. So much that caused me pain, and even more that brought me joy.

I blink, startled, as the storm whips another gust of wet wind across the porch. I realize I'm standing at the front door, lost in thought, mahogany cane in one hand, weird note in the other.

I do this now. I wander into memories. I go deep and lose track of where I am for a minute or even longer. And then — *snap*, I'm back. Dr. Franklin says I needn't worry. "Healing chooses its own path," he says. "You're doing well. Have patience."

The rain's really coming now, steady and relentless. The sky's darker, the wind moving restlessly through the trees.

I unlock the front door and step into the house. The instant the door shuts, the storm fades to background noise. The world becomes quieter.

Still dripping, I slip out of my running shoes, taking care to avoid movements that might upset my hip. Then I limp to the kitchen, grab a dish towel, and finish drying off.

With Ava and Beth not here, the house is silent. It's a modern, unblemished place with all the latest appliances and amenities. The walls are off-white, the floors are engineered hardwood, and the fridge and dishwasher are stainless steel. Upstairs are three bedrooms and two bathrooms. Downstairs has a living room, kitchen, dining room, and half-bath, along with a three-car garage and a back deck.

I don't like the house. It's not my style. It feels cold to me. Impersonal. Bland. Uncaring.

I see I'm complaining again. I need to stop doing that. The house is a perfectly comfortable place. It just has no soul. I wake up every morning dreaming of the day we can leave.

In my mind's eye, my daughter and I live in an old, ramshackle house full of character, with creaky floorboards, noisy pipes, and ancient windows that rattle in the wind. There's trim that needs painting and plaster that needs patching. I was planning to start an interior design business before the accident. I'm itching to get that going. I want to discover places that need love and attention and coax them back to life — to wrap my arms around lost causes and make them glow again.

I glance at the digital clock on the microwave. Ava and Beth will be home in an hour. I need a shower. My eyes land on the laptop on the marble countertop. Yes, I should check email.

I open the laptop and scroll through. A reminder for an upcoming appointment with Dr. Franklin. An invitation to a bake sale fundraiser for the town rec center. And then —

My heart skips a beat. An email from Ava's school, with the headline "Tragic news." I open it and read:

Parents,

*We are saddened to report the sudden death of Rory
Freeman, a member of the teaching faculty at Briarton
Academy for 18 years. Rory taught math and geography.
He was a respected colleague and a beloved teacher and will
be greatly missed. We extend our deepest condolences to his
wife, Susan.*

Grief counselors will be available this week to provide

emotional assistance for students. A substitute teacher will take on Rory's classes starting tomorrow.

We will share information about his funeral service as soon as we have it.

Please reach out to me if you have questions or concerns.

With deep regret,
Devlin Chatterton
Headmaster, Briarton Academy

The teacher's name isn't familiar, which means he didn't teach first-graders like Ava. I click to the school's website and scan through the faculty page. His photo shows a smiling man in his early forties, balding and pale, with a round, friendly face.

I read the email again and realize the headmaster didn't disclose how the teacher died. In announcements like this, isn't cause of death usually included?

If he died from something common — heart attack, cancer, car crash — then wouldn't the headmaster have mentioned it?

Probably. But the email said only that the death was "sudden."

A chill runs through me. I'm probably being silly — is being silly one of my new things, too? — but I can't help but wonder what "sudden" really means.

CHAPTER 3

'm out of the shower and still feeling unsettled when I hear Beth's car pull into the driveway. I hurry down the stairs, my hip jolting with pain.

I'm moving too fast but I don't care, because I'm no longer thinking about the teacher or the weird note or even my accident. My heart is singing, my spirit lifting with anticipation, as I carefully lower myself to my knees and ready myself for one of my favorite moments of the day.

The front door opens and a blur of six-year-old energy bursts in.

"Mommy!" my daughter cries as she rushes into my embrace, her tiny arms wrapping around my neck, her soft cheek pressed against mine.

"Ava," I murmur in her ear. "My darling girl."

This incredible child who is my everything — my joy, my soul, my life — dives breathlessly into a rapid-fire account of her eventful day that ends with, "I drew a horse!"

"I love horses," I say with a laugh. "What kind of horse?"

"Brown and very pretty," she says. "Her name is Georgina."

My daughter has a confidence that comes from deep within and a happy laugh that never fails to lift my spirits. Her hair — a frizzy light brown and hard to tame — seems to explode from her head. Her hazel eyes flash with whatever emotion she's feeling. Slight of frame with a wiry strength, she operates at two speeds: a whirl of energy one moment, a pool of stillness the next. She enjoys reading but loves being read to even more. Her current campaign is for Mommy to get her a dog or a cat or a hamster or a rabbit. No doubt she'll now be adding a horse to the list.

Beth follows her inside, loaded with bags of groceries, using her shoulder to push the door shut behind her.

"Sorry," I say. "I should be helping with that."

"All good," she says with a smile as she heads to the kitchen.

I turn to Ava. "Why don't you go upstairs and change out of your uniform? I'll be up in a minute."

"Okay!" she says cheerfully, then races up to her bedroom.

I get to my feet with difficulty — the shift from kneeling to standing is painful — and limp into the kitchen.

Beth's already putting away the groceries. "Thank you for doing this," I say, still uncomfortable about needing assistance.

"Of course," she replies. "About dinner — what are you thinking?"

"Josh is coming over, so…."

"Lean grilled chicken and veggies?"

I smile. "You remembered."

She shrugs. "Mr. Dupre seems to prefer eating healthy."

Indeed, aside from alcohol and an occasional cigar, Josh is all about healthy living. I'm not complaining — it's one of his good traits.

"What time is he coming over?" she asks.

"Six, six-thirty."

"If you'd like, I can slice the veggies before I leave and...."

"Thank you, that'd be great." Then I remember what I wanted to ask. I reach into my pocket and pull out the weird note. "Also, I found this taped to the front door. Is it for you?"

She takes the note and frowns. "5309?"

"It's not for you?"

"No. I mean, I don't think so. You said it was on the front door?"

"When I got home from my walk."

She shakes her head and hands it back to me. "Sorry, no."

"I was thinking it might be a message from one of your friends."

Another shake. "My friends would call or text."

Of course they would — why hadn't I realized that? So if the note wasn't from one of Beth's friends....

Beth seems to be thinking along the same lines. "The note's a bit...."

"Odd?"

"Yes." She's quiet for a moment. "Maybe it was a mistake? Like, maybe it got left at the wrong house?" She points to the neighboring house through the kitchen window. "I mean, maybe it's the passcode for one of those key boxes that real estate agents use? Maybe the other houses here are finally going on the market?"

Of course. That has to be it. Relief floods through me. "Oh my God, that has to be it. You nailed it. You're a genius."

She smiles. I've made her blush. "No, nothing like that."

"I can't tell you how worried I was. I had no idea what it could be."

"Glad I could help."

We spend a few minutes making sure I have everything I'll need for dinner. Then I head upstairs and lose myself in my daughter's world. I do this joyfully and with a full heart, aware of how precious and fleeting these moments are. If the accident has a silver lining, it's that it clarified how important my time with Ava is, especially with her still young enough to be sharing everything with me. I know the day will come when she starts keeping secrets, but for now I remain her trusted confidante.

After enthusiastically reviewing everything she can think of about her day and her friends and her homework, she goes quiet.

My daughter isn't able to hide what she's feeling. Something's on her mind.

"What's worrying you, sweetie?"

Her expression grows serious. "Are you okay, Mommy?"

I blink with surprise. "Of course, sweetie. I'm doing great. Why do you ask?"

"You were asleep in the hospital for a really long time."

I feel myself flush. "That's right. After the accident, the doctors put me in a coma so I could get better faster."

"A coma?"

"That's when you sleep for a long time and your brain doesn't wake you up."

"Why doesn't your brain wake you up?"

"Well, in my case, I needed the sleep to help me heal." I

touch the left side of my head. "My noggin got banged up in the accident. By staying asleep, I was able to get better faster."

She nods. I'm pretty sure she's following. "Is your noggin okay now?"

I smile. "All better." Which isn't completely true, but now is not the time for quibbles. "What I'm working on now is my hip."

Another nod. "Do you like your cane?"

"I do. I like it for a lot of reasons. First of all, it's very strong. Second, it's very pretty. The wood is smooth and has a really nice color."

"I helped you get it."

"You did. You've been incredibly helpful to me as I get better and I'm so thankful for that. The third reason I like it is, the cane is helping me get stronger every day."

That earns me a smile. She's reassured by what I'm saying.

"Did you go for a walk today?"

"I did. I got home right when it started raining."

"Did you go to the bayou?"

"I did. A good long walk, and gosh, it was hot!"

Her eyes light up. I know what's coming next. "Did you see a deer?"

I shake my head. "Not today."

"Did you see a frog?"

"I did. Lots of frogs. Ribbit, ribbit!"

"Did you see a pig?"

I scrunch up my nose. "Nope. But I heard them oinking in the bushes. Oink, oink!"

She laughs. "Did you see an alligator?"

I use my arms to mimic the jaws of an alligator. "I did, and I brought one home! Rawr rawr rawr!"

She scampers away, shrieking with delight. I begin to give chase but stop when my hip jolts a warning.

Our afternoon flows on like this, both of us lost in our time together. Before I know it, Beth is popping her head into the bedroom to tell us she's heading out. "The veggies are sliced and in the fridge."

"Thank you, Beth. See you tomorrow."

Ava dashes over and gives her a hug. "Bye, Beth."

I smiled, pleased to see the hug. Ava wasn't sure about Beth at first. It's taken her a while to warm up to her.

Beth hugs her back. "I'll see you first thing tomorrow, munchkin."

"We'll drive to school."

"That's right."

"Mommy's getting better. All better!"

"Of course she is," Beth says, shooting me a friendly smile. "See you two tomorrow!"

And then she's gone.

Ava turns to me. "I told her."

"Told her what, sweetie?"

"I told her you're getting better."

"Thank you, dear."

As she reaches for one of her toys, I'm struck by what my daughter just said. It's almost like she felt it was important to tell Beth that. Almost like she was....

Setting the record straight?

I frown. Why would Ava feel the need to do that? Had Beth said something about me?

If so, what had she said?

CHAPTER 4

mmediately I chastise myself. *Stop being so dramatic and suspicious. When did you become so paranoid?*

But maybe I'm feeling spooked for good reason. And the problem with questions like "What did she say to her?" is that there's no way to ever know the answer.

It was probably a harmless exchange. Beth's a kind, caring person. The last thing she'd want is for Ava to be worried about me. Maybe Ava asked a question about my hip. Maybe Beth responded in a way that inadvertently sparked Ava's concern.

By the time I hear a truck pulling into the driveway a few minutes later, I've pretty much convinced myself that I'm worried about nothing.

Ava hears the truck, too. "Daddy!" she squeals as she tears out of the bedroom and races down the stairs.

From the top of the stairs, I watch Josh step through the front door. He laughs as Ava leaps into his arms. He's in a dark suit, which means he's come straight from work.

I can't hold back a smile. My ex-husband loves our daughter and she loves him. That essential truth is a source of great comfort to me.

I told you earlier I'd get back to Josh. Well, now's as good a time as any, though I'm not sure where to begin. Actually, I do know.

What I'm about to say may sound mean, but it's true.

Josh is a peacock. Just like that beautiful bird that struts around, displaying his gorgeous feathers to attract the females, Josh knows he's good-looking and enjoys showing it. He's thirty-two, six feet tall, and handsome, with blue eyes, shaggy blond hair, and an athletic build. Working out is a religion to him. If there's an exercise that involves a lot of sweating — running, biking, swimming, lifting weights — he does it. He likes what all that huffing and puffing does to his body. He spends a lot of time in front of the mirror and deliberately wears pants and shirts that are just a bit too tight. He gets a charge out of walking into a place and knowing folks are checking out his ass. (For the record, he has a really great ass.)

He pulls off this "look at me, look at me" routine because he also has a naturally sunny disposition. He's quick to smile and quick to introduce himself. He asks people questions about themselves and really listens to what they tell him. He has the memory of an elephant — when he sees you again, he asks about what you talked about months or even years earlier. I've never known a person who's better at getting people to like him. If he ever goes into politics like his mother is planning, watch out.

We met eight years ago at Stella's Grill, the family restaurant in New Orleans where I worked. He was in his second year of law school at Loyola and I was the waitress for his group, which included him and five other stressed-out twenty-somethings at a table piled high with books and laptops.

The Grill is a short walk from the campus, so it gets a lot of study groups. And I'll be honest — I barely noticed Josh at first. It had been a long day and I was nearing the end of my shift.

But he certainly noticed me. He introduced himself and asked all the usual questions people ask when they hear my northern accent. Where you from? How long you been here? What do you think of our fair city?

I gave him the usual answers — Connecticut, four years, love it — then took their orders and didn't give him another thought.

Which may be why he came back the next day, and the day after that, and the day after that. Though he's always denied this, I think he kept coming back because I didn't pay him much mind at first. My indifference bothered him. I became a challenge. He set out to charm me. To win me over.

Eventually, of course, he did just that.

I guess you could say I have a daughter because I ignored her father.

Which isn't fair to either of us. (Snarky commentary — is that another of my new things?) What Josh and I had in New Orleans went far beyond that.

Also, about him being a show-off — that wasn't fair either. His fondness for himself is just a part of who he is. After majoring in partying in college, he buckled down in law school and ended up graduating in the top quarter of his class. He's now on the partner track at the big firm in Boudreaux. He was more than generous during the divorce and has been incredibly supportive since the accident. Most important of all, he's a good father. I'm truly glad he's in our lives.

As for why I divorced him, I'll get to that. Right now, I want to stick with the positive. I'm enjoying the warm glow that comes from seeing him and Ava together. When he swings her around and she screams with delight, I'm reminded of me and my own dad. I want them to always feel this way about each other.

I make my way down the stairs. He watches my progress and gives me a quick hug when I reach them.

"How you doing?" he asks, his blue eyes alive with interest. I catch a hint of his aftershave mixed with sweat.

"Good," I say. "Feeling stronger by the day."

"That's great."

"Mommy went for a walk," Ava says, still in Josh's arms. "She heard a pig in the bushes. Oink, oink!"

"Oh, did she?" he says with a laugh. "You get caught in the rain?"

"Almost," I say. "Made it home just in time." I gesture toward the kitchen. "So … are you guys hungry?"

"Starving!" they exclaim in unison.

I laugh — this little back-and-forth is one of our things. "Then let's get dinner ready."

We head together into the kitchen and Josh sets Ava down. "You got any homework, munchkin?"

"So much homework!"

"Why don't you bring it down and we can get started on it?"

She whoops enthusiastically and races upstairs. Having Josh help with her homework at the kitchen table is another of Ava's favorite activities. While Josh starts setting the table,

I grab the chicken and sliced veggies from the fridge and set the grill pan on the burner.

Quickly, before Ava comes back, I ask, "You see the email from the school about the teacher?"

He looks over from the table. "Yeah. Terrible."

"Do you know what happened?"

He glances toward the stairs to make sure Ava can't overhear. "Suicide."

I gasp. "The poor man."

"The firm handled his will. They sent me over today to offer condolences to Susan, his wife."

That explains the dark suit. "You know them?"

"Yeah. Nice couple. We'd run into each other every now and then and catch up."

"How did he….?"

He glances again toward the stairs before continuing. "Ate his hunting rifle."

I gasp again. "Where?"

"Near one of the walking trails in the state park."

"Why?"

He shrugs. "Gambling, apparently. Word is, he lost big in the back room at Lola's."

Lola's is a notorious strip joint just across the parish line. I've never been to it. By reputation, it's rough and wild.

"What do you mean by big?"

"Life savings big."

"That's terrible."

"Selfish," Josh says with sudden vehemence. "What he did was selfish. Cowardly."

I'm taken aback. "You think so?"

He shoots me a look. "You don't?"

I pause, wanting to make sure the words come out right. "I guess I think of killing oneself as … an act of desperation. You find yourself in a terrible situation and don't see a way out."

He gazes at me for a long moment. "You're doing okay, right?"

I blink, surprised. "Yes. I'm fine. Why?"

"Just want to make sure."

"Josh," I reply, perturbed by the sudden turn. "I'm fine. I'm doing really well. All's good here."

"I'm glad to hear you say that." After a pause, he adds, "Listen, I know I messed up being a good husband. I want to be the best ex-husband I can. You need anything — at all — for you and Ava, you let me know."

CHAPTER 5

There's something hiding behind his words, something he believes about me, something he's worried about. But before I can dig into what he just said, Ava rejoins us. She plops her school backpack on the table and the mood snaps back to the sunny zone where Josh lives most of the time.

Dinner is a happy, active affair. Josh wolfs down his chicken and veggies while Ava picks her way through her meal. Right now she's all about applesauce, slices of American cheese, and white bread. Fortunately she also likes grilled chicken, so she eats that without complaint after Josh carefully slices it into Ava-size bites. The grilled veggies, as expected, get a firm thumbs down.

"Okay," I say as the last of the chicken disappears. "It's time for...."

"My bath!" Ava exclaims.

Josh laughs. "Let's go, munchkin."

Ava tears out of the room, hollering with enthusiasm.

"Start the water, sweetie!" I call out after her.

Josh is beaming. "Our daughter is the best."

"The very best. Can you stay and read her to sleep?"

"Of course."

I almost bring up what we touched on earlier — I want to unearth what he's worried about. Instead, I hesitate. I've been enjoying our interlude of warm fuzzies. I want the mood to linger.

So does he, it seems. He almost says something — after eight years, I know him — but he changes his mind and pulls back.

For a brief moment, I wonder what it would be like for us to be together again. There'd be more moments like this. In so many ways, my life would be easier.

But with a discomfort that comes from knowing someone far too well, I'm aware of what I can count on Josh for and what I can't.

When it comes to doing what's right for Ava, I know I can trust him.

But when it comes to me? I'll always wonder.

"Go on up," I say quietly. "I'll join you after I get everything into the dishwasher."

There's regret, even sadness, in his eyes. He knows what he lost when we divorced. "All righty."

I point to his tie. "Better take that off. Bath water will ruin it."

"Thanks."

He slips it off and sets it on the counter next to his phone and keys. Once again, I almost ask him he's what's worried about, but don't.

"See you in a few," he says, then heads upstairs.

A sigh escapes my lips as I watch him go.

If only my ex-husband wasn't such a cheating tomcat.

If only I could learn not to care.

Even as the two thoughts collide, I find myself shaking my head.

He is who he is. You are who you are. Neither of you is going to change.

My eyes land on his phone. And like a proverbial thunderbolt, a shocking possibility hits me.

What if the number on the weird note is …?

It couldn't be.

But what if…?

Trembling and silent, I listen to the sounds floating down the stairs. Ava and Josh are in the bathroom, chattering away happily. I inch closer to the phone, eyeing it like it's radioactive.

I pick it up, then set it back down.

I shouldn't. I have no right.

For Ava's sake, you need to find out, I argue with myself.

It would be such a huge invasion of his privacy.

Fuck privacy.

I breathe in, surprised by how strongly I feel.

You need to find out if you're right.

After a final pause to make sure he's still upstairs, I pick up the phone again and tap it.

It lights up and displays the passcode screen.

Heart pounding, I type in "5309" and —

It works!

CHAPTER 6

Oh my God, I'm in his phone.

Adrenaline and triumph shoot through me.

Followed by a massive rush of guilt.

If the situation were reversed — if Josh was snooping on me — I'd be outraged.

Too bad, my inner voice says. *Hurry up.*

Before I can stop myself, I go to his text messages and start scrolling.

Most are from people I know — friends and work colleagues.

Boring, boring, boring.

I see texts from "Mama" and frown. *Ugh.* His mother and I aren't close and never will be. Quickly, I scan her messages, which are basically commands.

A legal question — call me.

Lunch at 1 on Saturday — be on time.

And so on. Nothing that pops out as surprising or alarming.

I keep scrolling. Newer messages give way to older ones. It's like going back in time.

And then, a name I don't know: "Tiff."

I open the texts. There are just a few of them, all from a few months ago.

JOSH

Hey baby.

TIFF

Hey, lover. Been thinking about you
all day.

JOSH

Can't wait for tonight.

TIFF

Left your name at the door.

JOSH

What's the new bouncer's name?

TIFF

Big Ed.

And then, a few weeks later:

JOSH

Done.

TIFF

Remember, no more texts. Call me at
my new number.

And that's it.

Hurriedly, I go to his phone call history and immediately see multiple calls to one number — 649-555-2394. The calls happen every day.

The new number is probably "Tiff." But he hasn't set her up as a contact in his phone. Why is that?

Because he's hiding her.

I blink with surprise.

Why would he hide her?

From upstairs comes a loud "Mommy!"

"Coming, sweetie!" I yell.

I set the phone down. For a moment, I don't move. I need to think this through. Starting with:

Someone gave me the passcode to Josh's phone.

Why did they do that?

What did they want me to see?

How did they get the passcode?

Oh, God. There's so much to unpack. None of this makes sense — yet it all just happened.

Mind awhirl, I make my way upstairs, one careful step at a time, and join Ava and Josh in the bathroom. After a few more minutes of washing and chatter, we get her dry and into her pajamas, then climb into bed with her. Ava smiles happily as Josh reads to her. Eventually, like a battery sliding into sleep mode, she nods off.

After dimming the light and closing her door, we head downstairs.

"So how are you doing?" I ask my ex-husband when we're back in the kitchen.

"Fine." He moves to the sink to start rinsing dishes. "Why?"

"It's been a while since I checked in with you."

He shrugs. "I'm good."

"How's work?"

"Busy."

I don't doubt that. His firm has a hand in pretty much everything that happens business-wise in Boudreaux Parish. Back when we were married, he used to tell me about some of it — the firm's involvement in land deals, zoning changes, inheritance disputes, even the occasional high-dollar divorce. He persuaded one of his clients, a developer who built the new houses on Sycamore Lane, to let me and Ava move in here after the accident.

"Any new and exciting clients?"

He smiles. "Here in Boudreaux? You know better than that. This ain't New Orleans."

I return the smile. This is one of our things — comparing Boudreaux to New Orleans, with New Orleans always winning.

"How's your mother?"

He gives me a skeptical look. "You're asking about Mama?"

"Yes. How is my favorite person?"

"She's looking forward to seeing you and Ava on Saturday."

I let out a small groan. I'd forgotten about lunch on Saturday.

"Oh, come on," he says mildly. "It'll be fine."

"I know, I know." I shift my hip and feel a jolt of pain. "And you're right. It'll be fine. Ava always has fun there."

"That's the spirit."

"But seriously, how are you?" Before I lose my nerve, I add, "Are you dating anyone?"

He blinks, taken aback.

Before he can respond, I rush in. "I'm sorry, maybe I shouldn't be asking. It's just, you know, the divorce is in the past and we're getting along well and we're finding our new rhythm and I — well, I want you to be happy."

He's still staring at me, still startled.

"If you're seeing someone, I want you to know that I think that's great."

Then I stop and feel myself flush. Have I said too much? Have I ventured where an ex-wife dare not tread?

He clears his throat, which is what he does when he's unsure about what to say. He opens his mouth, then shuts it, then opens it again. "Okay, um, gosh."

"I shouldn't have asked."

"No, it's not that. I mean, you asking is a little bit … awkward, I suppose?"

He's got that right. I stay quiet, waiting to see what comes next.

"I mean," he says, his blue eyes blinking uncertainly, "given our history, this isn't something I expected us to talk about."

"I get that. And if you don't want to, I totally understand."

"Well…." After a pause, he continues. "I am seeing someone. But it's not something I'm sharing yet — with anyone."

"With anyone?"

He shakes his head. "We're keeping it quiet for now."

"No one knows?"

"No one."

Wrong, I don't say. "I won't say anything, I promise."

"Thanks."

"What you share and when — that's totally up to you."

"Thanks."

I almost tell him about the weird note. Chances are the note means someone knows and wants *me* to know.

But again I hesitate. Telling him would mean admitting I snuck into his phone. And there's more than just that. Something's going on. I have no idea what, but I can feel it. I'm a pawn in someone's game. I need to think this through before I say anything.

"So you're really doing okay, aren't you?" he asks.

This again? "Yes."

"I'm glad."

"Is there something I don't know about?" I finally ask. "Some reason you're worried?"

"Oh, no," he says right away. "I can see you getting stronger by the day."

"I am getting stronger by the day."

He nods vigorously. "I can see that."

"It seems like you have doubts."

"Not at all. I don't mean to come across like that. I just…. I care for you. I want you to be all better."

I hear the sincerity in his voice. I see the same in his eyes. I believe him.

God, I'm tired of being paranoid. It's so draining.

"Good," I say with a smile. "I want the exact same thing."

We turn back to cleaning up the kitchen and a few minutes later he leaves. I watch from the porch as he climbs into his truck and drives away. The rains have come and gone. The night air is still. Sycamore Lane is quiet.

I close the front door and lock it with a sigh, suddenly aware of how tired I am. Getting better is exhausting.

Which is exactly what I'm doing, I tell myself. *I'm getting better.* Every day, my hip hurts a bit less and my head is a bit clearer. I just wish the healing would happen faster. I want to be the old me again, the previous me, the me that moved with confidence through life, the me that didn't worry about the pain that might come with each new step.

Tomorrow I'll push myself, I decide. I'll finally walk all the way to the old oak tree in the state park. And while I'm on the walk, I'll think through the odd note and Josh's phone and his secret relationship with "Tiff."

The thought reassures me. I shut off the downstairs lights and make my way upstairs. Bed beckons.

I'm in the bathroom brushing my teeth when I hear a noise.

I spit into the sink, turn off the water, and listen.

Nothing. Whatever it was, I imagined it. I'm about to resume brushing when —

I hear it again.

I freeze.

The sound came from downstairs.

It was a sharp sound. A familiar sound.

It sounded like —

Someone scraping a kitchen chair over the floor.

CHAPTER 7

Fear jolts me.

Maybe Ava went downstairs?

Hoping against hope I'm right, I go quietly to Ava's door and peek in. My little angel is safe and sound in her bed, blessedly asleep.

I close her door and remain still, listening.

The house is silent.

Then —

I hear it again. That same *scraping*.

I inhale sharply.

Is someone downstairs?

Heart pounding, I limp to my bedroom and grab my phone. Hands trembling, I'm about to call Josh when I force myself to stop.

Didn't I lock up as usual? Isn't the security system on? I retrace what I did before coming upstairs.

Yes, I locked the front door before coming up, just like I always do. Same with the sliding doors leading to the deck and the door leading from the kitchen to the garage. Also, the light on the security panel next to the front door was green, which means the alarm is on.

Someone breaking in would trigger the alarm. And no alarm has been triggered.

Josh has a key to the house. So does Beth. Maybe one of them forgot something and wanted to come in and get it without disturbing me?

Or maybe it's an animal? A raccoon or a squirrel? This is Louisiana, after all — nature's pretty bold. It would have been easy enough for an animal to sneak in through an open door when I wasn't looking, or even squeeze in through some gap in the roof or foundation. Crazy stuff like that happens here all the time.

What will Josh say if he races over and it turns out to be just some harmless animal?

Or — the thought unsettles me — what will he think if he comes over and doesn't find anything at all? What will that suggest to him about me and my recovery? About the wisdom of Ava living here with me while I'm on the mend?

How sure am I that the sound I heard is a scraping chair?

I mean, couldn't I have imagined the whole thing? Didn't Dr. Franklin warn me that "transient audio-visual hallucinations" might occur as I recovered?

My eyes land on my cane, leaning against the dresser next to the door.

Find out what's down there before you call, I tell myself. *Bring your phone downstairs with you. And your cane.*

My hand closes over its solid smoothness. I like my cane. It's comforting. If I run into someone downstairs, I can whack the shit out of them.

Adrenaline surges through me. Emboldened, I move

forward slowly, taking care with each step, trying to stay silent.

The carpet is soft under my feet. For the first time since moving in, I'm glad the upstairs has wall-to-wall carpeting.

The hallway is dark, but not so dark that I can't see where I'm going. Slowly, I make my way down the stairs.

The house is silent. Moonlight's coming through the living room windows and casting a silvery light over the entry foyer.

At the bottom I pause, the hardwood floor cool on my bare feet.

Still no sound.

Senses on high alert, I make my way into the kitchen. Pale moonlight floats through the windows above the sink.

The kitchen chairs are where they should be, tucked under the kitchen table.

No one scraped them across the floor.

I imagined it. I spooked myself. That's it. That's what happened.

No one is here.

I nearly cry out with relief.

I'm safe. *Ava's safe.* All is good.

And then I hear it.

No, *feel* it.

Air on my neck. A soft whoosh.

I turn and —

A man is there!

Behind me!

I stumble back, too shocked to scream.

My hip cries out in pain as I struggle to find my footing.

"Look at you," the man whispers.

A glint of moonlight in his hand. A knife!

I gasp in terror and take hold of my cane with both hands.

He's wearing a black mask.

He laughs, low and evil.

He lunges for me and I pull back.

He laughs. "Feisty. I like it."

Then he lunges again and —

I move to the side and —

I swing the cane with all my strength —

At his head!

He groans and collapses, face down, on the kitchen floor.

I nearly cry out, nearly scream, nearly faint.

I can hear my breathing, jagged and harsh.

The man is still. Is he even breathing?

Then, in the moonlight, I see blood flowing onto the floor from beneath him.

Oh, God. He fell on his knife. He's bleeding.

Did I just kill him?

I'm about to inch closer when I hear Ava call out.

"Mommy?"

CHAPTER 8

I whirl around, frantic. Did Ava come downstairs?

"Mommy?" she calls out again.

I gasp. Her voice isn't nearby. She isn't in the kitchen!

I race into the foyer and look up the stairs —

And there she is. On the top step, holding her stuffed bear, rubbing her eyes.

Relief floods through me.

She's safe.

I hobble up the stairs, hip throbbing, and get down onto my knees to pull her in for a hug.

"Mommy, I heard a noise." Her voice is soft and drowsy. She isn't scared or worried. She's just wondering.

I can't let her see the man on the kitchen floor.

"It's nothing, sweetie. I dropped something, that's all. Let's get you back into bed."

Reassured, she lets me lead her to her room. I tuck her in and watch her slip back to sleep.

Trembling, I brush a strand of hair from her cheek. So innocent. So precious. My everything.

Tears are coming but I push them back furiously. No, not now. Not yet. I need to be strong.

I take a deep breath and then another, waiting for the wave of emotion to pass. I have to figure out my next steps. I need to call 911. A man broke in and tried to attack me. I hit him with my cane. He fell and landed on his knife.

Oh, God, did I just kill him?

Call Josh first.

The instant the thought comes, I know it's right. Josh will know what to do. He's a lawyer. He knows Boudreaux. He knows the sheriff. He'll protect me and Ava.

I reach for my phone in my pocket and realize — the phone isn't there!

Panic shoots through me. Where is it?

Then I remember. It was with me when I went downstairs.

The phone's in the kitchen — with the man.

I inhale sharply. I have no choice. I have to go down.

But what if the man isn't dead?

What if he wakes up?

I reach instinctively for my cane and realize — *the cane's downstairs too!*

When Ava called out for me, I must have dropped it.

Oh my God.

I can't go in there again. I just can't.

I have to.

But I –

Do it now. Before the man wakes up.

Shakily, I get up from the bed. After a long. lingering

glance at my daughter, I slip out of her bedroom, shut the door tight, and head down the stairs.

The house is silent.

In the foyer, I look around. I need another weapon. In the living room, on the credenza, I see the heavy glass vase that Josh's mother gave us. God, I hate that vase. But as I pick it up and grip it in both hands, I'm glad it's so hefty and ugly.

I'll crack his skull if he comes at me again.

I blink at the anger surging through me. This capacity for violence — has it always been within me, or is it too one of my new things?

Vase in hand, I make my way to the kitchen.

The man is in the same place, still lying on the floor, moonlight reflecting on the blood seeping from beneath him. Is he breathing? I can't tell.

Heart pounding, ready to bolt at the slightest movement, I inch closer. I can't see my phone. It has to be here. On the floor somewhere.

But I see my cane. On the floor next to the man. I set the vase on the counter and grab the cane. The handle is sticky.

I shudder. *Sticky with the man's blood.*

And then, across the kitchen, on the floor near the fridge — I see my phone.

Relief rushes through me.

Josh will know what to do.

I'm reaching to get it when I feel it.

A slight prick in my neck.

I turn in surprise. There's a shadow behind me —

Another man?

Holding a hypodermic needle?

My vision goes blurry.

Even as I struggle to hold on, consciousness starts slipping away.

I gasp in panic. I can't go dark. I can't let that happen. Ava needs me!

I hear a moan and realize the sound is coming from me—

As I drop to the floor and my world goes black.

CHAPTER 9

awake with a start.

My hip is aching. I have a headache. My mouth is dry.

I'm on the floor.

The *kitchen* floor.

With a gasp, I remember the attack and bolt upright.

Frantically, I look around.

It's morning. Daylight's flooding in.

No one's here.

The man is gone.

His blood *is gone.*

My heart stops: *Ava!*

I scramble to my feet and climb upstairs.

Heart pounding, I open her door and —

She's in bed. *Thank God!*

She hears me. She's awake. She turns over and stares at me as I rush in.

"Mommy, are you okay?"

I rush to her and pull her in tight, a single thought echoing through me: *She's safe she's safe she's safe she's safe....*

"I'm fine, honey," I say, my mouth like sandpaper. "I'm fine."

She wriggles free of my hug. Was I holding her too tightly?

"Is it time for school?" she says.

I glance at her bedside clock and gasp. It's seven-thirty. We should be downstairs having breakfast. Beth will be here any minute to drive Ava to school.

But what about the man? And his accomplice?

A chill runs through me: *Are they still in the house?*

"Sweetie," I say, trying to keep my voice calm. "Did you sleep well?"

She nods.

"Did you see or hear anything...," I begin, but stop when I see the confusion in her eyes.

"Did I see what?"

"Nothing, sweetie." I get up from the bed. "Yes, it's almost time for school. Why don't you get dressed? I'll be back in a minute."

"I have to use the bathroom."

"Of course." I move to the bedroom door. "In just a minute."

She's looking at me, puzzled.

"Get dressed. Be right back."

I race to the hallway bathroom and look in — no one there.

I search the master bedroom and the third bedroom and the closets.

No one.

It's just me and Ava on the second floor.

"Mommy, I have to pee!"

"All clear," I call out.

She dashes past me into the bathroom.

I stand still for a moment outside the door, wondering what the hell is going on.

Think, Callie, think.

No one's upstairs. But what about downstairs?

Dread grips me as I realize my phone and cane are both downstairs.

I have to go down again.

Do it now — while Ava's in the bathroom.

Once again, I head downstairs. The house is quiet. Nothing seems out of place.

Quickly, I check the front door — locked — and the security system — on. Then I race through the kitchen to the dining area and check the sliding doors — also locked.

I make my way back to the foyer. As I do, I glance into the living room and gasp.

The vase is back on the credenza — *right where it was before I grabbed it.*

Dear God, what's going on?

I rush over and pick it up. It looks and feels exactly like it did last night.

Who put it back? And why?

I'm startled by the sound — the familiar sound — of a car pulling into the driveway.

I step to the front window and look out.

Beth.

Relief floods through me. Through the window, I watch her hop out of her car and make her way to the front porch. Everything she does looks completely normal.

She opens the front door and calls out "Good morning," just like she always does.

When she sees me in the living room, she jumps, startled. "Callie."

Suddenly I feel self-conscious. What do I look like? "Hey."

She's staring at me. "Is everything okay?"

I was attacked by two people, I almost blurt out. *I hit one and he fell on his knife. I might have killed him. Then a second person jabbed a needle into my neck and knocked me out. I woke up a few minutes ago on the kitchen floor. I have no idea what's going on.*

I almost say all of that. I come so close. My mouth is open, the words about to tumble forth, when something stops me.

Fear.

Yes, fear stops me.

Fear of what they'll think.

Of me.

Of my ability to be a responsible parent for Ava.

I haven't mentioned the fights yet. The arguments. The battle I fought after I woke up from the coma. I prefer sticking with the positive, keeping my focus on the here and now.

I'm doing my best to look past how things really work in Boudreaux Parish. How they'll pounce if I show the slightest weakness.

I know you don't understand. I know I sound paranoid. I can't go into that right now. I'll share more later.

As I stand there in the living room, ugly vase in hand, looking no doubt like a crazed wacko, the words that leave my mouth come from the gut, the result of a decision made on pure instinct, without an instant of conscious thought.

"Everything's fine," I say to her.

She stares for another few seconds, her brow furrowed. "Is Ava in the kitchen?"

"Sorry," I say apologetically. "We're running late this morning. She's upstairs getting dressed." I set the vase down and hobble into the foyer. As I do, I see myself in the hallway mirror.

God, I'm a mess. No wonder Beth was staring. My hair is standing up all over. My skin is red. I look like I drank myself to sleep.

Is that what Beth is wondering?

Still operating on instinct, I say, "Can you put some fruit and cheese slices in a container for Ava? She can eat it on the ride over."

"Sure," Beth says, still staring at me. I see the worry in her eyes.

I head into the kitchen. "Oh, and I'm going with you guys."

"You are?" she says, following me.

"I have a meeting with the headmaster."

A total lie. But there's no way I'm leaving Ava alone this morning.

I cast my eyes around the kitchen, looking for my phone and cane. I see the phone on the counter and the cane resting against the wall.

Before I go down the rabbit hole of wondering how they got from the floor to the spots where I found them — and before I begin what I know will be a massive freakout when I finally accept that a man attacked me and fell on his knife and vanished from my kitchen floor and another man jabbed me with a hypodermic needle — I turn to Beth and smile.

"I'm a mess. Gotta make myself presentable. Be down in a few."

Cane and phone in hand, I head upstairs, heart thumping, relieved beyond measure to have this solid piece of mahogany with me.

Ava calls out from her bathroom. "Mommy, my hair!"

"Be right there, sweetie."

I hurry into the bathroom and grab the brush. Ava's hair is naturally thick and frizzy and needs brushing out daily. It's a ritual with my daughter that normally I cherish.

"I'm going to school with you," I tell her as I start brushing.

"Why?" she asks, puzzled.

"I have a meeting with the headmaster."

"Why?"

"I'm going to see him about helping out with volunteer activities at the school while my hip is getting better."

The explanation, which I just pulled from thin air, sounds pretty good to my ears.

Ava scrunches up her face as she thinks about the school activities I could be involved with. "Are you going to mow the lawn?"

The thought of doing that makes me smile. The school is set back from the road and has a long driveway and a well-tended green lawn. "I doubt that. But who knows, maybe I will."

Her eyes widen. "Will you go on critter patrol?"

My smile widens. Believe it or not, there actually is such a thing. Due to its proximity to the state park and the bayou, the school inspects the grounds for alligators and other animals twice a day. "Maybe so, sweetie." I turn my arms into an alligator's jaws. "Rawr, rawr, rawr!"

Ava laughs with delight.

"Okay, hair's done. When you're finished in the bathroom, get into your shoes and head downstairs. Beth's putting together a breakfast treat for the car. I'll get cleaned up and be right down."

My daughter dashes off to her room. She likes knowing the actual steps of what's going to happen next. She likes plans.

So do I. *I need one.* I go to my bathroom and stare at myself in the mirror. God, my hair. I'd taken it out of the ponytail after Josh left. Now it's a tangled, stringy mess. Also, my cheeks are redder than usual. Perhaps sunburn from yesterday's walk? Or the stress of last night? Or a reaction to whatever drug I was injected with?

I lean closer to examine my neck, looking for an injection mark, but I don't see anything. If a mark is there, it's faint.

A horrible thought hits me. What if they ...?

My heart starts racing. I pull down my shorts and underwear and check. No, I conclude after a moment, I'm fine. When my inner voice doesn't object, I sigh with relief.

There's no time for a shower, so I splash water over my face and apply a cleanser, then wash it off and quickly throw on a moisturizer with sunscreen, then mascara and lipstick. One thing about the South — they like their makeup. If I'm meeting with the headmaster, I need to look presentable.

As for what to wear.... Given where I'm going and what I told my daughter I'll be doing, I should go with slacks and a nice blouse. Instead I find myself slipping in on a pair of shorts and an athletic shirt.

That way I can walk back home through the park, I tell myself. *I can finally make it to that old oak tree.*

I blink, surprised. There are a million reasons why that

plan makes zero sense. I've just survived a terrifying attack. I need to focus on my safety and Ava's. I have no idea what the hell is going on. But I'm apparently in no mood to listen, because before I can stop myself, I've put on the shorts and the shirt and pulled my hair back into a ponytail again.

I give myself another look in the mirror. The mascara looks wrong with the ponytail — too much for my taste — but I remind myself where I am and who the makeup is for and let out a sigh.

I slip the phone into my pocket — from now on, it's not leaving my possession — and grab my cane.

Before I can second-guess myself, I head downstairs and into the kitchen, where Ava and Beth are waiting.

In as bright a voice as I can manage, I say, "Okay, gang, let's get going!"

CHAPTER 10

A tremor goes through me as I ease into the front passenger seat and buckle in.

Clearly, for reasons I do not yet comprehend, I'm deciding to ignore the terror of last night. My response to what occurred is to pretend it didn't happen.

Am I making a terrible mistake?

Beth slips into the driver's seat and glances back at Ava, who's settling in. "Ready, munchkin?"

"Ready!" Ava says.

The school is on the opposite side of the state park, about a ten-minute drive away. Beth takes us through the gated community, past dozens of perfectly manicured lawns and identical stucco houses, before turning onto the parish road.

I swivel toward my daughter. "Ava, eat your breakfast."

She opens her container of fruit and cheese and tears into an apple slice.

Beth glances at me. "You want me to stick around and drive you back after your meeting?"

"No, I'll walk back."

Her eyebrows go up. "Through the park?"

"There's an old tree I've heard about but never seen. It's supposed to be near the school."

"An old tree?"

"It's supposed to be really big and really impressive."

She shrugs, not convinced. "Seems like your hip is doing well."

She's right about that, I realize. Despite the ordeal I've been through, my hip is holding up. The thought cheers me. "It is."

On one side of the road is the park and its endless expanse of swamp. On the other are farms, homes, and occasional roadside businesses. There isn't much to Boudreaux Parish these days. The population of seven thousand keeps dropping as people leave for jobs closer to New Orleans and Baton Rouge. Aside from the state park, a cute little downtown, and a couple of historical tours, the parish doesn't have much to offer visitors.

Or me, for that matter. Before the accident, I was preparing to move Ava and me back to New Orleans. Now the move is on hold, probably until next year. As much as I hate admitting it, my healing is going to take time. Plus, Ava is doing well at Briarton. Disrupting her school year isn't something I'm willing to do.

The school comes into view, its green lawn sweeping us up the long driveway to the antebellum plantation house that serves as the school's administration building.

Beth parks in the passenger loading zone next to the path that leads to the classroom buildings.

"Got everything?" she says as Ava unbuckles.

"Got it!" Ava says, grabbing her backpack.

I find myself blinking back tears. I'm so proud of my confident little girl. "Have a good day, sweetie. Love you. See you after school."

She leans forward and wraps a little arm around my neck. "Bye, Mommy. Love you!"

Then she's out of the car and racing down the path toward her classroom.

I watch her go, my eyes wet with emotion. She'll be safe here, I tell myself. Surrounded by teachers and students, she'll be protected.

Besides, they're not after her, my inner voice whispers. *They're after* you.

I shiver as the apparent truth of that sinks in. The person who injected me with a knockout drug could have gone upstairs to Ava's room while I was unconscious — but didn't.

I'm the target.

Why?

I turn from the window and see Beth gazing at me with compassion. Has she noticed the tears in my eyes?

"She's growing up so fast," I say softly.

"She's a great kid. She's lucky to have you."

I flush, self-conscious again. Earlier this morning, when Beth arrived at the house, I was a total mess. What do I look like now?

"You know," she says, "if something's going on, you can tell me."

I gaze into her kind eyes, considering. Part of me wants to do just that — to open the floodgates and confide everything. I feel safe here in the car. The low rumble of the engine is soft and soothing. Beth's presence is comforting. She's a good listener. I can trust her.

But another part of me says — *no, stop, don't.* Dragging her into this wouldn't be fair. The one thing I know for certain right now is that someone's messing with me. Until I find out who and why, I can't risk getting anyone else involved.

"Oh, I'm fine," I say. "Just impatient. I want to get better faster. It's hard to accept that getting better is going to take time." I can tell she's not convinced. I gesture to the administration building. "I should go. The headmaster awaits."

"You sure you don't want me to stick around and drive you home?"

"Nope, no need."

"It's gonna be a hot one today."

"I'll bring a water bottle with me."

Her tone is anxious. "Call if you need anything?"

I smile. "Will do. See you soon."

Cane in hand, I push open the door and climb out. Beth's right about the heat. Barely eight in the morning and already the muggy air is clinging to my skin.

After confirming that my phone and wallet are in my shorts pocket, I aim for the administration building. As I reach the front door, I glance back and watch Beth drive away.

I turn toward the door, steeling myself.

Time to tell some more lies.

CHAPTER 11

My hand is almost at the door when I realize I don't actually need to talk to the headmaster. That was just the lie I told to get Ava and me out of the house.

I could, of course, turn the lie into truth by walking inside and asking the receptionist for a few minutes with the headmaster, then going upstairs to his office, engaging in polite chit-chat, and offering to help with upcoming school events.

Until a few seconds ago, that was my so-called plan.

But now?

A wasp buzzes in my ear, startling me out of my reverie. Instinctively I duck down and back away from the door.

As I do, I hear a familiar sound. Somewhere nearby, a woman is crying. No, more than that — sobbing. After a few seconds of scanning, I see her in a car in the parking lot. The car window is down and she's blowing her nose, her eyes puffy and raw. She's white, probably in her forties, with shoulder-length red-brown hair.

I breathe in sharply. Without knowing how I know, I know the woman is the wife of the teacher who killed himself with his rifle in the state park.

I'd completely forgotten about that poor man.

What is his wife doing here? Maybe she came to get her husband's things? Clear out his desk? Would she do that so soon after he died?

Tears of my own threaten as I watch her cry. The poor woman. I know grief and it's just plain awful. When I lost my parents during my senior year of high school — Dad from prostate cancer, Mom from a heart attack two months later — I was beyond devastated. For months, it hurt to breathe.

Losing a husband would be equally terrible, perhaps even worse. Even though Josh and I are no longer married, if anything were ever to happen to him, I'd be beside myself.

The woman — I remember her name is Susan, assuming it's her — is rooting around for something in her car. Maybe in her purse.

When she finds it and holds it up, I catch a glint of metal.

I gasp. *A gun?*

Before I even know what I'm doing, I'm hobbling toward her as fast as I can.

"Susan," I call out. "Susan!"

She blinks, startled. When she sees me, her face crumples.

"Put the gun down," I say firmly. Where the hell is this take-charge-iness coming from? I have no clue, but I can't stop myself. "It's not what you want to do."

She's staring at me, shocked.

"I want you to place the gun on the seat beside you."

Almost like she's in a daze, she does what I say.

I'm at her window and she's looking up at me, her eyes bloodshot, her skin flushed.

"Is it okay if I sit with you in the car?"

Wordlessly, she nods.

I have no idea why I'm doing this, or even *how* I'm doing this. It's like I'm watching a movie of myself as I walk around the car and yank on the handle of the passenger door.

The door is locked.

"Unlock the door, Susan."

Still staring at me, she presses a button and the door *thunks* softly.

I pull open the door and the gun is right where she set it on the passenger seat, glinting in the sunlight.

As I reach for it —

Her hand darts out and grabs it.

Before I can stop myself, I slide in next to her.

She's aiming the gun right at me. *Dear God, what am I doing?*

"Don't point that thing at me," I say.

She gasps as she realizes the danger and turns the gun toward the windshield.

"Who are you?" she finally says.

"My name is Callie Crawford."

"What are you doing here?"

"I'm here to help."

She shakes her head, her eyes bugging at me.

"Let me hold the gun for you."

"No."

"I want you to let me hold it for the time being."

She shrinks back, her gaze unfocused, her gun hand trembling.

"Susan," I say, gently but firmly. "I need you to give me the gun."

Tears spill from her eyes. And then, like a balloon deflating, her resistance collapses, her hand drops, and the gun clatters to the floor, landing next to my left foot.

My heart is thumping in my ears. At least the gun is out of her hand. But what the fuck am I doing? How did I just do that?

"Thank you, Susan. You've done the right thing."

She starts sobbing again. I sit there quietly as her grief rolls out of her. A good minute passes, then two. The morning sun is beating down on me. Barely eight in the morning and already the heat is unbearable. I'm trying to figure out my next step when she takes a couple of deep breaths, reaches into the purse in her lap, and pulls out a tissue.

After wiping her eyes and blowing her nose, she really looks at me, as if for the first time.

"Who the hell are you?" She doesn't say it like she's angry. More like she's disappointed in herself for letting me stop her from whatever it was she came here to do.

"My name's Callie Crawford." I gesture to the administration building. "I was on my way to see the headmaster when I noticed you."

She doesn't respond, still staring at me.

"My daughter's in the first grade," I add, beginning to feel self-conscious. Her lack of response is unsettling, like the tables have turned and suddenly I'm the one who needs to justify my presence.

"Crawford?" she repeats, as if my last name doesn't make sense.

"That's right."

"You were married to Josh."

"That's right."

"Why the hell did you divorce him?"

Now she's staring at me like *I'm* the crazy one.

"He cheated," I blurt out before I can stop myself.

She laughs. Not a bitter laugh. More sad and knowing. "Oh, honey, like that really matters."

My mouth opens, but no words come out. Because what is there to say?

Her eyes flash with emotion. "I always figured that bitch Marian drove you away. Josh is a sweetheart, but that mama of his? Pure evil."

I blink, taken aback. Marian Dupre is certainly a strong-willed individual, but— wait, what am I doing? Was I actually about to *defend* my former mother-in-law? Marian is a cold, controlling, spiteful woman and I can't stand being around her.

"Yep, total bitch." I hear myself say. "*Huuuuge.*"

Susan's eyes widen — she wasn't expecting that — and a guffaw bursts forth, like she had all this pressure inside and I found a way to pop it.

"Tell me what you came here to do," I say.

"Oh, holy Jesus, who the hell knows." After a pause, she continues. "I've barely slept and I need answers and I know Devlin's gonna cover things up like he did with that man Bracken and I thought, maybe if I scare the shit out of him I can get the truth for once."

I tense. Her plan was *to bring a gun into my daughter's*

school. The very gun on the floor of the car, pressing against my left foot. If she reaches for it, I can try to stop her.

"Soooo," I say slowly, "you were going to confront him and…."

"Get him to open his goddamn mouth." She blinks at her word choice and her eyes fill with tears, and I remember what Josh said about her husband: *He ate his hunting rifle.*

Before she can collapse again, I try to distract her. "What do you think the headmaster is covering up?"

"He would never do that," she says.

"The headmaster wouldn't do what?"

"No, Rory."

I blink back tears as I realize what she's saying.

"Rory wouldn't do that to me," she says, crying again. "He loved me too much. I was his boo-bear. He was my everything."

The tears start flowing again, and now I'm about to join her.

"Susan, I am so sorry for your loss." I motion for her to come closer and I allow her to sob uncontrollably on my shoulder. Even as I breathe in her perfume and sweat, I can't believe I'm here, hugging a grief-stricken, gun-toting, accusation-hurling stranger in her own car.

"Listen," I say when the crying finally dies down, "if it's okay with you, I'm gonna call Josh."

She goes still and I sense her considering that.

"He can help us right now."

She lets me go, then reaches into her purse for a tissue. "Okay," she finally says.

I pull out my phone and text him: "With Susan at Briarton. Need your help. Call me."

Susan blows her nose, then says, "You're doing the right

thing, getting the hell out of Boudreaux. Poor Josh is stuck here — Mama Marian will never let him escape — but she doesn't want you here. She wants you *gone.*"

I'm surprised she knows that even though we've never met, until I realize — of course she knows. In Boudreaux, everybody knows everything.

Susan points to my leg. "How you doing? That leg of yours on the mend?"

It's my hip, I almost say. "Yes, I'm getting stronger by the day."

"They catch the bastard who ran you down?"

"Not yet." Despite the heat, my cheeks flush. The truth is, I don't remember the accident or anything from that day. I was out for a jog, I'm told, and got hit by a car. The impact sent me flying into a tree and fractured my hip and skull. According to Dr. Franklin, my first couple of days in the hospital were touch and go. More than once he's told me I'm lucky to be alive.

After I woke up from the coma, the sheriff told me he was treating the incident as a felony hit-and-run. "The driver left the scene of the accident. He shouldn't have done that. We're not stopping till we find him, Miss Callie. You have my word."

Susan's searching my face, waiting for me to say more. "It was probably Marian."

I gasp. "What?"

"She hates you. You know that, right? When Josh told her about you, she went ballistic."

"How do you know that?"

"Oh, everybody knows. She told the ladies at the Cotillion luncheon there was no way her son was marrying a waitress. 'Northern trash,' she called you. 'Barely graduated high school. No breeding.'"

"I don't —"

"She only put up with you because of your daughter."

Grief has loosened her tongue. God knows what she's like usually. "Susan, I —"

"Now her granddaughter is where she wants her — here in her precious parish, at her precious school."

I don't like my former mother-in-law and don't trust her an inch, but I can't see her running me down with her fancy silver Caddy. She likes that car way too much.

I try to shift the topic. "Susan, I'd like to help you with—"

"You've served your purpose. You gave her her precious grandchild. If you get in her way, watch out."

I swallow back a response as unease shoots through me. I mean, could Susan be right? Is it remotely possible that Marian…?

Stop. Don't go there. The very thought is insane.

Instead I say, "Susan, we need to talk about the gun."

She shrinks from me and blinks rapidly, her lips trembling.

"I think it's best if I take care of it for a few days."

"Why?"

"You've got an awful lot on your plate right now. Grief is a terrible thing. You're gonna have to dig deep to find the strength to make it through the next few weeks and months — probably deeper than you ever have before."

Her eyes fill with tears. "I can't believe he's gone."

"I'm so sorry for your loss." I give her hand a squeeze. "I want you to know — I'm here to help. You name it, I'll do it."

She clasps my hand tight. "You will?"

My phone in my lap buzzes. It's Josh.

"I know Josh is gonna help, too." I extricate my hand from hers and pick up my phone. "Both of us. Whatever you need, we're here for you."

CHAPTER 12

Josh roars in a few minutes later. After a few gentle words, Susan allows him to guide her out of her car and into his truck. He's good with her — kind, patient, encouraging. It's nice to see and I'm reminded again why I married him.

I clamber out of her car as he helps her into his truck. Then he leads me to a spot where she can't hear us.

His blue eyes drill into me, his mouth tight with tension. "What happened, Callie?"

I tell him about finding her but don't mention the gun, which is now in my shorts pocket, pressing heavily against my thigh. "She hasn't slept. She's in shock. She said the headmaster likes to cover things up. She said she was planning to confront him."

He exhales heavily. "Damn."

"She needs rest. Is there someone who can watch her, make sure she gets some sleep?"

"Her sister's driving over from Atlanta. I'll stay with her

until the sister arrives and find someone to pick up her car. You want a ride home?"

"No, I'm good."

He frowns. "You sure?"

"I'm walking back."

His frown deepens. "Through the park?"

"I need the exercise."

"It's gonna be hot as hell today."

"I'll bring water. I'm good."

He's about to argue but sees the look on my face and has the good sense to back off.

"What brought you here?" he asks instead.

I needed to get out of that house. I needed to make sure Ava is safe. And right now I need to think hard, really hard, about why someone is messing with me.

I clear my throat. "I came to talk to the headmaster about volunteering. I figured it would help me to be out and about while I get better."

"Oh." He likes the sound of that. "You sure you don't want a ride?"

"I'm sure. I'll call if I need anything."

We return to the truck and I say, "Susan, when you get home, I want you to get some sleep. You need to rest up. You got that?"

"You're a good gal."

"I'm here for you. I mean that. Josh will give you my number and I'll get yours from him. Call me after you get some rest, okay?"

Josh climbs in. After watching them drive off, I pick up my cane from where I dropped it next to Susan's car.

It's time for that walk that I apparently really want to do. But first I need water — Josh and Beth are right about the heat — so I head back to the administration building. I was inside once before, shortly after getting out of the hospital. If I remember right, there's a vending machine in the reception area.

It's only as I'm pushing open the front door that I realize there's something else I want to do. Susan's accusation about the headmaster has gotten under my skin. What she said — "Devlin's gonna cover things up like he did with that man Bracken" — sounds crazy, but what if it isn't?

The door closes behind me and blessedly cool air envelopes me. Thank God for air conditioning. Straight ahead of me is the building's gorgeous grand staircase. To the left is a room, probably the former mansion's front parlor, that's been turned into the reception area. A receptionist is smiling at me from behind her desk. "Good morning. Can I help you?"

I approach. "Good morning. I don't have an appointment, but I'm hoping I can see the headmaster for a few moments. I'm Callie Crawford. My daughter Ava is a first-grader here."

"Oh, yes, Ava Dupre. A wonderful child. Can I ask what you'd like to see him about?"

"About volunteering here."

Her eyes go to my cane — she knows what happened to me. "Of course. Let me see if he's available." After a few hushed words into her phone, she gives me a smile. "He's happy to see you."

"Great. Should I go upstairs?"

She glances again at my cane. "If that's all right?"

"Yes, totally fine."

Which isn't totally true, though there's no way I'm telling her that. I'm in less pain than even a few days ago, but certain movements remain difficult. Walking down stairs, for instance. Getting down on one knee. I still can't press the brake and gas pedals in my car without pain. But normal, regular walking is getting easier by the day. The limp is lessening. I just wish the healing was happening faster.

One careful step at a time, I make my way up the grand staircase. Halfway up I turn around and imagine myself in a beautiful gown, floating down the stairs to welcome a handsome suitor. "Miss Callie," my admirer says, his eyes shining with appreciation. "You look so beautiful."

On the walls, oil portraits of the school's former headmasters gaze down on me, their expressions serious, even reproachful. With a sigh, I let the moment go. The school has had six headmasters since its founding fifty years ago, all of them men, all of them white, all of them old. Now I'm about to meet the current one.

On the second floor, I make my way down the hall to the headmaster's office and knock on his open door. He leaps up from his desk with an anxious smile.

"Mrs. Dup — I mean, Ms. Crawford. What a pleasant surprise." He hurries to greet me, eagerness personified.

Devlin Chatterton is a thin man, about fifty, with graying hair and thick glasses. I first met him a month ago, a few days after getting out of the hospital. I'd missed the fall orientation for parents — being in a coma and all — and he graciously gave me a private tour. He'd acted nervous and jumpy that day and he's giving off the same vibe now. It's like he thinks I'm about to chastise him.

Irritation flashes through me. The man's lack of confidence bothers me. He's head of an institution with two hundred students and dozens of staff. Why is he behaving this way?

Because of who I am, I tell myself. *Or rather, who my daughter's grandmother is.*

"Please have a seat," he says as he ushers me in. Back when the building was a family mansion, his office was probably a bedroom. Now the walls are lined with shelves filled with yearbooks, trophies, and other school memorabilia. Behind his desk hangs a large oil portrait of the plantation, painted shortly after its construction nearly two centuries ago. Amidst the green of the fields, the white mansion seems to gleam.

The headmaster's beautiful antique desk is spotless aside from a laptop, with not a single piece of paper on it. As I settle into the chair in front of the desk, I catch a whiff of the wood oil he must use to keep the surface polished.

"Now," he says, his eyes darting nervously to my cane, almost like it's poisonous. "How can I help you today?"

"Thank you for squeezing me in, Mr. Chatterton. I'm sorry about showing up without warning."

"Oh, not a worry, Ms. Crawford. I'm here to be of assistance."

We smile at each other, both of us being ever so polite.

"I'd like to volunteer to help out around the school."

"Oh," he says, his shoulders relaxing. Clearly he'd been expecting something else.

"I'd like to be productive with my time. And I'd like to get to know my daughter's new school better."

He nods eagerly, like what I said was pure genius. "The involvement of parents is always welcome. We have a number of upcoming events and your participation would be greatly appreciated."

He picks up his phone. "Sherry, can you print a copy of our events calendar for Ms. Crawford?"

He sounds confident enough talking with Sherry. So why the nervousness with me?

He clears his throat. "I'm told your daughter is doing wonderfully."

"She is. She's thriving. She wakes up every day excited to come here."

He smiles, relieved. "That's gratifying to hear."

"So … about helping out. There's something I think I can help with right away."

"Oh?"

"I read your email yesterday about Rory Freeman."

He goes still. "Rory. Yes, very sad. All of us are in a state of shock."

"I was with his wife Susan a short while ago."

He blinks. "You were?"

"Josh and I were just with her. He's her lawyer and, well, I've lost loved ones, so I know the territory. I told her I'll be happy to help her out. I know how difficult even the little things will be for her in the coming weeks and months."

"Indeed. Such a terrible tragedy."

"She said she was planning to come here to see you."

"She did?"

Her gun in my shorts pocket feels heavy against my leg. "She doesn't believe Rory did what he apparently did."

"I see," he says slowly. "So you're aware of how he…?"

"Josh told me."

He sighs. "It's a terrible business, just terrible. Rory was very well-liked here. His fellow teachers, his students, everyone."

"She told me — and I'm only telling you this because I'm trying to help her and not because I think it's true—that you know what really happened to him."

His shoulders stiffen and his face turns red. "She said *what?*"

"I'm sorry, I shouldn't have —"

"Of course I don't know anything. How could I?"

"I apologize, I didn't mean —"

"I must say, I'm surprised and concerned that she would say that."

"I'm sorry I brought it up. I just thought you should know what she said."

He gazes at me for a moment, as if weighing my trustworthiness.

"Well," he finally says. "Thank you."

"Also, about Bracken," I add. "She's afraid you'll do to Rory what you did to Bracken."

He breathes in sharply and his eyes flash panic.

Holy fuck. For the record, I have no idea why I'm doing this. Not a single lick of this is my business. None, zero, nada, zippo. What am I now, a wanna-be cop? Callie Crawford, private investigator?

But boy, I've struck a nerve. The headmaster is acting like I slapped him. His gaze darts to a bookshelf, then back to me.

"What…," he begins, his voice nearly a whisper. "What did she say?"

"I'm sorry," I say, trying to sound clueless and meek. "I have no idea what she was talking about. I just thought you should know."

"I…." He stops, struggling with his words. "I have no idea why Susan would say that about me. We've known each other since Rory joined the faculty eighteen years ago. He and I started here at the same time. We were teachers together."

"I didn't know you were a teacher before you became headmaster."

"My first four years here, until my predecessor died of a heart attack. At this very desk, in fact." He says it almost proudly, like he's paying tribute to the man's work ethic.

"Was his name Bracken?"

"Oh, no, his name was Hiram Higgins."

"So who was Bracken?"

He shrugs. His panic is receding, but he's still nervous. "The name doesn't ring a bell."

Liar, I almost say. "Well, anyway, I was thinking I might be able to help out with the memorial service for Rory here at the school, if there is one."

"I see. Well, we will be doing something to commemorate his years of service, but I'm not sure of any details at this point."

"I understand. I was thinking it might be helpful if I could be a liaison of sorts with Susan, to help smooth the way and assist with communication and planning, if you will."

"I see." He can see the benefits of my offer, but clearly he's not ready to say yes.

"Also, I can help with preparing materials, getting things ready if there's an in-person event, and stuff like that."

"Thank you." He's back to eyeing me carefully. Not like he's suspicious, exactly. More like he's wondering why I'm so eager to help out.

"The accident really threw me for a loop," I say, answering his unspoken question. "I'm healing well, but it's taking more time than I want it to. I guess you could say I'm eager to get out and about and do more."

It helps that the words are true. He senses that, I can tell.

"I'm glad you're ready to volunteer. We encourage parents to participate in the school's events and activities."

As if on cue, a woman bustles in with a sheet of paper. "Here's the fall event schedule."

"Thank you, Sherry. It's for Ms. Crawford."

She hands me the paper but is still looking at him. "Also, I talked with Janice. Their copy's gone, too."

Once again, the headmaster's gaze darts to the bookshelf. And this time I pay attention. The shelves look ordinary and normal, and then I notice a gap in the row of school year-books. One of them is missing.

"Thank you, Sherry," he says, then turns to me. "About Rory's service, I'll need to get back to you. But let's take a look at the events calendar. I'm sure there are a number of activities you can volunteer for."

For the next few minutes, we look at the upcoming events and discuss each one, and I find myself agreeing to help out at several.

As he ushers me out of his office a few minutes later, I leave knowing in my heart that Susan is right.

Devlin Chatterton is hiding something.

What that might be, I have no clue.

But all of a sudden, I really want to find out.

CHAPTER 13

The day is hot as hell, just like Josh said, the air clinging to me as I limp along the bayou trail. Barely five minutes have passed since I left the Briarton campus and walked into the state park and already the school's lawn and manicured hedges seem like they're a million miles away. I'm surrounded by swamp and trees and by the buzzing of insects, the cries of birds, and the occasional rustling of animals in the brush. The stink of decaying vegetation fills my lungs.

The sun overhead is blinding and relentless. Instinctively, I hunch lower in a futile attempt to keep the sun from my face. The mascara I applied earlier is supposed to be waterproof, but I can sense it starting to melt in the heat, dripping away with my sweat.

I shouldn't be out here. I should be hunkered down at the school or huddled with Josh, trying to make sense of what happened last night. I should be at the sheriff's station reporting the crime. I should be at the hardware store, stocking up in preparation for a siege. At the very least, I should be coming up with a plan to protect myself and Ava from whoever the hell broke into my house and attacked me.

That's right — *attacked me*. My inner critic is revving up for battle like it always does, ready to lay into me, and this time it has powerful ammo. Two strangers *attacked me in my own home* and I haven't told a single soul. Not only that — I've done *nothing* to prevent the same horror from happening again.

I'm still in a state of shock, no doubt, still not ready to accept what I endured and survived. I understand more about trauma now than I did before my accident, so instead of doing what I usually do — immediately rejecting any possibility that I might need help — I let the trauma idea rattle around my head as I continue heading deeper into the park.

Boudreaux State Park is ten thousand acres of swamp and forest, a wild patch of land that's never been farmed, never paved for residential development, never anything other than the untamed swamp it's been since the last Ice Age. It's an alien environment to me. I grew up with well-tended woods, farmland, and towns. This place makes me feel like an outsider, a stranger. Still, I can feel its pull. It's like the wildness has its tendrils in me and is slowly reeling me in.

For weeks now, I've been gradually acquainting myself with the park's winding trails. I started slow and have gradually gone longer and farther. Each day brings a new bend or twist, each day a fresh discovery.

I learned about the old oak tree from Alice, the woman who works behind the counter at the gas station across from the park's main entrance, where I stop sometimes to get water for my walks. A few weeks back, after I'd been in a few times, Alice's curiosity got the better of her. She looked at my cane and sweaty face and asked what I was doing. When I told her I was exercising, she laughed. "You're crazy going out in this heat, but I applaud your spirit."

About a week after that she told me about the oak tree and I made it my goal to find it. "My grandma took me once," she told me. "A big old tree in the middle of a clearing. Creepy as hell, but there's something about it. It has a power."

A power. Maybe that's why I'm out here on this hellishly hot day. I need power and I want the old oak tree to lend me some.

Tree power — what superstitious nonsense, my inner critic immediately scoffs. *You're out here because you're too proud to ask for help.*

The realization stings. I've always been prone to believing I can do it all myself, even when I can't. I was offered all kinds of help after my parents died — from my aunt and uncle, from my neighbors, from my friends, from my friends' parents, from my teachers at school — and I pushed them all away.

The instant I graduated from high school, I sold my childhood home and everything in it, packed two suitcases, and bought a one-way train ticket to New Orleans. Everyone tried to stop me, dissuade me, get me to slow down. Everyone tried to get me to let my grief play out, but I wasn't having it. I was desperate for my fresh start and nothing was getting in my way.

When the train stopped in Atlanta, a young woman about my age got on and sat next to me. I wasn't in the mood for talking, but she struck up a conversation anyway. I learned her name was Gwen. She was twenty years old and a sophomore at Emory studying Business Administration. Black with a determined glint in her eyes, she was short and solid, with an open face and a warm laugh. She'd gotten on the train in jeans and a college sweatshirt, but after we pulled out, she slipped into the restroom and returned wearing a beautiful long-sleeve blue silk dress. "Daddy's picking me up at the station," she said, her eyes sparkling. "He's old-fashioned. He thinks we should dress up to travel. He likes seeing me in this. It was my mother's."

It was probably the affectionate way she spoke about her father that thawed my reserve. I allowed her to get me talking. By the time we reached New Orleans, she'd skillfully extracted my whole sad story.

"You need a job and Daddy's restaurant needs a waitress," she told me. "You're coming with me."

"Oh, no, I couldn't —"

"You don't know a soul in New Orleans and I'm not having you go to that shitty weekly hotel you booked a room in," she continued. "That place is a crime scene waiting to happen. You're moving in with my Auntie Ella. She has a spare bedroom and likes the company."

Then she whipped out her phone and called her aunt and her father and that was that. I suppose I could have tried to stop her, but I didn't, which was just as well because Gwen is basically a bulldozer when she sets her mind to something.

She became the first person since my parents' deaths to pierce the veil of my supposed self-sufficiency. I ended up boarding with Auntie Ella for two years until I got a place of my own. I was a terrible waitress at first — truly awful — but I gradually got better. And Gwen became my closest friend. Even while she was back at Emory, we talked nearly every day.

That is, until Josh entered the picture. She liked him well enough at first — I mean, who doesn't? — but that changed when she found out about his family.

"You didn't tell me he's from *that* Dupre family," she told me.

"What do you mean?" I replied, honestly puzzled. I knew so little about Louisiana back then. Now I know enough to know how much I still don't know.

"His family's old money," she said. "Going back two centuries."

"Okay," I said, still not getting it.

"His ancestors owned a big cotton plantation," she continued, waiting for me to catch up.

It took me a few seconds. "You mean, his family had slaves."

"That's right." As she waited for me to respond, something in her shifted. It's like she was realizing something about me — something that saddened her.

She continued, her tone deliberate and patient. "His family is one of the richest in the state. They established their plantation in Boudreaux in the 1830s. For decades, until the end of the Civil War, his family enslaved hundreds of people."

I'll be completely honest with you and admit that until that moment, I'd never tried, not really, to consider slavery from Gwen's point of view. I'd never attempted to put myself in her shoes. Her ancestors came to this country in chains. It's entirely possible that Josh's family brutalized and exploited *her* family.

As my friend's disappointed gaze settled over me, I realized she'd kept this reality — this part of herself — from me. She and her dad and her aunt and everyone in her family who had shown me such kindness had kept their pain, their anger, their sadness about slavery and its heritage from me because they knew that I, the northern white girl, wouldn't understand it the way they did.

"I'm sorry," I said, meaning it. "I didn't know."

"I know," she said sadly.

"But…." I was unsure what to say but felt the need to defend my new boyfriend. "You know that's not who Josh is."

"Oh, I believe that."

"He can't help who his family is."

"I agree."

In that moment, as my friend gazed at me with disappointment, I felt ashamed, guilty, uncertain — you name it — but also resistant. "Josh is different," I continued. "He's a good guy. He cares about people."

"I can see that. But here's the thing. He can't escape who he is."

"But he's —"

"No, Callie," she said, her impatience breaking through. "He can't. He doesn't stand a chance. His life isn't his. His family has a plan for him. He has no choice but to play the role they've assigned him."

"But that's not —"

"That *is* how it works when you come from money and privilege. His family will do anything to maintain and preserve their power."

"He doesn't want —"

"No, Callie. What he wants doesn't matter. Not to his

family. There's literally nothing they won't do to get their way."

"But he's not in Boudreaux now. He's here in New Orleans, at Loyola."

"Just like his daddy and granddaddy before him, right?"

A flush rose to my cheeks.

"He's a legacy, right? Like you said — he didn't get into law school because of excellent grades and test scores."

My flush deepened. I'd told her about Josh partying his way through college so that she'd see how much he'd grown and matured in law school.

"After he gets his degree," Gwen continued, "he'll put in a couple of years at a big firm downtown. And eventually he'll get pulled back to Boudreaux."

I tried arguing. "It's not like that now. Things aren't set in stone. He doesn't want to live in Boudreaux. He loves New Orleans as much as I do."

She shook her head. "It doesn't matter how much he loves it here. He'll get yanked back home. If you're with him when that happens, he'll drag you with him. He'll end up working to perpetuate the wealth and privileges his family has unfairly enjoyed for two hundred years."

I didn't know how to reply to that, but on some deep level, I feared she was right.

The conversation proved a turning point for me and Gwen. We weren't as close after that. I think I resented her bringing up the painful truth about Josh's family and their ongoing privilege. Plus, I didn't like being lectured. It felt like our friendship had taken a back seat to her proving her point.

Still, she was the first person I called when I found out I

was pregnant, and she supported my decision to stay that way. When Josh and I got married at City Hall, she was there as my witness, despite her misgivings. Through it all, she did her best to hide her fears about what my marriage meant for me.

After graduating from Emory, she returned to New Orleans to run her daddy's restaurant. She's now working to expand it to other locations. A year ago she met a jazz musician named Frank and six months ago they got married.

After my accident, when it looked like I wasn't going to survive, she drove here right away and camped out at the hospital three nights in a row, talking to me nonstop even though I couldn't hear her. After I woke up, she came back and stayed for a long weekend to help me move into the house. She calls like clockwork every three days to check in.

I know what you're thinking. No, I'm not telling her what happened, at least not yet. If I told her, she'd jump into her car and drive here and bulldoze me into packing up and getting me and Ava the hell out of Boudreaux for good. As I said earlier, I'm not ready to do that.

Gwen saved me once before. I can't ask her to do it again.

This time around, if any saving needs to be done, the person doing it will be me.

CHAPTER 14

A dragonfly lands on my arm and with a jolt I realize I'm standing still as a statue on the bayou trail, leaning on my cane, staring into the distance, looking at exactly nothing.

I've done it again — fallen into my memories and allowed my mind to take me from the here and now.

Which may have been a blessing, given where I am. The sun is frying my skin. Sweat is pouring from me. The not-so-subtle aroma of swamp rot is filling my lungs.

I wait until the dragonfly zips away, then open the water bottle I got at the school and take a deep swig. Two big gulps later, I'm wishing the bottle was bigger.

Not everything in this moment feels uncomfortable or wrong. The solid smoothness of the cane in my hand feels good. Also — and this is something of a surprise — the heavy weight of the gun in my pants pocket is giving off welcome vibes of reassurance. I've never liked guns and don't know much about them. But after last night, I'm glad I have this one with me.

I remain still for another moment, unsure what to do. There's nothing requiring me to continue on this walk. I'm not far from the school. If I turn back, I can call Beth and have her pick me up.

Aside from the humming of insects, the swamp seems quiet. I'm alone out here. For reasons I don't quite get, that knowledge doesn't frighten me.

Why is that? Why am I not more afraid of the people who attacked me? I mean, what if they followed me? What if they're lurking behind a tree, waiting to lunge at me again? Why did I deliberately come to an isolated place all by myself? Am I behaving as stupidly as every idiot in every horror movie ever made?

You're not scared because you don't need to be scared, I hear myself answer. *The big one's injured, maybe even dead. His knife got him good.*

I blink back a rush of emotion, surprised to be realizing that. I've been keeping myself at a distance from what happened, giving myself space to breathe. Am I really ready to start examining what I've been through?

I wipe a tear away and realize something else: I referred to the first attacker as *the big one.*

Is that right? Had I noticed a size difference? Was the second attacker shorter?

I start walking again, though not back the way I came.

The knife guy was bigger, I confirm as my steps take me deeper into the park. Taller and broader. His voice was terrifying, malicious, cruel. He'd been eager to hurt me. If I hadn't whacked him on the head, if he hadn't fallen on his knife, I'd be dead. Of that I have zero doubt.

But the second guy? I don't have as clear a sense of him. Even so, I've picked up things. He was quiet, for one thing. Before I even knew he was there, he snuck up behind me and jabbed me with the needle. He was also patient. He waited for me to come back downstairs before going after me. Plus, he was careful and organized. After knocking me out, he got the big guy out of the kitchen and cleaned up the blood. He even returned the ugly glass vase to the living room.

I breathe in sharply. *The vase.* He'd known where to put it — but how? Did he know the house?

Perhaps but not necessarily, I realize. He could have watched me take the vase from the living room. It's possible that I showed him where it belongs.

My pace quickens, my steps becoming more confident. Thinking about the attack is helpful. I'm getting a better understanding of the scene of the crime. I'm gaining insight into my two attackers.

The big guy is likely out of commission, at least for now. Does that mean the smaller guy is less likely to go after me alone?

And does that explain why I'm not more frightened right now? Is my subconscious ahead of me in figuring this out?

A weight lifts. My decisions this morning are starting to seem less stupid.

The trail curves ahead. As I round the bend, I let out a gasp.

I've reached the edge of a clearing, a field of barren dirt. And in the center stands a tree unlike any I've ever seen.

The thing is huge — easily the biggest I've come across in the park. As wide as it is tall, I can barely make out the whole of it. It seems impossibly old. From a base of thick, gnarled roots, a massive trunk rises up to support a tangle of branches that extend over most of the clearing.

As I move under its canopy, the air cools and I realize the ground isn't barren but instead is covered with a soft moss.

Suddenly I'm very glad I decided to come here. Alice was right — this tree is special. It possesses a power. It hums with energy.

As I limp closer, I spot knobby bumps on the tree's trunk.

But wait, the bumps aren't bumps.

They're *shoes,* nailed to the tree.

What the …?

I count at least a dozen pairs as I circle the trunk, all pointing upward, like the folks wearing them are walking up the tree into the sky. Boots, pumps, ballet slippers, men's dress shoes, sneakers.… Most look like they've been here for years, their colors faded, some even covered in moss.

Alice said the tree is creepy, but I'm sensing instead a spiritual purpose. The shoes are nailed to the tree for a reason. Perhaps they're meant to help earthbound souls who've lost their way. Maybe the tree is here to help them find heaven.

Poetic nonsense, my inner voice says, though without much conviction, because it too feels the power of this place.

The shoes nailed to the tree have stories to tell. The ballet slippers, for instance — what do they say about the young woman who once wore them? Was hers a tragic tale of a life cut short? Was she troubled and beautiful, defiant and reckless? Did she find a consoling joy in dance? Did her family bring her shoes here to help her find the peace that eluded her in life?

That's when I notice, at the far edge of the clearing, a

jarring slash of bright yellow. I inhale sharply when I realize it's crime-scene tape circling a small tree.

A shiver goes through me. That must be where the teacher, Susan's husband Rory, killed himself. Josh said it happened in the park near a walking trail. This part of the park is near the school. It makes sense that it happened here.

I hobble over for a better look. I can make out stains of dark red on the tree's trunk. Is that the poor man's blood?

I can almost visualize his final moments. Walking from the school along the same trail that brought me here. Sitting down against the tree. Putting the rifle in his mouth.

The last thing he would have seen before pulling the trigger was the big oak tree. Perhaps he chose this spot because he understood what the tree represents. Perhaps he feared he'd need the tree to help him find peace in the afterlife.

And perhaps, I say to myself as the morbid thoughts keep flowing, I need to stop dawdling and get a move on. My goal was to find the tree. Mission accomplished. I have a long, hot walk ahead of me to get home.

More importantly, I need to focus on what's going on with *me*. I need to figure out what I'm going to do next. I need a plan and I need it now.

The sooner I get moving on that, the better.

CHAPTER 15

hree long hours later, with the sun high in the sky and me wilting in the oppressive heat, I finally finish my walk through the park. Between the heat and a couple of wrong turns on the trails, it's fair to say I'm completely wrung out, depleted, exhausted.

Still, I've made it. The park's main entrance is just ahead, and beyond that the parish road and my house on Sycamore Lane.

I'm parched. Close to overheated. The convenience store across the road beckons. My pace picks up as I scoot toward it, my hip deciding not to complain too much.

My eagerness about the Boudreaux Quickie Mart doesn't mean it's special, because it's not. It's pretty much like every other roadside convenience store you've ever been in, with gas pumps out front and the usual retail items inside.

I'm at the door when a woman bursts out and barrels past me, almost a blur as she races to the passenger door of a pickup truck and jumps in. Barely a second later, the truck roars off.

I'm about to wonder why she's in such a hurry when cold air from inside hits my skin and all thinking comes to a halts. *Dear God, air conditioning.*

Hurrying inside, I gasp with relief as coolness washes over me.

"Lord, girl, you are a mess," a familiar voice says as I stand there in a daze.

Alice is behind the counter, grinning at me. She's about my age, Black and pretty, with a close-cropped afro and a quick smile. Today she's wearing a "Fight the Power" t-shirt, oversize gold hoop earrings, and a playful expression.

"Love your earrings," I say.

She tilts her head from side to side to let me see them better, then laughs. "For my glamorous life."

"Guess where I just was."

Her eyes widen. "The creepy old tree? You actually found it?"

"I did."

"Just now?"

"Just now."

"I will never understand you," she says with another laugh. "You are *weird.*"

I laugh with her, enjoying my first moment of lightness since dinner last night. The way she says *weird* sounds like a compliment. Besides, she's probably right. I am a bit weird. Is that a bad thing?

I head to the back where the refrigerated drinks are, open the door, and stick my head in.

"Heaven," I say loudly enough for her to hear.

She laughs. After five long seconds, I remove my head,

grab a water bottle and a sports drink, and return to the counter.

"It's actually rather impressive," I tell her as she rings me up.

"The tree?"

"Yeah. And all those shoes."

She blinks. "Shoes?"

"Nailed to the tree."

She frowns. "I don't remember shoes."

"A good dozen pairs."

"You're saying *shoes* are *nailed* to the tree?"

"Pointing up. Like the people wearing them are walking to heaven."

Her eyes widen. "And you don't think that's creepy?"

"Well...."

She shrugs. "Explains why Grammy took me. She wanted me to get closer — 'lay your lands on it,' she said — but I wasn't having it. It's years since I was there."

"If you ever want to go back, I know the way."

"Thank you very much, but hell no." She gestures to my cane. "How's the hip?"

"Holding up pretty well."

"Good. But I want you to listen to me. I don't like you out in this heat. Louisiana weather is not your friend. Before you know it, it'll sneak up on you and *wham*, you're out."

I tense — her words have struck a nerve — but she doesn't notice.

"Heat stroke," she continues. "You gotta be careful."

I crack open my sports drink and take a big, glorious swig. "God, I needed this."

Her attention is caught by something on the counter. "Damn, she forgot this."

"What?" I say, not following.

She picks up a package of gauze bandages. "She ran out so fast, I didn't even notice."

"You mean the woman who pushed past me when I got here?"

"Tearing out like a banshee? Yeah, that one."

"Seemed in a rush."

Alice is still frowning. "Something off about that one."

"How so?" I reply, starting to get interested. I hadn't caught much about the woman beyond that she was slim and white, with a head of thick, curly brown hair, dressed in cut-off jeans and an oversize t-shirt.

"Sometimes she's, I don't know, flashy."

"Flashy?"

"Trashy flashy."

I know what she means but want to be sure. "Like how?"

"Makeup, hair, clothes — way too much. I mean, who's she trying to impress?"

"And the other times?"

"It's like she doesn't want to be seen. In and out, barely a word."

"Like today?"

"Right." She looks at the package of bandages in her hand. "She's gonna miss this."

"Why do you say that?"

"She loaded up on bandages, ointment, a lot of it."

"Someone got hurt?"

"Her boyfriend, she said."

"What happened?"

"He cut himself."

A jolt goes through me. "How'd he do it?"

"Didn't say." She shakes her head. "I told her to take him to the hospital, but she said they can't afford it."

Or maybe they can't afford the *attention,* I'm suddenly thinking. Maybe they can't afford folks finding out he *stabbed himself in my kitchen with his own knife.*

I try to keep my voice normal. "Do I know her and her boyfriend?"

"Nah, they're new here — only seen them around the past few months."

"Try me. What are their names?"

Her brow furrows. "Sorry. Though I've seen him working the door at Lola's."

Lola's — the rough strip club across the parish line.

Alice lowers her voice and leans closer, even though we're the only ones in the store. "I think she works there, too."

"At Lola's?"

"As a dancer." From her tone, I can't tell if she approves or not. Am I sensing respect? Concern? Jealousy? Maybe all of the above?

Her eyes widen. "Wait, I do know her name. He was in here one time and she was out getting gas and he opened the door and called her."

My pulse quickens. "So what's her name?"

"Tiffany," she says with a vigorous nod. "He called her *Tiffany.*"

CHAPTER 16

ater that afternoon, as I stand on the front porch of my house and watch Beth drive off after a full day of helping me, the odd confidence that's carried me through my tumultuous day begins to melt away. The sun is fading fast. The woods surrounding the house, once so nestling and protective, now seem to be hiding something. For the first time since moving in, I'm aware of how quiet and isolated Sycamore Lane is.

I didn't have danger on my mind when I got home from my long walk through the park. I felt energized, excited even, as I considered the puzzle of the woman at the convenience store, the woman with the same name as the woman in Josh's phone, the woman who apparently was dating a man who'd just cut himself badly enough to require a bunch of bandages.

Was Alice right about the injured guy working the door at Lola's and dating Tiffany? Did he hurt himself by falling on his knife in my kitchen? Could the second attacker be Tiffany rather than a man?

Another unsettling question: Could Tiffany be the "Tiff" in Josh's phone? Could she be the one he's secretly dating?

I have no idea what the actual deal is with any of this. For each and every one of my questions, the correct answer is most likely *stop being so foolish*. In all likelihood, what I'm doing right now is grabbing random scraps of information that have no meaning and cramming them into a puzzle of my own devising — trying to turn nothing into something to help me feel better about what I'm going through.

Still, I can't shake the sense that I'm onto something. Even if I'm wrong about most of it, it's possible I'm right about part of it. Tiffany could be the woman Josh was texting a few months back. Boudreaux's a small place and from what little I saw of her as she ran past me, she was attractive.

But the rest? I should accept that I'm most likely dead wrong. At the end of the day, all I really know is that a man cut himself. That's it.

Convenience store speculations aside, my long, hot walk through the park had ended up being productive. I arrived home with a to-do plan — a response to last night's attack — that seems practical and achievable, a plan I can implement without anyone's help, including Beth's. I have no worries about her willingness to lend a hand, but bringing her into my mess doesn't feel right.

Besides, it's too late to ask her now, my inner critic points out as I watch her taillights vanish behind a row of trees. *She's gone for the day. You and Ava are stuck here alone.*

Despite the lingering heat, a shiver runs through me. I really hate my inner critic sometimes. A few seconds ago, everything seemed under control. But now, with a swiftness that startles me, every shadow is a menace, every sound a warning, every flutter of movement an imminent attack. The doubts about my decision-making that I've been dealing with all day — worried whispers scurrying through my head, fretting and simmering, poking and occasionally jabbing — explode with newfound force.

I hurry inside and shut the door, heart thumping. *You've been incredibly foolish today*, my inner critic continues. *You say you want to protect Ava, but what you're doing is endangering her even more. You need help. You can't do this alone.*

To which another voice responds, just as firmly, *You had no choice this morning and you have no choice now.*

Total crock, my inner critic shoots back.

Not at all, my other voice responds. *The instant you tell them what happened, they'll flip it around and make it about* you. *They'll question your judgment, decide you can't be trusted to take care of your daughter, call you an unfit parent. For better or worse, you have to do this on your own.*

The lock slides into the bolt with a reassuring *thunk*. I walk through the house to the sliding doors that lead to the back deck and latch them tight, then head through the kitchen into the garage. After making sure the garage doors are locked, I search the space thoroughly, even checking inside my car trunk to make sure no one's hiding inside.

Back in the kitchen, I listen for Ava and catch the faint sound of her singing to herself upstairs. Satisfied, I begin a search of the entire downstairs, going room by room, checking inside every closet and behind every door, grateful the house has no basement. I then go to every window on the ground floor and make sure each one is locked tight.

Finally, I turn on the alarm system, relief flowing through me when the green light goes on.

I head upstairs and peek into Ava's room, smiling at the sight of her playing happily with her stuffed bear, then check every room, every closet, and every window on the floor.

Finally, my tension eases. No one's hiding in this house. The only people here are Ava and me.

I pop my head into her bedroom. "Dinner time, sweetie. You hungry?"

"Starving!" she yells, then rushes past me.

With a smile, I follow her downstairs. Dinner tonight is leftovers — chicken, apples, and cheese slices for Ava, chicken and salad for me. After helping her with her homework, we return upstairs for her bath.

Then, just like we do every night, I climb into bed with her and read her to sleep.

For a long while after she falls into slumber, I remain with her, listening to her quiet breathing, hoping against hope that what I'm doing for us is right.

I remember I promised Susan I'd call her, so I text Josh. "Hey, can you send me Susan's number? How is she doing?"

A minute later, he texts back her number and adds, "Her sister got in this afternoon. She's in good hands."

I breathe a sigh of relief and resolve to call her in the morning.

Josh texts again. "How was the park?"

"Hot hot hot," I reply, "but the walk was good."

I don't mention the shoe tree or the spot where Susan's husband killed himself. Instead, I tell him about the upcoming school events I volunteered for.

"Sounds great," he texts. "Remember, lunch at Mama's on Saturday."

"Can't wait," I text back along with an emoji of a smiley face with a Pinocchio nose.

He puts a "ha ha" on my text and that's that.

Finally, when I can delay no longer, I slip from the bed and tackle the final pieces of the plan I put together while on the long walk back through the park. I head downstairs and check the doors, windows, and alarm one more time — all still good. Then I grab one of the wingback chairs in the living room. With difficulty, I drag it up the stairs, one step at a time, pausing frequently to make sure I don't stress out my hip. After reaching the top, I pull the chair into Ava's room, taking care to be as quiet as possible.

In my bedroom, I retrieve the duffel bag I've already packed with the items I've already decided I need to have with me. From the top shelf in my closet, I take Susan's gun from its hiding place under a stack of towels and stuff it in the duffel bag, making sure the safety latch (something I watched a video for online) is on.

After a final bathroom trip, I slip into Ava's room and close the door behind me.

I review my preparations to make sure I'm good. Aside from my daughter's whisper-soft breathing, the room is quiet. I pull the wingback chair to the door and jam it under the handle.

I set the duffel bag on the floor next to me and slip into bed with my daughter.

Flat on my back, head propped up by a pillow, senses on alert, I settle in for a long night.

At some point, I reach into the duffel bag and pull out a book. At some later point, still holding the book, I fall asleep.

Hours later, I'm awakened by the muffled sound of my

phone alarm in the duffel bag. I reach for the phone and turn it off.

It's seven. Ava will wake up at seven-fifteen. Beth will arrive at about seven-thirty.

I've survived the night. A new day has begun.

Emotion surges through me — relief and gratitude we're okay, along with a sense of completion for coming up with a plan and seeing it through.

Ava stirs next to me. She'll wake up soon. I slip from the bed and drag the chair to the corner near the window. I step back to look at it — is it positioned right? — then nudge it closer to the wall.

The chair actually looks pretty good in that spot. I should have brought it up sooner. Home improvement inspired by home invasion — go figure.

After grabbing my cane and slipping my phone into my pocket, I pick up the duffel bag and cautiously open the bedroom door.

The hall is silent. I limp to my bedroom and am getting ready to hoist the duffel bag onto the top shelf of my closet when I pause. Is the duffel bag the right place for Susan's gun?

I stand there a moment, trying to decide. If I had a safe, I could put the gun there, but I don't. Nor do I have a cabinet or drawer that locks.

The duffel bag is as good a place as any. Ava can't reach the top shelf. My plan is fine.

Still, for some reason, I don't want it there. I don't *trust* it there.

Bring the gun with you, my inner voice says. *Put it in your handbag. You never know — you might need it.*

I tense. The gun makes me nervous. Having it with me is the last thing I want.

Still, better safe than sorry. I don't want to be taken by surprise again. For my sake and Ava's, I have to defend myself. I have to be prepared.

I'll be careful. I don't like people carrying guns everywhere. I've always thought of those people as dangerous idiots. Now I'm one of them.

It's just a temporary thing, I tell myself. Someone's after me and I have no idea why.

Until I figure that out, I have to be ready for the next attack.

CHAPTER 17

An hour later, I'm once again in the passenger seat of Beth's car, heading to school with her and Ava. Unlike yesterday, today's drive isn't spur-of-the-moment. It was planned days ago. I have a doctor's appointment this morning and Beth's my ride.

After dropping Ava at school, Beth and I aim for downtown Boudreaux.

Beth glances over. "I noticed a chair missing in the living room."

I have my answer ready. "I moved it upstairs to Ava's room."

"Oh, how come?"

"My hip's been getting cranky about me spending all my time on the floor or the bed," I say, pleased to hear the lie roll out smoothly. "Having a chair up there to sit on is going to help."

The reason makes sense, despite the fact that my hip hasn't been complaining about the floor or the bed at all.

"Speaking of," Beth says, "how are you holding up after your big walk yesterday?"

"So far so good. Generally speaking, the walking is coming along well. The limp is lessening. It's the other stuff that's still bugging me."

"Stuff like?"

"Walking down steps. Getting down on my knees. Driving."

Beth gives me a sympathetic look. "It still hurts to press down on the pedal?"

"Yep." My mind goes to my car sitting neglected in the garage, waiting for me to get behind the wheel again. "I'll be talking to the doc about it. Maybe there's a new exercise I can do."

"About your doctor," she says. "What's he like?"

"Dr. Franklin? He's pretty good, I think. Why do you ask?"

She shrugs. "It seems like he's everybody's doctor around here."

"He's been fine. I mean, normally I'd prefer a woman, if you know what I mean."

"Totally."

"But he's good. He was really helpful dealing with all the specialists after the accident."

"I see."

"You want me to introduce you?"

"Oh, no," she says immediately. "I still have my doctor in Greensburg. I was just curious if you've had any issues."

Something about the way she says it makes me ask, "Issues like what?"

She frowns, as if disappointed in herself for bringing it

up. "I shouldn't be saying anything. It's just — well, I hear things."

"Like what?"

She sighs. "At the diner, some customers don't realize how much their voices carry. The other night a woman was complaining about him."

"What was she saying?"

"She said he couldn't be trusted."

I frown. "Why? About what?"

"Not sure, but it sounded like he was indiscreet about a medical thing?"

"Who was she?"

"I'd never seen her before." She glances over and blushes. "I'm sorry, I shouldn't have said anything."

Damn right, I nearly say out loud. When giving voice to accusations, you've got to bring the evidence.

A few minutes later, we reach downtown Boudreaux. There's not much to the town center — three blocks of local businesses, well-maintained with a small-town vibe. They keep it looking nice to appeal to tourists. Most of the businesses won't open until ten or eleven. The street is quiet.

Beth pulls into a parking spot in front of Dr. Franklin's office, a two-story red brick building. "What time do you want me to pick you up?"

I consider for a moment. "Well, I'd like to get in a walk around downtown after I'm done, before it gets too hot. Also, I need to go to the library."

She perks up. "The library? In the mood for a good book?"

"I actually read a bit last night before going to sleep, for the first time since the accident. I'd like to get back to that. How about we meet at eleven in front of the library?"

"Got it."

I clamber out into another muggy morning, then make my way into Dr. Franklin's office. I'm early, but the assistant ushers me right away into an exam room and Dr. Franklin joins a moment later. He's a grandfatherly man in his late sixties, white and plump, with shock-white hair[a shock of white hair?] and a red face that looks like he spends too much time in the sun. He's been Boudreaux's main doctor for decades.

"Callie," he says with a friendly smile. "How are you feeling today?"

"Good, thanks."

"Glad to hear. You're certainly looking well. Is that sun I see on your cheeks?"

"Sunburn, actually. I went on a long walk yesterday."

"A walk?" he repeats, pleased. "That's good. Where?"

"On the trails in the park."

"Good, good. Exercise is important for healing."

He opens a file on his desk, quickly reviews my scans and charts, then turns back to me.

"So tell me. IIow is your hip?"

"On the right track, I think. My walks are lasting longer and the pain is going down."

"Still the occasional jolt of pain?"

"Yes, when I do something my hip doesn't want me to."

"Still limping?"

"Yes, but less so."

"Still making good use of the cane?"

"That's right."

He makes a note. "Still not driving, correct?"

"That's right." I extend my leg and move my ankle

slowly. "I still feel pain when I try to press down on the pedal."

Another note. "No change there, then."

"No, and I'll tell you, I'm not happy about that. I want to be able to drive again. How much longer before I can?"

He gives me a patient smile. "It will come, Callie. In time. I have every confidence."

"Yes, but when?"

"When your body is ready for it to happen."

I sigh. "You're saying I need to be patient."

"Yes, I'm saying exactly that. Now what about stairs?"

"Still hurting when I go down, but maybe less?"

He jots another note. "Let's go out into the hallway. I'd like to see how you're walking."

We leave the exam room and I walk from one end of the hallway to the other a few times while he watches.

"Good, good," he says, then ushers me back into the exam room. "The limp is much less noticeable than it was two weeks ago."

I carefully sit down again. "I've noticed the same."

He writes more notes, then says, "I have to say, I'm very pleased with your progress. Your recovery is coming along well."

I like hearing that even though I want it all to happen faster. "You're just saying that because patience isn't one of my virtues."

He chuckles. "I don't often have to say this to my patients, but apparently I need to ask it of you. I don't want you overdoing it. Tell me about your rehab sessions."

"Oh, they're fine. Every Monday morning they kick my you-know-what, but in a good way."

"When it comes to rehabilitation, they're the experts.

What are they telling you?"

"That I'm doing well," I admit. "That I'm making progress."

"And your takeaway from their assessment is…?"

I sigh. "That I'm doing pretty well, all things considered."

"Good. It's important to allow yourself to accept that. Consistent, steady, gradual progress — that's the goal here."

"Got it."

"You're scheduled for your next hip scan — when?"

"In two weeks."

"Good, good." He makes another note, then looks back at me. "Now, let's talk about your head."

With the easy part of the appointment over, I tense up.

"Are you still having the headaches?"

"No, those have mostly gone away."

"Excellent. Anything new on the memory front?"

"Sorry, no. I still don't remember the accident or anything about that day."

"There's no need to apologize." He takes a deep breath. "Frankly, Callie, I will be surprised if you ever remember what happened that day. Traumatic events are often best forgotten."

He picks up a small flashlight. I know what he wants to do, so I lean forward and let him shine the light into my eyes.

"Any changes in vision, hearing, smell, taste, touch?"

"All of that seems fine."

"Good, good." He sits back and takes more notes. "Any changes in sleep patterns?"

"No."

"How many hours a night are you sleeping? Are you

sleeping well?"

Not the past two nights, I don't say. "I've been getting seven hours on average, which is definitely more than I used to get."

"Sleep is important for healing. If you can, I'd like you to try for eight or even nine."

"Okay. I'll do that."

"About your general mental processes. In our past visits, you mentioned sometimes feeling 'fuzzy' or 'hazy.' Where are we on that front?"

I take a moment to make sure I say this right. "Generally, I feel I'm improving. There's less haze, less fog. I'm thinking more clearly this week than I was even last week."

"How close to one hundred percent are we?"

"Ninety, ninety-five percent?"

"Good, good." More notes. "Any changes in behavior?"

"Well, I mentioned this the last time. I'm less inclined to hold back now. If I'm thinking something, I'm more likely to say it."

And do it, I almost say.

"Behavioral changes are not uncommon after the type of trauma you experienced. Nothing you're saying seems concerning to me at this point. Is there something in particular you're worried about?"

You mean, like all the impulsive things I can't stop myself from doing? Like sneaking onto my ex-husband's phone? Like not telling anyone about being attacked in my own house? Like confronting a distraught woman who was holding a gun? Like taking the gun from her and bringing it home? Like turning my daughter's bedroom into a fortress? Like bringing a concealed weapon to your office?

I almost tell him everything, but at the last second I can't.

It's not that I don't trust him — I do trust him, I guess, despite what Beth's customer said about him being indiscreet — but I find myself holding back.

"Well, I don't want to be rude to someone," I finally say. "I guess that's my concern — something unkind might slip out."

He smiles. "You're afraid you'll speak your mind?"

"I guess so."

"That concern sounds very normal to me."

"So I shouldn't be worried?"

"About that, no." He flips to a new page. "Just a few more questions. Any perceptual changes, or changes in outlook?"

I take a second before responding. It's an interesting question. He wants to know if I'm feeling anxious, depressed, paranoid, scared — things like that.

Well, I'm definitely perceiving my world as more dangerous than I was two days ago, and I'm definitely more anxious and scared as a result.

"No," I say.

"You're sure? I sense you might have a concern?"

Once again, I almost tell him — the opening he's given me is a mile wide. "No, everything seems fine."

"You mentioned during your last visit that Josh hired someone to help around the house. How's that working out?"

"Oh, Beth? She's actually pretty great." I pause for a moment. "I mean, I wasn't happy about needing the help. I've always relied on myself."

"But now?"

I sigh. "Okay, I get what you want me to say. Yes, she's a godsend and I'm glad to have her help. There, I said it."

He smiles. "It's okay to allow others to lend a hand every now and then, Callie."

"I agree. Lesson learned."

"You've been through a very difficult event. I'm pleased to see you recovering so well."

"I'm glad, too."

"And Ava? How is she?"

At the mention of my daughter, my spirits lift. "She's doing great. She's enjoying first grade at Briarton."

Dr. Franklin smiles. "I'm glad to hear that. She's scheduled for a checkup soon, I believe?"

"That's right. In a few weeks."

"Good, good." He sets down his pen. "Is there anything you want from me today? Any questions or concerns? I'm here for you, Callie."

He seems so kindly sitting there, so attentive, so ready to help. He's been the town doctor in Boudreaux since forever, according to Josh. He has the doctor-patient routine down pat. Not only that, he's been thorough with me. The questions he's asked are the same ones the various specialists asked when I was in the hospital.

The man is good at his job, in other words, and seems genuine and sincere. So why am I holding back? Why am I not telling him about the attack? Why am I not asking him to look for a needle mark on my neck?

Because you can't trust him, my inner voice whispers.

Ridiculous, I push back. *Stop with the paranoia.*

Remember where you are, my inner voice continues. *Enemy territory. At the end of the day, he'll side with them, not you.*

I place a smile on my face and rise to my feet. "No concerns right now, Doctor. Thank you so much for seeing me today."

CHAPTER 18

The Boudreaux Parish Library is in a plain wooden building a couple blocks from Dr. Franklin's office, one block off the main strip. The sky above me is cloudless, the morning air muggy and still.

I've been to the library dozens of times, mostly with Ava, so when I get inside I head right to the reference desk.

A woman with "Vivian" on her nametag looks up from her computer. She's Asian and in her thirties, with pleasant features and a warm manner. "Good morning. How can I help you?"

"Good morning." I take a breath to quell my sudden nervousness. "I'm doing research about Briarton Academy and I'd like to look at the school's yearbooks."

"Oh, that's easy enough," she says as she stands up. "Come with me."

She leads me to the back of the library. "We keep material about Boudreaux on the two shelves here." She gestures to a shelf filled with a long row of Briarton Academy yearbooks. "Do you know which year or years you're looking for?"

"Well, not exactly." In the headmaster's office yesterday, I'd only gotten a quick look at the shelf with the missing yearbook. Assuming the headmaster arranges his yearbooks chronologically, it's likely the missing one is from about fifteen years ago. "I'm looking at a range — 2005 through 2010."

"Here we go." She pulls the yearbooks from the shelf one by one, then frowns. "That's odd."

"What's odd?"

"The yearbook for 2008 isn't here." She runs her finger along the shelf to make sure it hasn't been put in the wrong place, her frown deepening when she doesn't find it. "The yearbooks are for reference only. They can't be checked out."

A tingle goes through me. Is this the same yearbook missing in the headmaster's office? Also, hadn't his secretary Sherry said that "Janice" is missing hers as well? Is Janice the school librarian at Briarton?

Are three copies of the same yearbook missing from three different locations?

"Maybe someone put it on the wrong shelf?" I offer.

She shrugs, clearly not satisfied. "That's probably what happened. Are you okay with these five yearbooks?"

"These will be great, thanks." As she leads me to a nearby table, I add, "Also, do you have old copies of the *Boudreaux Herald*?"

"We do, though the *Herald*'s website might have what you need."

"I checked the site already and the news archive doesn't go back far enough."

"I see," she says. "The paper copies are offsite in storage, but we do have microfilm copies here. Are you familiar with how the machine works?"

"My high school had a microfilm machine. We used it for research for term papers."

"If you'd like, I can help you find what you're looking for."

"Is the microfilm searchable? Can I look for a certain word?"

She shakes her head. "No, and unfortunately, the owner of the *Herald* isn't interested in digitizing them."

"Why's that?"

She shrugs. "No idea. You should ask her."

"Her?"

"Your former mother-in-law."

I blink, taken aback. I had no idea that Marian owns the *Herald*. And no idea that Vivian knows who I am.

I blush. *Of course she knows.* "I wasn't aware of Marian's ownership of the paper."

"She has a controlling interest." Vivian looks like she wants to say more but bites her tongue. "If you'd like, I can bring the film you want to the machine. What time period are you interested in?"

"Same time period. Maybe I can start with 2008?"

As she heads off, I sit down at the table and open the 2005 yearbook. I'm looking for the man Susan mentioned, the man named "Bracken." My Internet search yesterday afternoon had yielded no clues. There are a fair number of Brackens in the world, but none with any apparent connection to Boudreaux.

My inner critic pipes up. *Why are you doing this? Why do you care?*

Because I'm curious, I reply.

My inner critic isn't buying it. *Why? Because Susan said something cryptic? She's a grief-stricken woman. You can't rely on what she says right now.*

Well, I still want to know.

I can almost hear my inner voice snort. *You're doing this to avoid your own issues — to distract you from the scary situation you're in.*

Anxiety churns within me. My inner voice is right about that. I'm in a frightening nightmare and instead of dealing with it, I'm digging into a minor local mystery — a mystery that has zero to do with anything going on right now.

Still, my other voice says, trying to calm me down, *you're here, so you might as well keep going.*

With a sigh, I flip through the yearbook pages, looking for anyone named Bracken. The yearbook is nicely done — better than the one my high school had. Every kid has a photo and so does every teacher. So do all the sports teams and school clubs. They even have a photo for the "Critter Club," a group of older students and teachers who patrol the grounds for alligators and the like.

There's no one named Bracken in the 2005 yearbook. I flip through 2006 and 2007 and strike out as well. I'm about to start on 2009 when Vivian comes over.

"I pulled the film for the *Herald* from 2008," she says. "Anytime you're ready."

I get up from my chair and limp over to the microfilm machine. She reminds me how to use the knobs to move the newspaper pages up and down and backward and forward through different editions.

"The *Herald* published weekly back then," she says. "Usually about twenty-four pages per issue."

"Sounds like I'm in for a lot of looking."

I can tell she's curious about what I'm after, but she's professional enough not to intrude on my privacy. "If there's anything I can help with, let me know."

"Thanks."

She leaves me and I begin scrolling, looking for anything related to either Bracken or the school. The *Herald*'s coverage isn't exactly hard-hitting. There are a lot of upbeat pieces about local tourist attractions and puff profiles of local businesses that coincidentally happen to be the paper's main advertisers.

But the *Herald* also covers a fair amount of local crime, and in a story from June 2008, I strike gold:

Arrest for Briarton Fire

Boudreaux police have arrested a local man for setting a fire that damaged a storage building on the Briarton Academy campus on the night of June 5.

John Edward Bracken, 42, a former handyman at Briarton, has been charged with arson and is being held at Boudreaux Parish jail.

Boudreaux Parish Sheriff Hoyt Denton told the Herald that Bracken "was burning garbage in a garbage bin next to the building and the fire got out of control. The building has been there a long time and now it's heavily damaged. In matters such as this, the law is clear. There must be consequences."

Briarton Academy headmaster Devlin Chatterton issued a brief statement. "I want to thank Sheriff

Denton for his quick and thorough investigation. The Briarton community is eager to move forward from this unfortunate incident."

Chatterton confirmed to the Herald that Bracken was employed as a handyman at Briarton until shortly before the incident. "All I can say about that is, at the time of the fire, he was no longer working at Briarton."

That's all there is. I look through the rest of the 2008 archive hoping to find out what happened next, but the *Herald* didn't run any follow-up stories.

I sit there for a moment, poking at what I've learned. Why is there nothing more? What happened after Bracken was arrested? Did the case go to trial? Did he plead guilty? Was he convicted? Did he serve time? Is he still in Boudreaux?

I think back to what Susan said yesterday about the headmaster covering up the truth about Bracken. Is it possible the man was innocent? Did someone else start the fire?

To find out more, I'll need to go to my source. I get up from the table, return the yearbooks to their shelf, thank Vivian, and leave the library. Once outside, I pull out my phone and dial Susan.

A groggy voice picks up. "Hello?"

"Susan, it's Callie. We met yesterday at the school."

"Callie?" She lets out a small groan, like she's lying down and is moving into an upright position. "How can I help you?"

"Would it be okay if I swing by your place in a little while? There's something I'm hoping we can talk about."

There's a long pause. "Okay," she finally says. "Do you know the address? I'm at 17 Clementine."

"In the neighborhood near downtown?"

"That's right."

I'd been planning to call Beth and ask her to drive me, but I realize I don't need to. Susan's house is close enough that I can walk.

"Thanks, Susan. Is it okay if I head over now? I can be there in fifteen minutes."

"Yes, that's fine."

"Thank you, Susan. I really appreciate it. See you in a bit."

CHAPTER 19

Thirteen minutes later, I'm almost there. The walk from downtown has taken me down a few roads and past a creek and into a neighborhood I've driven through a few times but don't know too well. The homes are mostly single-story ranch-style dwellings with two-car garages, most dating to the years after World War II. Though many are in good shape, others are rundown and neglected.

The street sign for Clementine is ahead and thank goodness for that. Though the walk was short, the muggy morning air has lacquered me with sweat.

Two minutes later, I'm there. The house is one of the nicer ones on the block, painted a crisp white with dark blue trim, the green lawn recently mowed, the flower bed well-tended. Susan and her husband have taken good care of the place. Clearly they loved living here. This is — was — a happy home.

Emotion sneaks up on me. The pride of ownership on

display here reminds me of my childhood home in Connecticut, the home I couldn't bear to stay in after losing my parents, the home I abandoned the instant I could. The people who tried to stop me from selling it — my aunt and uncle, my friends, my neighbors — were worried I'd regret my decision. They tried to convince me that I'd one day be able to look past the pain and find comfort again within its modest walls. They worried that without my home as a foundation, I'd be adrift, alone, rootless, a wanderer who didn't fit in anywhere.

Well, they'd been right about that. Grief propelled me to New Orleans, marriage dragged me to Boudreaux, and now my accident has left me damaged and stuck in a place I have no connection to.

As I knock on Susan's front door, I wonder what she'll decide to do with the house now that her husband is gone. Will she stay — or run away like I did?

There's a hint of movement through the front window and then the door opens and Susan is there, tired and pale, her eyes puffy and red, dressed in jean shorts and a wrinkled blue blouse. "Hello, Callie."

"Susan," I begin, realizing how wrong it is for me to be here. The poor woman just lost her husband, yet here I am intruding on her grief — and for what? To ask about a lie the headmaster supposedly told about a man who damaged a storage building fifteen years ago? I mean, seriously, who cares?

I clear my throat. "I wanted to check in and see how you're doing."

She stares at me for a few seconds, then opens the door wide. "Come in."

I step past her into a small foyer. After shutting the door, she leads me through the living room into the dining area next to the kitchen. "I've made coffee," she says, gesturing for me to take a seat at the table. "Would you like some?"

The aroma is tempting. "Only if it's not too much trouble."

She reaches into an overhead cabinet for mugs. "Cream? Sugar?"

"A bit of both, if that's okay."

As she gets the coffee ready, I ease into a seat at the oak dining table and take in my surroundings. The house has a cozy, autumnal vibe — the walls a warm mocha, the hardwood floors a rich golden brown, the living room furniture soft and over-sized. In the living room, an upright piano has family photos arranged on top. On the walls are a mixture of landscape portraits and music festival posters. The kitchen cabinets are painted a creamy white and accented with a tiled orange-red-blue-green backsplash.

Susan brings in the mugs, sets them on the table, and takes a seat opposite me. Her reddish-brown hair looks good in this house. The colors work together. I wonder if she's aware of that.

I close my hands around the mug. "Thank you for letting me come by."

She picks up her coffee and takes a sip, her eyes not leaving me.

"Josh said your sister arrived yesterday."

"She'll be back in a little while. She went out to do some shopping."

"Were you able to sleep last night?"

"Thankfully. I needed the sleep. I know that."

"I'm glad you were able to get some."

She takes a deep breath. "About yesterday. I'm sorry I

frightened you. That was not my intent. I was not at my best."

"There's no need to apologize."

"I suppose you want to talk about the gun."

I blink, surprised. I hadn't been thinking about the gun at all. "Well," I reply, trying to figure out how to respond. "I'm totally fine talking about it if you'd like to talk about it, but that's not why I called."

Her brow furrows. "Then why did you call?"

"To offer my help. Anything you need, you let me know."

Her gaze doesn't falter. "And?"

No doubt about it — she's definitely sharper mentally today than she was yesterday.

"Well, I'd like talk more about the headmaster. About him covering up what happened with 'that man Bracken.'"

She doesn't reply and doesn't move. It's like she's trying to decide what my deal is.

I'm suddenly nervous. Have I upset her? Offended her?

Finally, she sets her mug down. "The problem with Devlin is — he's weak. It's a birth defect. The man was born without a spine."

I nod encouragingly, hoping she'll say more.

"Of course," she continues, "that's why Marian made him headmaster. She likes her puppets."

It's odd hearing my former mother-in-law so openly disparaged. But I get where Susan is coming from. For Marian, control is everything.

"I did a bit of research about Mr. Bracken," I tell her.

Her eyes flash and for a second she seems almost amused. "Oh, did you now?"

"I didn't find much. I mean, there isn't much online about

him at all. I learned he worked as a handyman at Briarton and was arrested for setting fire to a building in 2008."

"What year did you say? 2008?" She lets out a big sigh. "Hard to believe it's been that long. What else did you find?"

"Nothing, unfortunately. The *Herald* didn't run any stories about what happened after that."

"Well, they wouldn't have."

"Why not?"

"The *Herald* isn't in the bad-news business."

My pulse jumps. She knows something. "Bad news? What happened?"

"You really don't know, do you?"

"Sorry, no."

"You sure you want to know?"

"Yes, I'm sure."

"Bracken died in jail."

I breathe in. "Oh my."

"The sheriff put him in a cell with a violent criminal. The man murdered him. Beat him to death. Bashed his head against the wall, over and over and over, until he was dead."

Nausea fills me. "That's awful."

"Made for a big old fuss, at least for a while. State investigation, the works. There was talk of Hoyt resigning as sheriff. But then, like magic, it all just faded away. Hoyt got reelected and that was that."

"What do you mean, like magic?"

"You know exactly what I mean."

I'm pretty sure I do. "You mean … Marian stepped in?"

She shrugs. "She runs this parish. What she wants, she gets."

I have to admit — the accusation sounds paranoid, even

to my jaded ears. I'm about to gently push back when she adds, "I don't have any evidence, of course, aside from what happened afterward."

"What happened afterward?"

"The state investigation went nowhere after Marian made a couple of calls to Baton Rouge, Hoyt stayed on as sheriff with Marian's full support, and the *Herald* didn't print a word about it. Soon enough everyone forgot the tragic event ever occurred."

I'm still not convinced. "How do you know Marian made calls?"

"She told the ladies at the Cotillion committee."

I must have looked skeptical because Susan added, "Marian doesn't hide her power, Callie. She wants everyone to know who's in charge."

"You're saying she did all that to protect the sheriff?"

Susan shakes her head. "Of course not. You need to ask the right question."

I frown. "What's the right question?"

"In Boudreaux, the right question is always: What's in it for Marian?"

I almost sigh. She sounds like a broken record.

"Okay," I say. "Why did she want Bracken arrested?"

"Because," she says with a dramatic pause, "he saw who started the fire."

"Who did he see?"

"Marian."

"No way," I say immediately. I mean, come on. Her fixation is going too far. "Why would she do that? Set fire to a garbage bin? At the school? *Her*?"

"Now you need to ask the next question."

"All right," I say, deciding to humor her. "What's the next question?"

"What was Marian burning?"

The question is interesting. "What did the sheriff say Bracken burned?"

"He never did say."

"Then how do we know what was burned?"

"Because Devlin told Rory, years later."

Finally, we're circling back to the headmaster. "What did Devlin tell Rory?"

"A few years after Bracken died, Rory and I hosted a barbeque for the teachers and staff. It was here in the backyard, right before fall term." Her eyes fill with tears and she brushes them away. "Devlin got sloppy drunk — the man can't handle his liquor — but everything was fine until someone brought up Bracken."

"What happened then?"

"Folks were saying nice things about the poor man and Devlin was listening and got upset. He said what happened was water under the bridge, we had to move on, things like that. Then he stormed off. Rory followed him to make sure he was okay and found him crying in the woods."

"Crying?"

"He told Rory he had no choice — Marian forced him to lie."

I inhaled with surprise. "Lie about what?"

"Devlin was clearing out the storage building and found some old papers and told Marian about them. She came out to the school right away and had Devlin take her there and look through it with her."

"Look for what?"

"More papers."

"Papers about what?"

"Rory wasn't sure, except they related to the property before it became the school."

"What happened then?"

"Marian took the papers out to the garbage bin and burned them."

"So you're saying Devlin was with Marian when the garbage bin caught fire."

"Just as the fire in the bin got going, Bracken showed up and asked what the hell they were doing and tried to put out the fire, but it was too late — it had already spread to the building."

"Marian and Devlin decided to blame Bracken for the fire?"

"Devlin said he went along with it because he felt he had no choice. Marian told him Bracken would plead to a misdemeanor and serve a few days and leave Boudreaux and that would be that."

"But that's not what happened."

She shakes her head. "The sheriff put him in a cell with a violent criminal and got him murdered."

With a jolt, I realize what she's saying. "Wait. You think the sheriff did that *deliberately*?"

She looks at me like I'm hopelessly naive. "Of course."

"The sheriff wanted Bracken dead?"

"No. Marian did."

"You're saying *Marian* had the sheriff kill Bracken?"

"Honey, you've been exposed to more than your fair share of that woman. Don't tell me you don't believe her capable."

I don't know what I think about Marian being a murderer — I've never gone down that particular rabbit hole. But I do know I like evidence and I'm not hearing it.

"Why would Marian want Bracken dead?"

For the first time, Susan seems uncertain. "That, I don't know."

"I mean," I say, trying to keep my tone neutral, "if the fire happened the way Devlin said it did, then all that happened was Marian accidentally set fire to a building she owned. She might have an issue with insurance if she filed a claim, but that kind of thing isn't something you'd kill someone over."

Susan nods reluctantly. "You're not wrong about that."

"Then why would she want Bracken dead?"

She shrugs. "Just because we don't know the answer doesn't mean the answer isn't out there."

I try not to show my frustration but it must be apparent because she says, "I know I'm not making much sense. I'm sorry about that. I'm not my best right now."

"It's okay. What happened after Devlin told Rory all that?"

"Nothing." Susan takes a sip of her coffee. "Rory went to talk with Devlin the next day and Devlin looked at Rory like Rory was crazy. He denied saying anything."

"So with Devlin denying it and with no other proof...."

"Rory called a guy he went to high school with who's an investigator in the Attorney General's office in Baton Rouge and told him about it, and the guy said he'd look into it."

"Did he find anything?"

"We saw him a few months later at a class reunion and he said, 'Boudreaux's tighter than a virgin clam.' His words, not mine. The words stuck with me because they bugged me. I mean, aren't all clams virgins?" She stops short as her eyes fill with tears. "Rory laughed when I said that. He likes when I notice things like that."

She's about to cry again. I feel an urge to walk around the table and give her a hug. "Susan, I'm so sorry for your loss. I shouldn't be asking about all this and dredging up painful memories."

"No, Callie," she says, shaking her head. "You don't understand. I will always treasure that memory. The reason I remembered it just now is because you're here being nosy."

"Oh," I say, surprised.

"I'm glad you're here and I'm glad you're being nosy. Because I need your help."

"You do?"

"You're good at being nosy. I can see that about you. I want you to help find out what really happened to Rory."

Oh, geez.

She leans forward, her eyes shining. "Devlin's doing another coverup. I know it in my bones. I want you to find out why."

I'm weighing how to respond when we hear the rumble of a car outside.

"That's my sister," Susan says.

"I should get going." I rise to my feet. "I've kept you long enough."

"I'm serious about wanting your help."

"Which I'm happy to provide, any way I can." I check with myself to make sure I really want to do this, then continue. "One idea is, maybe I could help with the memorial service at the school — act as a liaison or a coordinator or something like that."

"I like that," she says immediately. "A buffer between me and that goddamn liar."

"Plus, helping with the memorial will give me a good reason to interact with the headmaster and spend more time at the school."

Susan's sister steps into the kitchen carrying bags of groceries.

"Tammy," Susan says, "this is Callie. She was married to Josh."

"Pleased to meet you," Tammy says as she sets the bags on the counter. She's a slightly older version of her sister, with the same features and hair. "I met Josh yesterday. Such a nice fellow."

"I'm here to help, too. Anything you need, don't hesitate to ask."

"Thank you."

Susan turns to me. "You said you need to get going?"

"I did."

"Let me see you out."

"Nice meeting you, Tammy."

"You, too."

At the front door, Susan pulls me in for a hug and squeezes tight. I can smell her perfume and sweat. "You're a good gal, Callie. I like you."

"Thank you." As the hug continues, I find myself wondering how long I should wait before extricating myself.

Finally she pulls back, takes hold of my shoulders, and looks me in the eye. "I want you to be careful."

"Careful about what?"

"Careful about *you*."

I try to keep my expression neutral. I know she's about to spout more Marian conspiracy nonsense and I'm just not buying it.

My face must be pretty bad at hiding things because she

says, "I know I sound like a crazy lady when it comes to Marian, but you have to believe me, I'm not."

"I know you're not, Susan."

"Marian Dupre is capable of anything." Her gaze intensifies. "You need to remember that."

CHAPTER 20

Two mornings later, I'm still thinking about what Susan said, still nowhere near to being on board with her nonsense about Marian being a murderer, but still unable to fully expel her paranoia from my mind.

I'm in my bathroom, fresh from the shower and wrapped in a towel, staring at myself in the mirror. Lunch with Marian is looming. I've just finished putting my hair up and now it's time for my face. Unfortunately, my usual quick-and-easy approach — a bit of mascara, a dash of lipstick — is insufficient for the occasion. To protect myself, I'll need to do more. Looking good, as defined by Marian, is an important layer of my defense, and it takes work.

From downstairs come the happy sounds of Josh and Ava playing. He got here early and they're having fun. I don't need to rush. With a sigh, I pick up the concealer and start dabbing the dark circles under my eyes.

Somewhat to my surprise, not much has happened since I

left Susan's house two days ago. No more attacks, no more home invasions, no more teachers killing themselves, no more grieving spouses, no more weird notes on my front door — nothing. I've continued my new habit of carefully searching the house each night before locking it tight and barricading myself in Ava's room. Susan's gun has found a semi-permanent home in my handbag. After emailing the headmaster to tell him I'd be helping Susan with the memorial, we'd settled on a service at the school on Monday afternoon. Susan and I have talked several times about what she wants for the memorial. From my own experiences with grief, I know it's good for her to be engaged and making decisions.

I set down the concealer and examine my handiwork. The darkness under my eyes is barely visible. I pick up the foundation and get going.

I've spent a lot of time weighing whether to confide in Josh and Gwen about the attack. My need to share is growing, like a water balloon about to burst. But telling them has downsides. Gwen would shift immediately into super-heroine mode and mount a rescue operation to extract me and Ava from Boudreaux. And that is *not* what I want, at least not yet.

And Josh.... Not only would he be upset and angry about the attack if he found out, he'd be worried about Ava staying here with me. When I insisted on her living with me when I left the hospital, he supported me, and I'm grateful for that. But I can tell he has doubts about my mental and physical health. If I tell him about the attack, he'll question my judgment. He'll wonder why I didn't tell him sooner. It's entirely possible he'll conclude I'm not ready to take care of Ava on my own.

For now, at least, I need to keep what happened to myself.

I examine my cheeks. The foundation's looking good — smoothly applied, not too thin, not too thick. I brush it with powder to set it, then start with the eyeliner.

Even with all my pondering, I still haven't come close to figuring out what the hell is going on. At least four different mysteries are swirling around me and I don't have a clue about any of them.

Top of mind is the attack. My list of questions is a mile long. Who are the intruders? How badly injured is the big one? Did the two of them break in to steal or were their motives darker? Was I a target of opportunity or was the attack premeditated? After the smaller one jabbed me with a knockout drug, why did they leave me and Ava alone? Why did they clean up before they left? Did they steal anything? Are they coming back?

I blink several times, then lean closer to the mirror. With the eyeliner done, it's time for eye shadow. I take a deep breath. This step is always the trickiest for me. If I don't put on enough, I might as well not bother. If I put on too much, I look hot-to-trot. I want slightly smoky, not a four-alarm fire.

Aside from the attack, the most disturbing part of all this is the possibility that Josh is somehow tied in. Why did someone leave a note on my front door with the passcode for his phone, just a few hours before the attack? If I was given the passcode so that I could get into his phone and snoop on him, then what was I expected to find? Did they want me to see the texts from Tiffany, or something else entirely?

Which brings me to Tiffany. Is the Tiffany who dashed past me at the convenience store also the "Tiff" in Josh's phone? Is she the woman Josh is dating and keeping quiet about? If so, then what's the deal with the man driving the pickup truck? Is Tiffany dating him as well, like Alice thinks? Are his injuries the result of falling on his knife in my kitchen? Could Tiffany be the second attacker?

I examine the eye shadow carefully. I know I'm engaging in a massive amount of speculation with exactly zero evidence, searching for patterns where none may exist, most likely as a way of coping with what's going on. It's human nature to do that. People choose to believe the dumbest things when they feel powerless or lost. I need to keep that in mind as I stumble my way through this mess.

Yes, the eye shadow is good. Time for mascara and lipstick. I'm not a fan of overthinking. It leads me down unproductive paths, like it's done with Susan. I get why she's angry at the headmaster and my gut tells me she's right about him lying about Bracken — his reaction when I brought him up was telling. The missing yearbooks from Bracken's year at the school are another puzzle. Perhaps there's a photo in it that someone doesn't want someone to see?

Even so, I'm not buying Susan's suspicion that the head-master is covering up the truth about Rory's death. Sometimes, out of the blue, people kill themselves. Sometimes, despite our best efforts, we never learn why. All I know for sure is that Susan is consumed by grief and not thinking clearly. She's looking for a target for her anger and she's found it in the headmaster.

Most of all, I warn myself as I give my face a careful review, I'm not going to let Susan's rantings and ravings about Marian gain a foothold in my head. I'm no fan of my former mother-in-law — okay, fine, I can't stand her — but I can't see her setting fire to a building, arranging to kill a witness, and running me down with her fancy car. Susan's wrong about all of that. Marian may be vain, controlling and manipulative, but she's no murderer.

You better hope not, my inner voice says.

I head into the bedroom and slip into the dress I've picked for today, taking care to keep the fabric from my face. It's a one-piece with cap sleeves and a knee-length skirt, made with a soft floral print of golden yellow with hints of white and orange. It has a faintly autumnal vibe, which is probably why I like it. It also happens to be a gift from Marian, which today is a big point in its favor.

Almost done. I put on the gold earrings my parents gave me for my sixteenth birthday, followed by the pearl necklace that Josh bought me after Ava was born.

After slipping into the black flats that are my substitute for heels until my hip gets better, I grab my cane and handbag and return to the bathroom for a final check.

You can do this, I tell the image in the mirror, trying to quell the anxiety running through me. *After everything you've just been through, lunch with Marian will be a walk in the park.*

CHAPTER 21

On the ride over, a silly thought comes. "Lunch with Marian" would make a great title for a gothic horror film. Instantly I can envision the whole thing. The movie poster with the title in big, jagged, scary letters. The ominous soundtrack — the tense thumping of a cello, the frantic screeches of a violin. The climactic scene on a windswept night, lightning slashing through the darkened mansion as Marian rushes down the stairs, knife in hand, crazed and murderous, screaming at the top of her lungs, "How dare you! He's mine! All mine!"

Next to me in the back seat, Ava tugs at my hand and I return to the here and now. Through the car window, an endless vista of swamp is flowing by in a blur of green and brackish brown. "What is it, sweetie?"

"When we get to Grandma's, I'm going to see the horses!"

"Yes, you are."

All morning, Ava's been bursting with excitement about the horses. "I'm going for a ride!"

"Yes, you are. Right after lunch."

"Can I go before lunch?"

"We'll see. We'll ask your grandmother when we get there."

I'm in the back with Ava because Beth's driving us and Josh is in the front passenger seat. When I'd come downstairs, I'd been surprised to find Beth in the living room with Josh and Ava, but Josh had explained that he'd invited her. "I thought it'd be good for her to get to know Mama better, being new to Boudreaux and all."

Which makes sense, I suppose. A word from Marian could open a lot of doors for Beth in Boudreaux. Or shut them.

From up front, Josh glances back at Ava. "We'll probably do our ride after lunch, munchkin, but we'll see what Grandma says. One thing I know — there will definitely be time to swing by the stables before lunch to say hi."

Ava beams at the prospect. "My favorite is Midnight Star."

Josh grins. "She's a beauty."

Through the car window, I see we're passing Briarton and its immaculate green lawn, which means we're almost at Dupre Farms. Marian's not-so-humble abode sprawls across two thousand acres of farmland, woods, and swamp along the bayou. It's one of the largest private estates in Louisiana. Josh's family has owned it for close to two hundred years.

At the gated entrance, Beth pulls in next to a keypad on a stand and Josh gives her the code to enter. A few seconds later, the gate swings open and we're in.

The gravel drive from the entry gate takes us through a

grove of old cypress trees before crossing a wide-open meadow. Up ahead, posed proudly on a slight rise, stands the big house.

If you've ever visited a Southern antebellum estate, then you know what Dupre House is all about. It's a classic two-story mansion, painted a crisp white, with imposing columns and front porches. Beyond the big house are the stables and a barn.

As we pull in front, Marian emerges to greet us. The mistress of the house is a slim, elegant woman in her early sixties with perfectly coiffed silver hair, cheekbones to die for, and intense blue eyes. Today she's dressed in a loose-fitting pearl silk blouse-and-slacks combo that looks casual but probably cost a fortune.

"Grandma!" Ava yells as she rushes up the porch steps into Marian's arms.

Marian hugs her tight. "It's so good to see you."

"Grandma, can I go see the horses?"

"Of course, dear."

"Can I go for a ride?"

"First thing after lunch."

"Can I go right now and say hi?"

"Of course. Mr. Barnett is there. He'll help you."

With a whoop, Ava races off to the stables.

After I clamber out of the back seat, Josh points Beth to a spot under a big tree at the end of the gravel lot. "Why don't you park there?" Then he hops out and dashes up the steps and gives his mother a quick kiss on the cheek.

Marian's watching Beth park the car. "She's staying?"

"I invited her. She's new to Boudreaux. I thought it would be good for her to get to know you."

Her lips compress — she's not pleased — but then her

eyes dart to my cane and I can see her wondering if Josh invited Beth because I need Beth's help.

"Of course," she says smoothly. "I'll have Edmond set another place at the table."

She turns to me as I join them on the porch. "Callie, how are you?"

"Doing well, Marian, thank you."

She doesn't attempt to hug me and I'm grateful for that. Marian isn't one for pretense and neither am I. Her eyes sweep over me, cataloguing everything about my appearance in a millisecond, lingering only on my flats.

I relax, just slightly. My dress and makeup have passed muster. The flats should really be heels, of course, but for those I have a valid medical excuse.

"Tell me," she says, "how is your recovery coming along?"

"Pretty well, thank you," I say as Beth joins us. "The pain is lessening and I'm getting stronger."

"That's wonderful." She turns to Beth. "My son tells me you're joining us today."

"I hope that's all right, ma'am."

Marian looks her over quickly — in black heels, black slacks, and a soft pink blouse, she's quite presentable. "Of course. Let's head inside."

Josh gestures toward the stables. "Should I check on Ava?"

"Hank is there," Marian replies, referring to the stable manager. "He'll bring her to the house in fifteen minutes."

In that moment, I must admit a reluctant appreciation for my former mother-in-law. Not only has she anticipated her granddaughter's excitement about the horses, she's scheduled time for her to visit the stables before lunch and given

Hank instructions on exactly when to escort her to the house.

"If you'd like, I can go make sure she's okay," Beth says.

"No need for that. Hank and Ava get along well."

We follow Marian inside. "Have a seat in the front parlor. I'll tell Edmond about the extra plate."

Josh leads me and Beth into a beautiful room, large and graciously proportioned, with high ceilings, tall windows, and lovely natural light. The marble fireplace, crystal chandelier, and oak flooring are all original. In the center of the room are facing sofas clad in a soft cream chenille, joined by Wedgwood side chairs, anchored on a blue-and-yellow Persian carpet. At the far side of the room is the door that leads to the study.

The effect is serene and assured. Despite knowing that this place was built with slave labor, I can't help but respond emotionally to the room's beauty. The budding designer in me appreciates what Marian has done with the place.

We're settling onto the sofas when our hostess returns carrying a tray with a pitcher of iced tea and four tall glasses.

Josh jumps up to help but she shoos him away. Setting the tray and pitcher on the antique French coffee table, she takes a seat next to me.

Beth's sitting across from Marian, watching anxiously. They've met at least once before — Josh told me that Marian insisted on meeting Beth before he hired her to help me — but if I were in Beth's shoes right now, I'd be nervous as hell. I'd feel like an interloper at a family gathering, unsure of my welcome, praying to make it through without screwing up. Despite being a newcomer to Boudreaux, I have no doubt Beth understands that the woman pouring the iced tea is the single most powerful person in the parish.

"Thank you, ma'am," Beth says as Marian hands her a glass.

"You're welcome."

Marian pours for me, Josh, and herself, then settles back onto the sofa. "Tell me more about your recovery, Callie." Though her tone is polite, I'm being given a command.

"It's coming along. Not as fast I'd like, but I'm making progress. I've been walking a lot, gradually increasing the distances."

"Are you using the cane for that?"

"Yes. I'm actually quite comfortable with it now."

"How far do you go on these walks of yours?"

"The other day I walked from Briarton to the house. About three miles in total."

Her eyebrows rise. "Three miles? Through the park?"

"I'm actually enjoying the walks along the bayou, despite the heat."

She eyes me for a moment. "I'm surprised to hear you say that. I've always thought of you as a … city person."

What she means is: *An outsider. A trespasser. A Northerner.* "Well, Boudreaux does have its charms."

"And your head? Your memory? Your headaches?"

I try not to tense. This is where the terrain gets tricky. "Also on the mend. I'm feeling more like myself every day."

"Any memories of the day of the accident?"

"Not yet, no. Dr. Franklin says I may never get those back."

"That may be for the better." She turns to Beth. "You're new to Boudreaux. How are you finding our parish?"

"I'm liking it a lot, ma'am. Folks have been very welcoming."

"She's been a huge help to me and Ava," I chime in.

"Always willing to pitch in. She'll make a great nurse someday."

Beth gives me an appreciative glance. "I'm just glad I can be of assistance."

"Indeed," Marian says. "Having support at a time like this is important for Callie and Ava." She swings her gaze to me. "I still do not understand why you insisted on moving into that house."

Here we go — I've been expecting this. "Well, the house is quite nice."

"Not as nice as here. Here you'd have your pick of the guest rooms. Edmond and Ella are here, Hank is here."

And you're here, I don't say. "I'm grateful for the offer. I just felt the house was a better place for me to focus on getting better."

Her eyes flash — she really hates not getting her way — but Josh intervenes. "Callie's doing great there, and so is Ava."

Marian glances again at my cane. "Still, it would be better if —"

"Mama, that's in the past now." He gives her a *let it go* look. "You know, I'm hoping you can give Beth your quick talk about this place."

Still frustrated, Marian nevertheless backs off and launches into a well-practiced overview of the plantation's history. She gives this mini-speech a lot, at various dinners and receptions. She's good at it. She enjoys it.

Of course, the history she shares is only a slice of the truth. When she tells us how Jeremiah Dupre founded the plantation in the 1830s and built a vast cotton empire, she doesn't mention the hundreds of enslaved men, women, and children who harvested the cotton for him. When she talks about his descendants expanding after the Civil War into other lines of business — banking, insurance, manufacturing — she doesn't discuss the lynch mobs and racist laws they used to suppress competition in the parish and maintain control for more than a century.

Instead, she talks about the fancy balls that were thrown here and the illustrious guests who slept here. She details the historic nature of the mansion and her efforts to preserve it. She brags about the corn and soybeans farmed today, the foundation she's established to restore the bayou, and the scholarship program at Briarton.

Through it all, Beth listens attentively.

And I find myself growing irritated. I want Marian to acknowledge that her empire is built on a foundation of exploitation and misery. I know she'll never do that — she'd scoff at the very notion — and I know the best thing for me to do right now is to nod appreciatively and keep quiet. My goal, as always with Marian, is to survive the encounter and live to fight another day.

So I surprise myself when I clear my throat and say, "About Briarton. I've been helping plan the memorial service for Rory Freeman."

"Yes," Marian says, turning to me. "Devlin mentioned that."

"I've been searching for information about past memorials to see how they were handled, but I haven't found much of anything."

"Handled? By that you mean...?"

"Well, when the previous headmaster died, what did the school do to honor his memory? Also, there was a handyman at the school who died around the same time. Did the school do anything for him?"

I'm hoping my question about Bracken sounds innocent and sincere, but the instant the word "handyman" leaves my mouth, Marian goes still. "Callie, what exactly are you looking for?"

"Programs, printed materials, things like that. Basically, anything that can help plan the memorial for Rory."

Marian shakes her head. "There's nothing complicated about a memorial."

"Well, are there any school traditions we should follow? When those two members of the staff died, what did the school do to honor them?"

"Hiram Higgins had been headmaster for seven years when he died at his desk. He gave his life in service to Briarton. His memorial was an important event for the school."

"And the handyman?"

"That was different."

"Different? How so?"

Her nostrils flare — she's not used to me pushing like this. "Callie, I'm puzzled by your interest." Josh and Beth are giving me curious looks as well.

I shrug. "I want to do a good job for Susan and the school. The memorial is the first thing I've done since the accident that isn't about getting better. Focusing on it has given me something to do."

The answer seems to satisfy her. "I'm sure the memorial you and Devlin are planning for Rory Freeman will be more than suitable for the occasion."

"Oh, I hope so. And I'm sorry to keep pressing, but what made the situation with the handyman different?"

"I prefer not to discuss that."

"But I'm hoping —"

"Callie, when I say no, I mean no."

Josh jumps in. "What Mama's too polite to say is that the handyman was involved in a crime."

"A crime?" I ask, pretending surprise.

"I was in college when it happened and don't know much about it, but apparently he set fire to a building at the school."

"Oh, gosh. Is that how he died? In the fire?"

"No, he died in jail."

"In *jail*? What happened?"

He shrugs. "Honestly, I don't know."

"He picked a fight with the wrong inmate," Marian says, unable to keep quiet. "Caused no end of trouble for Hoyt."

"That's terrible," I say right away. "And I'm sorry I brought this up, Marian. I didn't mean to cause upset."

"Well, you have."

"I'm sorry about that."

She isn't done with me. "When I say I don't want to talk about something, I expect you to listen."

Fortunately, at that moment we hear the pounding of happy feet on wood floors and Ava bursts into the room.

"I love horses so much!" she proclaims.

"Perfect timing," Marian says, rising to her feet. "Lunch is ready."

CHAPTER 22

Lunch is like a board of directors meeting, or at least how I imagine a board of directors meeting might go. From her seat at the head of the table, Marian directs the discussion with a firm hand. We delve extensively (and, yes, aGwenbly) into Ava's visit to the stables and what she likes most about each horse. Marian then quizzes Beth about her plans for nursing and me about the interior design business I'm planning. She brings up a fundraiser at the school and asks Josh several questions about business matters related to the law firm.

We're at the table in the formal dining room, with Ava and me on Marian's right and Josh and Beth on her left. The lunch, served on antique china, is trout with steamed vegetables prepared and served by Ella and Edmond, the Black couple who have been with Marian for thirty years. They come and go silently, like a whisper. I've often wondered why they stay here — there's no warmth or affection in their interactions with their employer. Maybe she pays them well?

Or there aren't any better jobs around? Or simple force of habit?

Or she has something on them and they're trapped?

I hold back a sigh. I really need to stop indulging in Susan-style paranoia about Marian. Crazy thoughts like that do me no good.

Having dispensed with the law firm business, Marian turns again to me. "Callie, you mentioned the memorial service for Rory Freeman. The arrangements have all been finalized?"

"Yes," I reply, sitting up a little straighter. "Monday afternoon in the school auditorium, during the last class period."

"Parents have been notified?"

"The headmaster emailed the entire Briarton community list and the parent list yesterday."

Marian nods. She must know all of this already — I can't imagine Devlin not running everything by her for her approval — but checking on things is standard operating procedure for her and in this case I can't argue. If I owned the school, I'd probably do the same.

"The speakers are set?"

"The headmaster will open the service and two of Rory's colleagues will speak, followed by the school choir and the minister from Rory's church."

"Josh can speak as well."

Josh shifts in his chair. "Mama, I —"

"Now, now," she says. "You were his lawyer."

"I didn't know him all that well."

"You'll be representing the firm."

"I wouldn't know what to say."

"I'm sure you'll come up with something. Think of it as practice."

"Practice for what?"

"For the future."

He frowns because he knows — we all know — what she means. She's talking about his future in politics. She wants him to speak in front of hundreds of people because she wants folks to start seeing him as a local leader.

"Mama," he says, still reluctant.

"You'll do wonderfully. Isn't that right, Callie?"

After a short pause, I say, "He'll do great." The thing is, Marian's completely right about Josh. He'll do wonderfully up there. He's a natural at things like that.

My ex-husband holds my eyes for a long second before finally sighing. "All right. But only if Susan agrees."

"I'll run it by her this afternoon," I volunteer.

"Good," Marian says. "I'll let Devlin know."

Josh turns to Ava. "Munchkin, are you excited about your ride on Midnight Star?"

Ava beams. "So excited!"

"What do you want to do first? Go for your ride or have dessert?"

Her eyes widen, temporarily flummoxed at being asked to choose between two amazing options. "Can I have dessert after my ride?"

"If that's what you want."

"Ride first!"

"You ready to change into your riding outfit?"

"So ready!"

She's about to bolt from the table when Josh says, "Hang on, honey. What do you say to Grandma?"

Ava turns to Marian, barely able to contain her excitement. "Grandma, thank you very much for lunch. It was delicious. May I please be excused from the table?"

"Of course, dear."

With a whoop, she leaps from her chair and races out of the room.

Smiling at her enthusiasm, I reach for my cane. "I'll go with her."

"Actually, if you could stay a minute," Josh says. "There's something I want to share."

Surprised, I settle back down. "Okay."

I glance at Marian and find her giving her son a puzzled look.

Josh clears his throat and I tense up. I know that sound. It means he's about to confess something.

"I want the two of you to be the first to know," he says, looking at me and then Marian. "I've met someone."

I go still. Is he about to tell us he's dating the Tiffany I found on his phone?

To my shock, he reaches over and takes Beth's hand in his.

"Beth and I are together."

I gasp. Marian breathes in sharply.

"And we're engaged to be married."

CHAPTER 23

*B*oom. That's what it feels like. A bomb exploding in my face. I hadn't seen it. Not even a hint. How is that possible?

The air has left the room. Marian's eyes widen and her mouth opens, but no words come out.

"What did you say?" she finally whispers.

"Beth and I are engaged to be married." His gaze is steady, but I can tell he's nervous.

Next to him, Beth looks completely terrified.

Marian grips the table and rises to her feet. "Over my dead body," she declares, then rushes from the room.

"Mama," Josh says as she stomps down the hallway. A few seconds later, we hear a door slamming shut.

He looks at Beth and then me. "I should go talk with her."

Beth nods and he goes without another word, leaving me and Beth alone, staring at each other across the dining table.

We listen to his steps and then the fainter sound of a door

closing, followed by the muffled sounds of Marian yelling — screaming — at him.

I don't know what to do. I don't know what to think. But I do know how I feel. *I'm fucking pissed at Josh and Beth.* Anger's building in me, about to explode.

I mean, *seriously, how dare they?*

I can't just sit here and do nothing. I can't even look at her.

Abruptly, I stand up and limp over to the window and gaze out at nothing, willing myself to not lash out.

Seconds pass in silence. Beth pushes out her chair and walks around the table toward me.

"Callie," she begins, her voice trembling. "I'm so sorry I didn't let you know sooner. I can't tell you how much I've been wanting to share this with you."

I keep staring out the window, too unsettled to reply, my mind awhirl, my stomach in knots, my heart thumping.

"The instant I met you," she continues, "I realized it would be better for you to know. Keeping it from you didn't feel right. But Josh thought it was important to stay quiet until the time was right, especially given how his mother might...."

Finally, I summon the will to look at her. "He told me a few days ago he was seeing someone. But he didn't say who."

She blinks back tears. "You were the first person he shared that with. When he told me, I said good, I'm glad. I told him it was time for everyone to know."

I gesture in the direction of Marian's yelling. "And that's why...?"

"We decided today would be the day."

She glances anxiously toward the yelling before turning her attention back to me.

The silence seems to expand between us, goading me to fill it. "I know we're just beginning to get to know each other," I say, desperately wishing I had time to think this through. "But keeping something like this from me — that's huge."

"You're absolutely right and I'm so sorry. I just hope you can find it in your heart to forgive me."

"For the past month, you've been coming into my house and helping me out — why?"

She flushes. "I wanted to. I knew Josh was looking for someone to help you and I volunteered."

"Why?"

She takes a deep breath. "Working at the diner and being a waitress is fine, don't get me wrong, but that's not what I want to do permanently. I'm more interested in health care and nursing, so I thought that helping you out would be a good experience for me."

I stay silent, waiting to see what else she says.

"Plus," she continues, "I wanted to get to know you and Ava better."

Under false pretenses, I almost say. "When did you and Josh start dating?"

"Five months ago. We met at the diner."

In other words, months after he and I separated and right around the time our divorce became final.

That's when I realize something.

Josh's texts with "Tiff" were from *three* months ago.

So if what Beth's saying is true, then Josh was dating Beth at the same time he was hooking up with Tiff.

Unease shoots through me, because now my head is

going to the weird note I found on my front door. Was the point of the note to inform me that my tomcat ex-husband is still a tomcat, cheating on his new girlfriend the same way he cheated on me?

But wait, did that idea even make sense? I mean, wouldn't it be a huge stretch to expect me to figure out what "5309" was, and then gain access to Josh's phone, and then find the texts between him and Tiffany? A lot had to line up perfectly for that to happen.

Plus, why would someone want *me* to know? Aside from feeling disappointed in my deeply imperfect ex-husband for continuing to be deeply imperfect, how was I expected to respond? Was I supposed to get angry and decide to fight for my man and stomp my way in and break them up? Is that what the note was about — getting me to interfere in Josh's new relationship?

Or maybe, I realize with a jolt, the note wasn't for me — but for *Beth*?

I blink when I realize Beth's staring at me with concern. I've done it again — gone into my head and left the real world behind.

"Callie, are you all right?"

"I'm fine," I reply, feeling myself flush. "Just got lost in my thoughts for a second."

Unbidden, a new question arises. Do I tell Beth what I know about Tiff — woman to woman, in acknowledgment of her entry into the Sisterhood of the Cheating Tomcat? Do I owe her that? Or do I owe her nothing, given how she lied to me?

Footsteps sound in the hall and Josh returns to the dining room, his manner subdued. "We should get going," he says to Beth.

She steps toward him, her hands clenched. "Is she…?"

He shakes his head. "She'll come around. She just needs time."

Dream on, I almost say.

"I'm taking Beth home," he says to me, "but I'll be back later to pick up you and Ava."

You're going to leave me alone with Marian? I almost say before realizing he has no choice — he has to get Beth out of here. "You'll be back soon?"

"Soon, promise."

Beth swivels toward me. "Callie, if you don't want me coming to the house anymore, I'll totally understand. But I hope I can keep coming. I like spending time with you and Ava. I'm hoping we can find a way to move past what I've kept from you?"

I take a deep breath and weigh my response. The moment feels important and not just for me. "Let's take a break tomorrow and I'll see you Monday."

She blinks back tears of relief. "Thank you, Callie, thank you. See you Monday."

Josh is appreciative, too. *Thank you*, he mouths as he leads Beth out. "I'll see you in a bit."

"In a bit."

I step back to the window and watch them get into her car and drive away.

Behind me, I hear footsteps and turn to find Marian staring at me. Her pale skin is flushed, but otherwise she seems her normal controlled self.

"Callie, come to the study. We need to talk."

CHAPTER 24

I follow Marian out of the dining room, down the hallway, through the front parlor into the adjoining study. It's a smaller room than the parlor and unlike the rest of the mansion, it's thoroughly masculine. The dark blue wallpaper, mahogany bookshelves, and leather chairs give the room an aura of power — a place where important matters are decided.

Before he died in a hunting accident ten years ago, the study belonged to Josh's dad. Now the room is Marian's. Aside from adding a vase of fresh-cut flowers on the antique oak desk — yellow tulips today — she hasn't changed a thing. It's her way of showing she's comfortable operating in a man's world.

She settles into her swivel chair and points me toward a chair in front of the desk. There's an intensity in her gaze that's frightening.

"Tell me what you know about this."

She's in control of herself, but barely. I've never seen her anger this close to the surface.

I need to be careful — *extremely* careful. "A few days ago, he told me he was dating someone. But he didn't say who."

"What do you know about her?"

"Well," I say, trying to decide how much to share. "Not a whole lot, to be honest."

Marian snorts. "She's been helping you for a month. Surely you know something."

"I mean, I know she's helpful. She runs errands, drives us places, does the laundry, helps with the cooking...."

She waves me to stop. "That's not what I mean."

I know that's not what she means. She's on a fishing expedition, searching for something — anything — she can use as a weapon.

I'm trying to decide how to respond when I realize there's another layer to this moment. For the first time ever, Marian is enlisting *me* in a cause of hers. Recruiting *me* to join her in battle.

It's a strange spot to find myself in. I've always been Enemy Number One — the undeserving interloper, the scheming harlot who trapped her son in marriage, the inconvenient mother of her precious granddaughter.

But now she has a new enemy. A dangerous threat to the bright shiny future she's planned for her son.

And that makes me — what? A temporary ally? A fresh pawn for her chessboard?

I hold back a sigh. Poor Josh. She's always had plans for him and mostly he's played along: law school, a stint in corporate law in New Orleans, and now back in Boudreaux. Next up, if she gets her way, is politics. State representative, congressman, senator — that's the intended path. Crucial to that is marriage to a bride of her choosing. A daughter of a connected, wealthy family. Someone she can mold into the perfect political wife.

What Marian doesn't understand about her son is that Josh will always be with who he wants to be with. Sex is his rebellion and his escape. When he plays the field, he isn't just cheating on whoever he's currently with. He's also cheating on *Marian*.

Which, I know, is totally gross. Took me years to figure out.

Bottom line, my tomcat ex-husband has a deep-seated need to be loved. He never got what he needed from his mama, so now he gets it from the women who flock to him.

That's when the thought hits. *The cheating.* I remember what Alice said about Tiffany — and I remember where Tiffany and her boyfriend might work.

Suddenly, I know what I have to do next.

"Beth is pretty quiet," I say to Marian. "We've only been starting to get to know each other. Mostly she keeps busy doing errands. But I can try to find out more."

Marian is frowning at me, clearly disappointed.

I sit up straighter. "But on a different topic, can I ask a favor?"

She blinks. "A favor?"

"Would it be all right if Ava stays here tonight with you?"

Her eyes widen — I've surprised her. "Of course. She's welcome anytime. Why?"

"Honestly, I need a night off." I gesture to my hip. "I'm getting better and stronger, but to be frank, the healing process is exhausting. After today's curveball from Josh, all I want to do is draw a bubble bath and pour myself a glass of wine and dive into a good book and forget about everything, just for a little while."

"Of course," she says immediately. She likes this idea — she's almost purring. "I understand completely."

"Plus, I'd love for Ava to spend more time with you." Which isn't true, but I know it's what Marian wants to hear. "You're the only grandparent she has. I want you and her to be close."

I almost can't believe it, but Marian's eyes start glistening. "I'm glad to hear you say that." After a pause, she adds, "Callie, there's something I want to say. It's possible I misjudged you. I want to … acknowledge that."

I blink, unable to hide my shock. Not once have I heard Marian Dupre admit to a mistake.

I keep my tone level. "Thank you. I believe we both want what's best for Ava." I point in the direction of the stables. "Speaking of, perhaps we should…?"

"Yes, of course." She gets to her feet. "And about what just occurred. There's no need to worry."

"There isn't?"

A steely glint has appeared in her eyes. She's thought of something. A plan of attack.

"In my experience," she says, her words crisp and ominous, "these matters have a way of resolving themselves."

CHAPTER 25

almost shudder at Marian's pronouncement. Her confidence is back with a vengeance. Whatever she's planning, Josh and Beth won't like it.

We reach the hallway and she gestures toward the stairs. "I'm going to change."

"See you outside." After making my way down the hall and through the family room, I head out onto the back porch and down the path to the stables.

The sun is bright, the heat intense, the air carrying a hint of the nearby bayou. Up ahead, Ava and Hank are walking a horse.

Ava sees me and waves. "Mommy, I helped put a bridle on Midnight Star!"

I smile, thrilled to see her so excited. In her riding helmet, jodhpurs, and short riding boots, she looks aGwenble. "Looks like you did a great job!"

Hank gives me a tip of his hat as I reach them. He's a grizzled dude in his sixties who looks like a broken-down cowhand. Like Edmond and Ella, he's been with Marian for decades. "Good to see you, Callie."

"You, too, Hank."

"How's the hip coming along?"

"Pretty well, thanks."

He turns to Ava. "You ready to ride, young lady?"

"So ready!"

He lifts her onto the horse and the horse turns her head to watch as he gets her boots into the stirrups. Midnight Star is a dark beauty with a star-shaped patch of white on her nose. I don't know much about horses, but she seems patient and gentle.

Hank helps Ava get her feet into place. "You comfortable?"

Ava's beaming. "Mommy, I'm on Midnight Star!"

She looks so small on that big horse. If she were to fall…. *Stop*, I tell myself. *Don't even think that.* Pushing back the tremor of worry, I pull out my phone. "Time for a picture. Hank, get in there."

With a self-conscious grin, Hank stands in front of the horse and the three of them pose.

"What's the plan?" I ask Hank.

"Mrs. Dupre will be here in a bit."

As if on cue, Marian hurries out of the house and down the path. She's changed into riding gear — form-fitting cream riding breeches with a tailored blue jacket and tall black boots.

"Is Isobel ready?" she calls out to Hank.

"Waiting for you."

She heads briskly into the stables and emerges a moment later atop a beautiful white horse.

"Ava, how are you and Midnight Star doing?" she asks.

"Really good."

"You ready for a walk?"

"So ready!"

With a smile, Hank starts walking Midnight Star, with Marian and her horse walking alongside.

"Mommy, I'm riding!"

"You're doing great, honey!"

I snap more photos as they head toward the open meadow.

Perhaps inevitably, my thoughts turn to Josh and Beth and what they just revealed. Despite the hurt and anger they caused me by keeping their relationship a secret, I can't help but feel a twinge of concern for them. One doesn't cross Marian Dupre without suffering the consequences.

From the direction of the house comes the sound of a car engine and a minute later Josh is heading over. He smiles and waves when he sees me and despite my anger, my heart quickens. My ex-husband is way too attractive for his own good, and it's not just his athletic build and charming smile I'm referring to. His *sunniness* has always tugged at me. His upbeat view of life, the natural optimism he carries with him, the genuine interest he has in everyone he meets — *that's* what made me fall for him. I needed his brightness in my life. I still do. Maybe that's why, even after the pain he caused with the cheating and the divorce, I remain in his orbit.

He joins me at the fence and for a long minute we watch our daughter. She and Marian and Hank are at the far end of the meadow. Even at that distance, I can hear Ava happily talking up a storm.

"Callie," Josh says. "I'm really sorry."

"Words I hear from you way too often." My anger is

simmering, ready to be unleashed, but I'm still not sure what I want to say.

"I mean it."

I turn to face him. "I know there's more going on. There always is with you. So go ahead, get it out. Get it off your chest. Tell me."

Surprise flashes through his eyes — along with panic. *Oh my God.* I made the accusation because I wanted to see him squirm, not because I actually thought he was still hiding something.

But am I actually *right*?

"Callie...."

My heart starts thumping. "What are you holding back, Josh?"

He blinks rapidly, unsure what to say.

And that's when I figure it out.

"You're already married."

The guilt in his eyes is the only confirmation I need.

Holy shit. I take a deep breath as the implications ricochet through me.

He's done it again. Seven years ago, he married me without telling Marian and now he's gone and married Beth for the exact same reason — to outmaneuver his mama and prevent her from stopping him.

"I almost feel bad for your mother."

He looks miserable. "I didn't want it to be like this."

"Yet here you are. Again."

"Well, it's different this time."

No, it's not. But I say, "How so?"

"We told her we're engaged."

"Which is a lie."

"But a good one."

"No, Josh," I say, trying to keep my voice level. "It's a terrible lie."

"Callie, we did it for a reason. I learned my lesson the first time. The way Mama treated you was awful, and that was my fault."

Emotion surges within me. For months after we got married, Marian refused to meet me. She accepted me as a member of the family only after Ava was born, and then only grudgingly.

I shake my head. "She's going to shut out Beth the same way she shut out me."

Josh swallows. "We're hoping not."

A shocking thought hits me with a wallop. "Is she pregnant?"

"No," he says immediately. "No, that's not why we're doing this."

I stare deep into his eyes. He's telling the truth, I think. But how can I be sure?

"We're hoping we can persuade Mama to come around faster this time if we get her involved in planning the wedding."

I inhale sharply. "The *wedding*?"

"Yeah. She likes planning events. It's something she can work with us on."

Dear God, what he's saying is so wrong. "You really think a *wedding* is going to matter to her?"

He opens his mouth but no words come out.

"She's upset, she's furious, she's pissed as hell because you've committed yourself to someone she doesn't approve of. *Again.*"

"That's not —"

"Josh, you married the help. *Again.*"

His cheeks flush.

"Two waitresses, two marriages."

He flinches at my words.

"She has someone else in mind for you."

He throws me a quick glance. "You know about Penelope?"

"I don't know a thing about *Penelope*," I snap, newly irritated. "I haven't heard a peep about *Penelope*. But this is how your mother operates. She's picked out some rich, connected gal for you. Someone she can mold into your perfect wife."

He shrugs. "Well, she ain't getting her way on that."

I shake my head. He's acting like the matter's already decided. Like his future with Beth is a done deal. Surely he knows his mother is plotting right now to break them up. Surely he knows she'll never stop trying to control him.

We're silent for a moment. In the distance, Ava and Marian are laughing.

"Does Ava know anything?" I ask.

"No. We wanted to talk with you first. Figure out the best way to tell her."

The whole situation is so aggravating. I take a breath and gather my thoughts. "We'll tell her at dinner. This week, at the house. You and Beth, me and her."

He blinks back emotion. "Thank you. What night?"

"There's a lot going on the next couple of days — tomorrow's the funeral for Susan's husband and Monday's the memorial at the school…. How about Tuesday?"

"Sure."

"This whole thing is awkward as hell for me — you know that, right?"

"I do and I'm sorry."

"I can't believe you let her come into my house and kept your relationship with her a secret from me."

He nods vigorously. "You're completely right. I shouldn't have done that. I was a total idiot and that's all on me. It wasn't Beth's doing at all." He looks so abashed, so contrite, so regretful, his eagerness to make amends practically gushing from him. As I stare into his gorgeous blue eyes, I feel myself softening. He's so appealing when he's begging — so damned good at it. He's had a lifetime of practice.

But there's no way I'm letting him off easy. "You don't trust me."

"No, no, no." His tone is urgent.

"You didn't tell me because you thought I couldn't keep your secret."

"No, it wasn't like that."

"And that's not all," I add, my momentum building. "You secretly think I'm not getting better fast enough. You're worried I'm not healthy enough to take care of Ava on my own."

His head is shaking even though I see a flash of recognition in his eyes. "Never. I've never thought that."

"That's why you've been asking where my head's at. It's like you think I'm on some bad path mentally."

"No, Callie. I swear, no."

"Bottom line, you don't trust me."

He's frowning at me now. "I swear, that's not true. You've never given me cause to doubt you. Not once, not ever, not even after I let you down. You've always been there for Ava and me. Always. I trust you with my life."

His sincerity is flowing strong and I like what I'm hearing. I can't deny the warmth his words stir up inside me.

But I'm not done being pissed. "I just wish I could say the same about you."

He blinks, taken aback. "Callie, I —"

"What else are you holding back?"

He blinks. "Nothing."

What about Tiffany? I almost say, the accusation on the tip of my tongue, ready to explode into the air.

Somehow, just barely, I manage to stop myself.

"I wish I could believe you," I finally say.

"Callie, I —"

"You know what? I don't want to hear anything more from you right now. I'm fucking pissed at you and I might say or do something regrettable if we keep going with this, so I'm gonna give you a piece of advice and I want you to take it."

"What's that?"

"Stop talking."

"Callie, I —"

"Seriously, just stop." Deliberately, I turn away from him and focus on Ava in the distance. "This is one of those moments when it's best for you to simply shut the fuck up."

CHAPTER 26

After an early dinner at Marian's, Josh drives me back to the house and together we pack an overnight bag for Ava's sleepover with Grandma.

"I have to ask," he says as he slips several of her favorite books into a duffel bag, "why are you letting Mama keep her tonight?"

There's no way I'm telling him the real reason — *because I want to meet the woman you cheated on Beth with* — so instead I say, "Believe it or not, I want my daughter to have a relationship with her grandmother."

He shoots me a skeptical look.

"I mean, I'm fine with *me* not having a relationship with her. But it's important for Ava to have that tie, that bond."

"What's the other reason?" He's smiling as he says it — he knows me well enough to know there's more going on.

I give him the same lie I gave Marian. "Well, frankly, I could use a night off. Some honest-to-goodness me time. An evening with nothing but a bubble bath and a good book."

"You certainly deserve that."

"Damn right I do." The fierceness of my words surprises me. "Especially after what you did today."

He blinks back sudden emotion. "Callie, I'm so sorry I didn't tell you sooner, and I'm even sorrier I let Beth come here without letting you know first."

I will myself to hold his anxious gaze. Though my anger is real and fresh, already in my heart of hearts I know I'll be forgiving him.

But not yet. Not today.

"You hurt me, Josh. There's no getting around that. I need to be able to trust you and right now I'm wondering — can I?"

"You can. I'll make it up to you, I promise."

I let out a sigh. "Let's just finish with the overnight bag so you can get it over to her."

"Anything you want to talk about, we can talk about. Whenever you're ready."

I stare into his pleading eyes and feel my resolve weakening. Damn him for being so appealing.

"Fine," I say, trying to sound more irritated than I actually am.

We finish packing her things and I follow him downstairs.

"I'm picking you up tomorrow for Rory's service, right?" he says as he loads the duffel bag in his truck.

"Yes, and thank you for that. The funeral's at noon."

"I'll be here at eleven-thirty."

I watch from the front porch as he drives away, my mind racing. Part of me wants to call him right now and have him come back so I can sit him down and yell at him more about the difficult position he's put us all in. Another part of me wants to help him finally succeed at being a good husband. But what I want most of all is to be reassured that he's always going to be here for Ava and, yes, for me.

For the millionth time, I can't help but wonder what my life would be like if I'd never met him.

Simpler and easier, my inner voice reminds me. *But you wouldn't have Ava.* It's the same answer I get every time I ask. When it comes to Josh, the good outweighs the bad.

I head back inside, pull out my phone, and stare hard at it, weighing my next step. Do I really want to do what I'm about to do? Wouldn't a bubble bath and a good book make for a much more enjoyable evening?

You know you need to. You need answers.

With a frustrated sigh, I dial the number for Lola's, the strip joint where Big Ed works as a bouncer and where Tiffany might work as a dancer.

A man picks up on the first ring. "Lola's."

"Hey," I say, adopting a friendly, breezy tone. "Is Tiff on tonight?"

"Lemme check." A few seconds later, he says, "Starting at ten."

Excitement jolts through me. "And is Big Ed working the door?"

"That's right. You a friend of theirs?"

Instead of answering, I say, "He feelin' any better after his accident?"

"You know about that?"

"Yeah, I heard he cut himself."

"And you said you're a friend of theirs?"

"I'll be swinging by later. Thanks!"

Before he can ask me anything else, I hang up.

I stand there for a moment, considering. Thanks to the

call, I know two things I didn't before. When the man asked if I was a friend of "theirs," he was telling me that Tiffany and Big Ed are close enough to each other to share friends. Does that mean they're girlfriend and boyfriend? Also, the man didn't correct me when I told him I'd heard that Big Ed cut himself, which suggests Big Ed probably did just that.

What I still don't have are answers to my three big questions:

One: Did Tiffany hook up with Josh?

Two: Did Big Ed injure himself in my kitchen when he fell on his knife?

Three: Is Tiffany the second attacker?

The answers to Two and Three are almost definitely no, but I still want confirmation, if only for my peace of mind.

As for One…. I'm hoping the answer is no, but Josh being Josh, it's entirely possible the answer will end up being a big fat yes.

I let out a sigh. *That bubble bath sure does sound nice….*

Decision time. Should I stay or should I go?

CHAPTER 27

A bit before ten, with a mixture of reluctance, excitement, and trepidation, I head into the garage and carefully slide myself into my car. My hip immediately tells me it isn't happy, so I shift into what I hope is a position that will allow me to drive without too much pain.

Before starting up, I run through my mental checklist. House locked up tight — check. Mahogany cane in the seat next to me — check. Phone, ID, cards, cash, and house keys in my jeans pocket — check.

I adjust the car mirror so I can stare at myself. I'm wearing a dark oversize hoodie and loose jeans to avoid attracting interest, but there's no hiding the tension in my eyes. I've never been to Lola's or any other strip club. All I know about those places is what I've seen in movies and on TV.

I'm hoping I can zip in and out without a problem, but

what if I can't? What if someone pays me too much atten-tion? What if someone threatens me?

If that happens, you'll deal with it, my inner voice says with more confidence than I feel. *If you need help, ask for it.*

In the mirror, I notice myself frowning. The idea of needing someone's help shouldn't bother me, but clearly it does.

Get over yourself, my inner voice says. *And get going.*

Irritated, I start the car and head out. Lola's is just over the parish line, about ten minutes away. The night is dark, the passing swamp a blur. A pothole in the road sends a jolt of pain to my hip, but I grit my teeth and keep going.

Ten minutes later, my hip's starting to really ache when I see the big neon "Lola's" sign and pull into the gravel parking lot. It's a big, ramshackle building. The lot is half-full. At the door, a line of folks are waiting to get in.

I pull into a spot near the door and shut off the engine. The bouncer is a huge white guy who looks like a linebacker with a square face and close-cropped brown hair. He's probably in his twenties and dressed in jeans, a stained white t-shirt, and a faded black leather jacket.

Am I looking at Big Ed, the guy who cut himself and who might be Tiffany's boyfriend?

Apprehension twists my gut. *Am I looking at the man who attacked me in my kitchen?*

My heart starts racing. What in the hell am I doing here? In what universe is it a good idea for me to walk up to a stranger who might be the dangerous pyscho who broke into my house and tried to kill me?

He most likely didn't do that, my inner voice says, trying to reassure me. *You're just looking for patterns that don't exist.*

Even though I'm here, I don't have to do this, I remind myself. I can drive home and slip into that bubble bath I supposedly want so much.

Of course you can do that. But if you leave now, you won't find out the truth.

But what if it's actually him? Won't he recognize me?

My inner voice has an answer: *If he recognizes you, then you'll know who attacked you. You're in public — he can't do anything. You can call the sheriff right away and tell him every-thing. When the sheriff investigates, he'll find evidence.*

The thought of the sheriff investigating is reassuring.

You can do this, my inner voice says.

I take a deep breath and reach for my cane, then pause. I want to be inconspicuous. The cane is anything but.

Don't advertise your presence. Leave it in the car.

Reluctantly, I move my hand away and clamber out. After waiting for my hip to settle down, I shut the door and make my way to the back of the line at the door.

The line's moving fast. Big Ed — assuming it's him — is checking each person's I.D. quickly and efficiently, with minimal conversation.

Before I know it, I'm there. My stomach's in a knot as I hand him my I.D. and say, in a voice that sounds casual, "Hey, do we know each other?"

He squints at me. "Not sure. Do we?"

"I think so. Big Ed, right?"

He looks again at my ID, then back at me. "Not ringing a bell."

I try to stay calm, even though my heart is pounding. "I could swear we ran into each other recently."

"Don't think so." As he hands me back my I.D., I search

his face for a clue, a flicker of emotion, anything — but it's like looking at granite.

He gestures to the line behind me. "You going in?"

"Sorry."

As I hurry inside, I can't help but feel a jab of disappointment. I'd sensed no reaction from him. Either he doesn't know me or he has a great poker face.

Loud country music washes over me as I try to get my bearings. The club is only dimly lit — no surprise — but it's bigger than I expected. A bar runs along one wall and the other side of the space is dominated by a low stage. A runway extends from the stage into the middle of the room, surrounded by chairs and tables. I pick up faint hints of beer and sweat in the air.

The place is packed. Most of the patrons are men, but I'm surprised — and reassured — to spot a fair number of women as well.

I blink as my gaze lands on the woman dancing on the runway stage. She's facing away from me and dressed in heels, a thong bikini bottom, and nothing else. Purple lights play over her toned body as she sways to the beat. Her moves are confident and smooth — she dances beautifully. A man approaches, dollar bill in hand, and she kneels down and lets him slip the money into her g-string.

When she stands up and turns around, I see she's also wearing a jeweled Mardi Gras face mask.

Tension jolts me. Could this be Tiffany? It's certainly possible — the dancer is white, slim, and has thick, curly brown hair, just like the woman I saw running out of the convenience store.

I head to the bar and flag down a bartender. Getting up

on my tiptoes — much to my hip's displeasure — I lean over the counter and yell in his ear. "Is that Tiffany?"

He glances at the stage. "Sure is."

Excitement jolts me. "Thanks!"

Heart thumping, I navigate my way through the chairs and tables to the edge of the stage. I could hang back and wait for her to finish her performance, but for some reason I want to be up close.

The woman doesn't notice me right away, but when she does, she falters just for a second.

Surprise jolts me. Did I just see what I think I just saw? Did she recognize me?

She makes her way toward me and starts dancing in front of me. She has a great body. Her skin is smooth, her stomach toned, her breasts on the smaller side but beautifully shaped. There's a confidence in her, a bravado, that I can't help but admire. If I were in her high heels, I'd be a self-conscious mess, but she's handling herself with skill.

She bends down and brings her face close to mine.

"Hey," she yells over the music.

"Hey," I yell back.

"Haven't see you in here before."

"First time."

She laughs — it's like I've pleased her somehow.

"What brings you here?"

"I was hoping we could talk."

She stares at me for a moment, like I've puzzled her, then leans into my ear again. "You don't know, do you?"

I pull back. "I'm sorry, what?"

"You don't know."

"I don't know what?"

She laughs again, then raises her mask and —

At first I don't understand what I'm seeing. But then I realize *I know her*.

Shock wallops me. It can't be true — but it is.

I'm staring at —

Beth!

CHAPTER 28

I can't believe what I'm seeing.

I can't believe *who* I'm seeing.

My shock and confusion must be obvious because she laughs again.

"I know what you're thinking!" she yells over the thumping music.

I can only gape at her, speechless. What the *fuck* is going on?

"Meet me in two minutes," she yells, pointing to a spot at the side of the stage.

Then she's off to grind her hips at some dude waving money at her.

Oh my God, how is this possible?

Over the loudspeaker, a man says, "Hey, everybody, next up is — Crystal!"

And then another dancer sashays onto the stage and Beth's pulling me by the arm through a side door next to the stage into a backstage dressing room.

It's a shitty space with a couple of makeup stations and costumes hanging on racks and two women on a sofa having a heated argument and even after Beth shuts the door, the music is still way too loud.

But none of that matters right now.

She tosses her jeweled mask onto a makeup table and laughs again and I can only stare, still thoroughly discombobulated. The way she's strutting around is very un-Beth-like. It's like she's a different person — coarser, louder, more confident.

"Beth," I begin.

She laughs again. "Gonna stop you right there."

"But —"

"You think I'm my sister."

Wait — *what?* Did she say *sister*?

She gestures around the room. "You think Beth would be caught dead here?"

I'm still catching up. "You're saying —"

"I'm saying, Beth's my sister."

I can only stare. *Beth has a sister!*

"Happens a lot. We're twins. Identical." She steps closer, gazing at me with an unsettling intensity. "But we ain't the same person. Not by a long shot. She's prim and proper. Sad and *boring*."

Inexplicably I feel an urge to defend her. "She's very nice."

"*Nice*," Tiffany repeats with a sneer. "I hate that word. Miss Goodie Fucking Two Shoes can have all the nice she wants. I take it you're a friend of hers?"

"Yes," I say, even as I realize how little I actually know about the woman who just married my ex-husband. Not once has she mentioned having a twin sister — why is that?

Tiffany's eyes narrow. "She ask you to come here?"

"No."

"She didn't have you come here to tell me to leave Boudreaux?"

"No."

"She did that a couple years back. Sent a whole posse to the club I was working in Greensburg. Too scared to do it herself."

I shake my head. "She hasn't mentioned you."

"She got me fired from that place."

"I'm sorry about that."

"Are you?" Her gaze intensifies. "My dear sis doesn't like me much."

I can see why, though of course I don't say that.

"According to her, I'm a 'disruptive influence.'" She frowns. "So if she didn't send you, why are you here?"

I open my mouth and immediately shut it. Do I still want to ask her about Josh?

"Well," I say, after deciding I do. "I wanted to ask about a guy you dated."

"Ah," she says, visibly relaxing. With a sly smile, she sits down at a makeup station and looks at me through the mirror. "I have to be back on in five minutes."

"Got it. His name is Josh."

"Josh." Her eyes flash with amusement as she applies fresh mascara. "You mean Josh from around here? Josh Dupre?"

"Yes."

"You dating him?"

I shake my head. "We're divorced."

Her eyes widen. "You're the ex-wife? Why the hell do you care who he's dating?"

I flush. "We have a daughter together."

She cocks her head. "A custody issue? You looking for dirt?"

"No, no," I say immediately. "Nothing like that."

She picks up her lipstick. "Then what is it?"

"He's dating a … friend of mine."

She shrugs. "And?"

"When we were married, he cheated on me, so I want to find out if…."

"If he cheated on your friend with me."

"Right."

She stares at me in the mirror, deciding whether to take pity on me.

"Okay, fine." She gets to her feet and turns to face me. "We met a few months ago. It didn't last long. A few weeks."

Her timeline matches the texts on his phone. "You met here at the club?"

"He slipped a twenty under my g-string."

"And then you…."

"I fucked him." She sighs almost wistfully. "Cute as hell, but of course you know that. Great in the sack. Ate me out like nobody's business."

God, she's so crass. Not at all like Beth. I swallow back my distaste.

"You tell your friend that Josh and I are over. We had our fun and now we're done."

"Thank you."

Her gaze hardens. "And you tell Beth to leave me alone. What I do with my life is my business, not hers. I don't want her bothering me, got it?"

"Got it."

"My sister is a small, tedious, unimportant person. You tell her that, too. A fucking loser. A total waste of space."

I blink, stunned by her anger.

With a final snarl, Tiffany says, "You tell her to stay away from me — or else."

CHAPTER 29

wake up Sunday morning still rocked by what I learned last night at Lola's. *Beth has a twin sister.* I have so many questions — endless questions. After throwing off the blanket and easing myself out of Ava's bed, I move the chair away from the bedroom door and go downstairs.

As I do my morning walkthrough, I'm struck by how quiet and lonely the house is without my daughter's happy energy. I head back upstairs to shower and get dressed. By the time Josh arrives to pick me up, I'm ready to go.

We're quiet on the drive to the church, the tension from yesterday still between us. It's possible his silence means he's taking my advice about keeping his mouth shut. As for me, I'm completely unsure what I want to say to him about last night's revelations. Do I tell him I met Beth's identical twin sister? Do I tell him that I know he slept with her? Do I tell Beth? Marian would definitely be interested, but there's no way I'm telling her about any of this. As upset as I am with Josh and Beth for lying to me, unleashing Marian on them is something I'd never do.

No, my allegiance — if that's what you want to call it — is to either Josh or Beth or maybe both. As the church draws near, I'm tempted to cut to the chase and tell Josh what I know. That's probably the simplest path: Reveal all and make him promise to tell Beth so the two of them can sort it out for themselves.

Yes, that's what I'll do. After the funeral. But right now we have to focus on our friend in her time of terrible grief.

The church is crowded and hot. Josh and I slip into a pew in the back and settle in. Susan and her sister are up front. The minister steps to the pulpit, folks quiet down, and the service gets under way.

One thing quickly becomes clear: The minister isn't comfortable offering up the usual funeral platitudes. He doesn't say anything about Rory Freeman living a full life, being a good role model, or getting welcomed into the pearly gates of heaven. He can't bring himself to say any of that about a man who, if the rumors are true, lost his life savings at a poker table in the back room of a strip club and then blew his brains out in a swamp.

Fortunately for everyone, the minister asks Josh to come up and say a few words.

Josh gets to his feet, walks up to the pulpit, and for a long moment gazes out upon us. He looks so handsome up there in his dark suit, his expression solemn and subdued.

"I want to tell y'all a story about Rory," he begins. "It's a fishing story but really more about what kind of friend Rory was. A few years back a group of us, me and Rory included, get up at the crack of dawn, ready for some fishing on the bayou. We're eager to reel in the big ones, but man, when we get out on the water, the fish are *not* biting. It's like they took one look at our motley crew and said no way, no how, not now, not ever."

He takes a beat to make sure the congregation is with him, then continues. "As the morning drags on, the sun gets hotter, and the bayou turns into a steam bath. A few of us, including yours truly, are getting pretty grumpy. But not Rory. He was always looking out for folks and he was good at it, because he cared about people. He cared about his students, he cared about his family, and he cared about his friends, even when we were whining about this and whining about that. So what does Rory do? He starts cracking dumb fish jokes, jokes we've all heard a million times. 'Why are fish so smart?' 'Because they live in schools.' 'Where do fish keep their money?' 'In a riverbank.'"

Someone in the congregation chuckles and he keeps going.

"'How do you communicate with a fish?' 'Drop it a line.' 'What's the difference between a piano and a fish?' 'You can't tuna fish.'"

More chuckles come, mixed with a couple of good-natured groans.

"And Rory just keeps going, rattling off joke after joke, dozens of them, and he's relentless. He doesn't stop until he's turned our frowns upside-down. Because that's who he was. We ended up having a pretty great time on the water that day and even caught a few fish — because Rory Freeman was looking out for us. He cared about us — all of us — a lot. I know everyone here has memories of him looking out for you or helping someone you know. When you remember him, I ask that you keep those memories close to your heart."

He takes a breath and continues.

"I want to share one more story about Rory, this one from a few years back. A bunch of us from Boudreaux were in New Orleans for Jazz Fest, including Rory and his beautiful wife Susan. I'm sure you all know how much Rory and Susan love music, especially live music. And on this day, at the festival, the band starts playing a favorite number and Rory — well, he just lights up. He grabs Susan and they start dancing. He's twirling her around and she's laughing and I'll tell you, that moment will always stick with me because of the way he was looking at her, gazing at his wife with complete and total devotion and love."

He focuses in on Susan in the front row.

"Rory loved you so much, Susan. He loved you completely, fully, unconditionally. He knew how lucky he was to be with you that day, dancing with the love of his life."

Up front, Susan's sister puts her arm around her.

"I can only imagine the depths of your loss, Susan. I am so sorry he's no longer here with you. I can only pray that the love he had for you offers solace. I can only hope, as time does what time does with sorrow, the memories of your years together become a blessing."

He glances toward the minister. "I know Rory's colleagues and students at Briarton Academy are also going to miss him terribly. His friend and colleague Nancy would like to say a few words about what a wonderful, caring teacher he was."

As he steps down from the pulpit, Susan leaps up and pulls him in for a hug. "Thank you, Josh," she says as she sobs into his shoulder. "Thank you so much."

Susan's sister gets up and gently eases her back into her

seat. Josh returns to me and I give him an appreciative smile. My ex-husband has his flaws for sure, but just now he helped everyone here move past the manner of Rory's death by bringing them into the emotional zone they need to be in to grieve the loss of their friend.

When the service ends, Josh and I hang back and wait for the crowd of well-wishers surrounding Susan to disperse, then make our way toward her.

She pulls Josh in for another hug. "Thank you so much. Your words were so beautiful."

Then it's my turn for a hug. "And Callie, thank you for all your help this week."

"Just want to let you know everything's set for the school memorial tomorrow."

"Two-thirty, right?"

"That's right."

"You're sure all I have to do is show up?"

"That's all you have to do. I'll call you tomorrow morning to check in."

She lets me go and looks at us. "Shame the two of you couldn't work it out. You make such a good team."

I flush and catch Josh blinking with surprise. In the awkward pause that follows, I feel an urge to say something — but what?

Susan takes pity on us. "Oh, please, I'm just messing with you. You two are grownups. You know what's best for yourselves."

I find my voice. "Call if you need anything. Anything at all. We'll see you tomorrow."

After leaving the church, we drive to Marian's and pick up Ava. Our daughter's bursting with stories about Midnight Star. Marian seems pleased about having had

Ava for the night, but she's also clearly ready for a long nap.

Josh has agreed to hang out with us today, so we head home and play with Ava in her bedroom and then watch one of her favorite movies (the one about two princesses in a cold climate, which I've seen so many times I know every line of dialogue by heart). Then it's dinner and bath time and bedtime.

Finally, after reading her to sleep, we head downstairs.

Josh and I haven't been alone since we drove to the funeral. He looks at me awkwardly. "Well, I guess I should get going."

"You all set for the school service tomorrow?"

"Yep. You need a ride there?"

"No, I'm good. Beth will drive me."

It's the first time all day I've mentioned Beth and he notices.

He takes a deep breath. "Thank you again for letting her keep coming here to help out."

"Well," I say with a sigh, "I can't really blame her for how this unfolded."

"That's right. The blame's on me. All of it."

"I know that."

It's decision time: Do I tell him I know about Tiffany?

He gestures toward the kitchen. "Need any help cleaning up?"

"No, I'm good."

"You sure?"

The decision comes: *You can tell him later.* "Go ahead, scoot. Get home to your new wife."

Even though my tone is mild, he blinks and his cheeks flush. "Callie, I —"

"I mean it. Scoot."

With a trembling voice, he says, "Callie, are you and I gonna be okay?"

I'm silent for a moment. "When I'm done being angry with you, I think we'll be just fine."

His blue eyes shine with emotion. "I'm so glad we're still in each other's lives, even after all the stupid things I've done."

I hadn't expected him to say that. Now it's my turn to get emotional. "Same here."

He swallows. "Okay, I'm outta here."

"See you tomorrow at the memorial."

"Thank you, Callie. I don't know what I'd do without you."

And then he's gone. I watch him drive off, emotions swirling. I need to tell him I know about Tiffany — I don't have a choice — but the moment hadn't felt right.

Tomorrow, I tell myself as I lock the doors and begin my nightly walkthrough.

I'll tell him tomorrow.

CHAPTER 30

Monday gets off to a fast start. Beth arrives at seven-thirty to drive Ava to school and I tag along because the headmaster and I need to go over last-minute details for the memorial. While Beth waits outside in the car, I head up to the headmaster's office to review the program. The plan is for him to begin with a few words and then introduce each speaker. After the final speaker, the school choir will sing and the minister will close us out.

It's all straightforward. The headmaster tells me the speakers know what they're going to talk about and the choir has decided what it's going to sing. I glance at his office bookshelf and notice that a yearbook is still missing.

I gesture toward it "Still haven't tracked down your missing 2008 yearbook, I see."

His eyes dart over. "No, we haven't."

"The town library is missing their copy as well."

He frowns. "I didn't know that."

"How about the school library? Is that copy still missing, too?"

"How did you hear about that?"

"Sherry mentioned it last week. Seems like someone's going to a lot of trouble to keep folks from looking at that yearbook."

"Oh, I doubt that."

"Well, it's odd the thief is stealing only the 2008 yearbooks."

He's about to disagree when Sherry sticks her head in and reminds him about his next appointment.

"I won't keep you any longer," I tell him. "I'll be back at two to help with the setup."

"Thank you, Callie."

"Call if you need anything. See you this afternoon."

And then I'm out and a minute later back in Beth's car. My weekly rehab session is coming up and it's a short drive away.

Beth looks over anxiously as we head out. "It's going to be a busy day."

"Definitely."

A blush comes to her cheeks. "I'm glad I can be here to help."

"I'm glad, too." As the words leave my mouth, I realize I actually mean them.

"Again, I'm so sorry about not telling you sooner."

I take a deep breath. "I get why you two kept it quiet and I'm pretty sure that, once I'm done being upset with Josh over how it played out, you and I are going to be just fine."

"Thank you," she says, her voice filled with relief. "I'm so glad about that."

We pull into the clinic and Beth agrees to pick me up at

noon. Then I head inside and the staff put me through my paces. They're good at their jobs — painfully so — and by the time they're done with me, I'm an aching mess.

But there's no time to rest and recover because after Beth drives me back to the house, I barely have time to shower and get ready for the memorial service.

Shortly before two, Beth drives up and I climb in. Ten minutes later, we're at the school and I'm ready to help with any final prep.

At two-fifteen, students start flowing in, including Ava. I give her a hug and guide her toward a seat near the front. She's quiet and attentive and I'm grateful for that.

"You're being really good today," I say, leaning down to kiss her forehead. "Thank you."

She looks up at me with solemn eyes. "People are sad because Mr. Freeman died."

"That's right."

"It's sad when people die because we can't be with them anymore."

"Yes, honey," I reply, touched by her words. "It can be very sad."

"Everyone is going to die."

Emotion surges through me. "That's true. Death is part of the cycle of life. We're born, we live, and someday we die."

"When will we die?"

"Not for a long time. We have many, many, many years of life ahead of us."

"How many years?"

"So many years."

"More than ten?"

"So many more than ten."

"More than twenty?"

"So many more."

Her eyes widen. "More than a hundred?"

I smile. "That's a big number, but you never know."

"Do horses live a long time?"

"They do. They have nice long lives."

"How long?"

"Well, I tell you what. When we get home, we'll find a book that's all about animals and how long they live. Some animals live a really, really, *really* long time."

"Which animals?"

"Well, there are tortoises — big turtles — in the Galapagos Islands who live for nearly two hundred years."

Her eyes widen. Not only have I just introduced her to a cool new animal, but they live on islands that sound exotic and exciting.

"How big are the tortoises?"

"They're *huuuuge*," I say, holding my arms wide. "So big that we can't wrap our arms around them."

She's fascinated and, more importantly, thinking about something other than death. Out of the corner of my eye, I catch Susan walking in. She has the headmaster in her sights and is making an angry beeline for him.

Uh oh.

"Ava, I need to talk with the headmaster. I'll be right back."

I hurry over. By the time I get there, Susan's already said something and he's responding with, "No, Susan, I cannot and will not. There's nothing to say."

Her face is mottled. "I know that you know, you miserable coward." Though her voice is still low, folks nearby hear her and turn toward us, alarmed.

"Susan," I say, taking hold of her arm. "I have a seat reserved for you up front."

"Callie," she says, startled. "I need to —"

"You need to sit down." I tug at her — no easy task given my hip — but fortunately she lets me pull her away.

"What I need is the truth."

I glance around the auditorium. "Is your sister here?"

"She had to go to Atlanta. She'll be back later this week."

"I'm sure she'd agree that now's not the right time to tackle Devlin. The folks here today need this memorial. They're grieving, too. They lost a teacher, a colleague, a friend."

Susan's eyes fill with tears. "You're right. I'm sorry."

"Nothing for you to be sorry about." We've reached the front row. "We'll deal with Devlin, I promise. We'll find out what happened. But not here."

She nods. "Thank you, Callie."

"If it's all right, Ava and I are going to sit with you."

"Thank you."

I retrieve Ava and, after quickly introducing them, I have her sit next to Susan. Ava's presence seems to calm Susan, which is what I was hoping for. I glance at my watch — the service is about to begin — and look around to make sure everything's set. The headmaster, the minister, the teachers, and the students who are part of the program are all here.

But Josh isn't. Where is he?

In the back of the auditorium, I see Beth slipping into a seat. I catch her eye and mouth the words, "Where's Josh?"

She shrugs, then gestures to her phone and mouths, "I'll call him."

I sit down and the service gets under way. The headmaster opens with heartfelt remarks and introduces each speaker, all of whom have wonderful things to say about Rory. It's a lovely memorial and I can tell that Susan is touched. The highlight is when the students in the "Critter Club," the school group that had Rory as their faculty advisor, get up and unfurl a big banner with a drawing of Rory wrestling an alligator beneath the words, "We love you, Mr. Freeman."

There isn't a dry eye in the place when the service comes to a close. The minister ends with a prayer and dozens of folks come up and offer Susan their condolences.

"Thank you, Callie," Susan says to me when the crush finally eases. "I needed this and I didn't even know it."

"I'm glad I was able to help."

"You're a good gal."

"Anything I can do? Can we give you a ride home?"

"I drove. I'll be fine."

I stand there for a moment, considering. With Susan's sister back in Atlanta, she'll be alone tonight and I don't like that. "Ava and I would like to invite you over for dinner."

She glances down at Ava and smiles. "Why don't you two come over to my place instead? Folks have buried me in casseroles. I have too many to count. We can have us a smorgasbord."

"Does that sound okay, sweetie?"

Ava nods and I say, "I'll have Beth drive us over around six."

Susan pulls me in for a hug. "Thank you again. The service was beautiful. Rory would have loved it."

And with that she makes her way out of the chapel.

My phone buzzes and I see a text from Beth. "At the car when you're ready. No rush."

I reach down and take Ava's hand. "Okay, sweetie, time to head home."

A few minutes later, we reach Beth's car. I help Ava buckle up, then carefully climb into the front seat, my hip still aching from the morning rehab session.

"Were you able to reach Josh?" I ask Beth as we pull out.

"No. He didn't answer."

"Hmm."

"It's probably nothing," she says, though I can sense she's worried.

We're quiet on the ride home. Even though I didn't know Rory, the service left me feeling somber, maybe even a bit raw.

As we pull into Sycamore Lane, I'm surprised to see Josh's truck in the driveway.

"What's he doing here?" I say.

Beth shakes her head. "I don't know."

And then I see the front door.

Wide open.

Alarm shoots through me.

"The door's open," Beth whispers.

"Stay here with Ava. I'm going to check."

Ava pipes up. "Mommy, I want to go in."

"In a second, sweetie." I clamber out of the car. "I want to make sure everything's okay."

I grab my cane and handbag, shut the car door, and glance around, my senses on high alert. Everything is quiet. There's no breeze. Even the bugs are silent.

The wide-open front door seems — it seems *ominous*.

Fear floods through me. Heart pounding, I walk up the porch steps, listening carefully.

"Hello?" I call out. "Josh?"

More silence. I look back toward the car — Beth and Ava are both staring at me.

Get this over with, I tell myself.

I take a deep breath and walk inside. Everything seems fine in the foyer. I glance up the stairs and into the living room — completely normal.

I set my handbag on the sideboard, then walk into the kitchen and at first I can't accept what I'm seeing because it's not possible but then I hear myself gasp and I freeze and —

I can't breathe —

Because *Josh* is there.

On the kitchen floor.

In a pool of blood.

His blood.

His eyes wide open.

Staring at nothing.

Completely still.

"Josh?" I hear myself cry out, even though I already know —

He's dead!

CHAPTER 31

gasp as terror rockets through me. I'm frozen in place, unable to comprehend what I'm looking at, my eyes locked into the horror I'll never be able to unsee.

This isn't real. It can't be. He can't be dead. We're talking about *Josh*. My Josh. Ava's father. So full of life. He can't be lying on my kitchen floor in a pool of his own blood....

I break into a sob. This can't be happening. It can't.

Somehow I stumble outside and collapse onto the front porch.

I can't breathe. My stomach heaves and without warning I throw up. The vomit jets out of me, acrid and sharp. I feel faint, about to pass out.

Beth calls my name and races out of the car.

She's leaning down to help me when I push her away and gesture toward the house. She freezes, her eyes widening, then turns and goes inside.

Seconds later I hear her cry out and a horrifying thought rips through me:

Is the killer still in the house?

I gasp out loud. "Beth!"

Then an even more terrifying thought hits —

What if the killer's *outside*? Out here with Ava and me?

Ava — I have to protect her!

I stumble to my feet, hip screaming in pain, and look around wildly.

No one.

No one's here.

No one except us.

But the woods are so close.

So many trees.

How can I be sure?

My daughter's staring fearfully at me from the back seat and my heart leaps into my throat. I race to her, yank open the door, and rush into her arms.

"Mommy, what's the matter?"

Oh my God. What am I going to do? I can't let her see him. How can this be happening?

She starts crying. "Mommy, you threw up."

"It's okay, sweetie," I whisper as I clasp her tight. "It's okay."

"Are you sick, Mommy?"

"I'll be fine, sweetie."

I have to be strong. I have to get her away from here. Somewhere safe. As far away as possible.

Beth stumbles onto the porch. Her hands and dress are bloody. Dear God, she must have touched him. Her eyes are glassy. She's in shock.

Ava is staring at Beth fearfully. I slide into the back seat, unbuckle her, and pull her onto my lap, holding her close. "We're gonna stay in the car."

"I want to go inside."

"We can't do that right now."

"Why not?"

What do I say? I'm hugging her so tight I can feel her little heart hammering away in her chest. "Somebody broke into the house, sweetie. We're going to call the sheriff."

"The sheriff?"

"He's going to come here and check the house."

I take a deep, ragged breath. I can smell my own vomit. I need to keep it together. I need to call 911. I need my phone.

Where's my phone? In my handbag. *Where's my handbag?* I look toward the front seat.

I remember: It's *inside.* On the credenza in the entry foyer.

I have to go back in the house.

Fear shoots through me, but I have no choice. I take a deep breath, then let go of my daughter. I unfasten the car seat, pull it out of the car, and set it on the ground. "I'm gonna go get my phone, sweetie. It's in my handbag. I want you to lay down here in the back seat."

Reluctantly, she does as I ask, her eyes filled with confusion.

"I'm scared, Mommy."

"I want you to lay down and stay quiet. I'm going to get my phone and come right back."

She stares at me anxiously as I slowly shut the door.

I look around carefully — still no one.

Beth's on the porch steps, crying.

I hurry past her and through the open door and grab my handbag on the credenza. I reach inside and pull out my phone.

I can't believe this is happening. None of this is real. The air is heavy and still. Other than Beth's sobs, I can't hear a thing. The house is silent in a way that would seem normal and comforting except —

A gasp escapes me as my eyes land on bloody shoeprints on the polished hardwood floor. Are the prints mine? Beth's?

The prints are glistening, wet, fresh.

I'm looking at Josh's blood.

With trembling fingers, I dial 911. The line rings once, then twice, then a woman picks up and asks what my emergency is.

And somehow, despite a new surge of nausea and a pounding heart, I manage to say:

"I need to report a murder."

CHAPTER 32

What unfolds next is a slow-motion horror show. A sheriff's deputy pulls up and makes a beeline for Beth sobbing on the porch. Beth gestures for him to go inside and he comes out a minute later, his face pale. More deputies arrive, followed by an ambulance, then the sheriff, then more deputies. Yellow crime-scene tape goes up. A barricade is set up in the road. Before I know it, the place is swarming with law enforcement.

I've been watching all of this from the back seat of Beth's car. Aside from checking to make sure we're okay, the deputies have left me and Ava alone. My daughter's lying down, her head on my lap. I'm trying to persuade her to go to sleep but she isn't having it. She's very quiet, which isn't normal for her, and clinging tightly to my arm.

I hear a man say "Miss Callie" and turn to find Sheriff Denton at the car door, his concerned eyes taking in both of us. He's an older white man in his sixties with thinning gray hair and a paunch. He doesn't look like a sheriff, even in uniform. He looks too average. "Are you and Ava all right?"

"We're not injured, Sheriff, but if I can get some water or even some apple juice…."

"Of course."

"I need to get my daughter away from here."

"Of course. But I'm afraid I'll need you to —"

"If it's all right with you, I'm going to call my friend Gwen. She's Ava's godmother. She can be here in two hours."

He looks at Ava with sympathy. "That sounds fine."

"Until she gets here, I can have Ava stay with Susan Freeman."

He frowns at the mention of Susan. "Mrs. Freeman's going through a lot right now."

"She is, but I know she'll help out."

"You sure you don't want Ava's grandmother to…?"

Oh, God — *Marian.* Calling her hadn't even crossed my mind. She's going to be devastated.

I shake my head. "Marian isn't going to be able to … focus on Ava right now."

He blinks back sudden emotion. It's like he forgot that Josh is Marian's son. "Yes. Of course. You're right about that."

Ava's been listening to all of this. I gaze into her anxious eyes. "Honey, I need to make a couple of calls. I'll be right back."

"Mommy, stay with me."

I nearly start crying — she's so scared — but I force myself to keep my voice calm. "I'll be just a few feet away, sweetie. I'll be right back, I promise."

The sheriff tells a deputy to get a blanket and over Ava's

objections, I climb out of the back seat, then walk behind the car and pull out my phone. The sheriff comes with me.

My first call is to Susan. She picks up at once.

"Callie?"

"Susan," I manage to say, suddenly trembling.

"Callie, is something wrong?"

"Yes," I finally say. "I can't explain now. But I need to ask a big favor."

"Callie, tell me what's going on."

I want to tell her but the words refuse to come out. "Can I ask you to look after Ava for a few hours?"

I sense her surprise, but right away she says, "Of course."

"My friend Gwen, Ava's godmother, will be driving up from New Orleans. So it'll only be until she gets here."

"Of course I'll help. Callie, what happened?"

"Can I ask you to come to my house and pick her up? I'm at 14 Sycamore."

"I'll drive over right away."

"Thank you." I take a deep breath. "It's about Josh."

"About Josh? What happened?"

A sob escapes me. "He's dead."

She gasps. "What?"

"He's dead."

"Oh, Callie, I'm so sorry. What happened?"

I wipe tears from my cheeks. "Listen, I've got to call Gwen."

"Of course. I'll be there right away."

"Thank you." I hang up and turn to the sheriff. "Susan's on her way."

He nods. "Did Ava go inside the house at all?"

"No, she stayed in the car. The front door was open when we pulled up. I went in to investigate."

"Does she know that Josh is…?"

"No."

"What did you tell her?"

"I told her someone broke in."

"You said you're gonna call her godmother?"

"Yes." I dial Gwen and get sent to voicemail. "Gwen, it's me. Please call me. It's about Josh. It's bad." I take a deep breath. "He's … he's dead. Can you drive up tonight? I need to make sure someone can look after Ava. Please call me."

The sheriff's looking at me intently as I hang up. "Miss Callie, my deepest sympathies for your loss."

I blink back tears. "I can't believe this is happening."

"The paramedics are gonna take a look at you and Ava. We want to make sure you're both okay. I'll let you know as soon as Mrs. Freeman arrives."

"Thank you."

"Then we'll sit down and get your statement."

"Of course."

"Who else have you talked with?"

"You mean, aside from Susan and Gwen? No one."

"About Marian…. Would you like me to tell her?"

"Yes. Please."

He seems to sag at my answer. All of a sudden he looks old. "I should do it in person," he says, as much to himself as to me.

That's when we hear a car engine. At the barricade, Marian's silver Caddy screeches to a halt. Marian rushes out and tries to duck under the yellow tape but a deputy stops her.

"Damn it," the sheriff mutters as he hurries toward her.

Marian's struggling with the deputy. "Get out of my way. Let go of me."

"Marian," the sheriff says as he reaches her.

She whirls on him. "What the hell is going on, Hoyt?"

He leads her by the arm to a spot away from everyone. Then he says something to her, too quiet for me to hear, and she goes still.

She starts shaking her head. "No."

"I'm so sorry, Marian."

"No!"

"Marian, I'm so —"

"No!"

She breaks free and rushes toward the house. When another deputy stops her, she looks around wildly, frantically.

Then her eyes lock onto me.

"You!" she screams. "You did this! You murdered my son!"

CHAPTER 33

O h, God. In all my years, I've never witnessed such hatred, such fury, such unhinged grief and rage. If the deputy wasn't holding her back, she'd be attacking me right now. She'd be on top of me, dragging me to the ground, scratching my eyes out.

I realize I'm not shocked or offended by her accusation, maybe because I'm used to her constant loathing, and maybe because I can't imagine anything worse than what she must be feeling right now.

Plus, in some awful cosmic way, I can't help but think — maybe she's right. If I hadn't met Josh, if I hadn't married Josh, this wouldn't be happening. He wouldn't be inside my house right now, lying dead in a pool of his blood. He'd be somewhere else. He'd be *alive*.

The sheriff leads Marian to the ambulance. A deputy brings a juice for Ava and a bottle of water for me and another deputy gives a bottle to Beth, who's sitting on the porch, watching everything with grief-stricken eyes.

I'm still with Ava when Susan drives up a few minutes later. I get out of the car, grab the child car seat and my handbag, and take my daughter to Susan's car. A deputy offers to help me get the car seat buckled into the back but I tell him I'm good. While he's not looking, I reach into my handbag, take out Susan's gun, and shove it under the front seat. No way I want that thing with me right now. The sheriff might need me to go to the station and if he sees the gun, I'll have to explain where I got it and I don't want to be dragging Susan into this.

I clamber out and help Ava get buckled in. My daughter looks at me anxiously. "Mommy, I want to stay with you."

"I know, sweetie. But right now I need to help the sheriff. Mrs. Freeman is going to babysit you for a little bit while your Aunt Gwen is driving up from New Orleans. She'll be here in a couple of hours."

"I want to see Daddy."

It takes every ounce of control I have to keep my voice steady. "I know, sweetie. He can't be here, so Mrs. Freeman and Auntie Gwen are going to help out."

"Mommy, where's Daddy?"

I nearly lose it then — I almost start crying. She must have heard Marian's accusation. "I promise I'll explain later. Right now, I want you to be a good girl, okay?"

She nods reluctantly.

"I want you to eat dinner with Mrs. Freeman and then I want you to go to bed and get some sleep. Will you do that for me?"

"You'll come soon?"

"As soon as I can, promise." I pull her in for a hug. "I love you, sweetie."

"I love you, too, Mommy." Her little arms around my neck are tight with tension. I almost can't bring myself to break away but I finally manage it and gently close the car door.

I turn to Susan. "Thank you for doing this."

"Of course."

I keep my voice low. "Please don't say anything to Ava. If she asks, just tell her I'm helping the sheriff investigate the break-in and I'll tell her more when I get there."

"Break-in?"

"That's what I told her."

"Got it."

"She's a bit picky with food, but she's always okay with chicken and apple slices."

"Got it."

"I'll text you Gwen's number and give yours to her."

"Your friend Gwen can stay with me. So can you."

"Thank you."

She pulls me in for a tight hug. "Callie, I am so terribly sorry. If you need anything — anything at all — you call me."

"I will." And then I whisper in her ear, "Your gun is under your front seat." She tenses, startled, and I add, "I didn't want them finding it in my handbag and pulling you into this."

"Thank you," she whispers back, then lets go and gets into her car. "Anything comes up, I'll let you know right away."

"Thank you."

I watch, my heart in my throat, as she and Ava drive away.

The sheriff joins me. "Now, Miss Callie," he says, his manner sympathetic and encouraging. "Let's get your statement."

CHAPTER 34

He takes me to the front porch of the house next door and sits me on the steps, then calls over a deputy to take notes. There's less bustle over here. At my house, crime scene people are walking in and out in a constant flow. Two deputies are talking with Beth on my porch. A paramedic and a deputy are at the ambulance with Marian. Dr. Franklin has arrived and a deputy is pointing him toward Marian.

The investigation seems like it's been going on forever, but with a jolt I realize the afternoon sun is still high in the sky and the air is still uncomfortably hot. Maybe an hour has passed, if that, since I called 911.

The sheriff's watching me watch everyone. I point to Dr. Franklin. "What he's here for?"

"He's here as the coroner." He blinks as a thought hits him. "Is he your doctor? Do you want me to bring him over?"

"Yes, he's my doctor. No, I don't need to see him."

"All right." His gaze is sympathetic. "Then let's get started on your statement."

"Okay."

"Let's start with you telling me about your day."

"My day?"

"To help us establish the timeline."

Of course. The timeline. I take a breath and do my best to focus. "Ava and I woke up around seven-fifteen. Beth got here a little after seven-thirty and drove us to school at about seven-forty-five."

"You went with Ava and Beth to the school?"

"I was helping with the planning of the memorial for Rory Freeman and I needed to go over last-minute details with the headmaster."

"How long were you at the school?"

"Not long. Maybe twenty, thirty minutes. Then Beth drove me to the rehab clinic."

He points to my leg. "You mean, for your injury?"

"That's right. I go every week."

"How long were you there?"

"About two hours. My appointment was at nine-thirty. Then Beth drove me back to the house."

"What time did you arrive back here?"

"Around noon."

"Did you notice anything strange or unusual?"

I think back. "No."

"Okay, what did you do then?"

"I showered and got ready for the memorial."

"When did you leave the house to go to the memorial?"

"At about two."

"You and Miss Beth drove there together?"

"Yes."

"And the memorial was at two-thirty."

"Right."

"And lasted about forty-five minutes."

"Right."

"When the memorial ended, what did you do next?"

"Beth drove me and Ava back here."

"Arriving at about three-forty-five."

"Yes, that sounds right."

"Your call to 911 was at three fifty-two."

I blink back sudden tears. "Right."

"Miss Callie, thank you for taking us through this. This is very helpful."

I can tell he's trying to keep me calm and focused and I appreciate that, but I can't ignore the dread welling up in me. He's about to ask what I saw next and I'm desperately wishing I didn't have to go there. The last thing I want to do is relive that awful moment.

"This is going to be difficult, I know, Miss Callie. But I'd like you to take me through what happened when you got here."

I swallow back a surge of nausea. I need to push through this. "I was surprised to see Josh's truck out front."

"He wasn't supposed to be here?"

"He was supposed to be at the school. He was supposed to be a speaker at the memorial."

"You mean, like he was at Mr. Freeman's funeral service yesterday?"

"Right. It was Marian's idea."

"He didn't show up at the memorial?"

"Right."

"What did you do when you saw Josh's truck in front of the house?"

"Well, I was about to get Ava unbuckled when I saw the front door was open."

"The front door was open?"

"It made me nervous, so I told Beth and Ava to stay in the car and I went inside."

"What were you nervous about?"

"Well, it's not like Josh to not show up for something, and it's not like him to leave the front door open, so…."

"I see. Go on."

"I went in and didn't see anything at first. But then I walked into the kitchen and…."

I can't help it — tears come and I can't get them to stop.

The sheriff hands me a tissue. "What you're telling us is very helpful, Miss Callie. I want you to know that."

I try to stop crying and blow my nose. "I'm sorry."

"There's no need to apologize. What did you see when you went into the kitchen?"

"Him on the floor. All that blood. His eyes wide open, looking at nothing."

"Did you approach him? Touch him?"

"No."

"Was anyone else there?"

"No."

"Did you notice anything missing?"

I try to recall. "No."

"What did you do then?"

"I kind of … froze there for a minute. Then I made it outside and lost it."

"Lost it?"

"I threw up. I'm sorry about that. And I kind of just collapsed onto the porch."

"And what happened then?"

I blink back more tears. "I got scared. I was thinking, what if the killer is still here? So I got up and ran to the car."

"To Ava."

"Yes. Then I went and got my phone and called 911."

"And Miss Beth?"

"She went into the house and stumbled out covered in blood."

"And what did you take from that?"

"She must have touched him."

"You didn't touch him?"

I shake my head. "No, I froze up. I just stood there. I knew he was gone."

He reaches out and gives my hand a squeeze. "I'm so sorry, Miss Callie."

"I can't believe this is happening."

His voice gets husky. "Josh was a good kid and he grew up to be a fine man. I promise you, we're going to find the maniac who did this. I promise you that."

"Thank you, Sheriff."

"I need you to stay here a bit. I'm going to have more questions. I've sent a deputy for coffee and I'll bring you some when it's here."

"Thank you."

His leans down, his face suffused with sadness. "We're gonna get the bastard that did this, Miss Callie. I promise you that. We're gonna get him good."

CHAPTER 35

The sheriff and the deputy are called away and for the next few moments I'm left to myself, watching the scene unfold.

Unbidden, a memory stirs of a moment that's always been close to my heart — a moment that I realize, with a piercing pang of sadness, will forever be accompanied by the shadow of loss.

I'm washing dishes in the apartment in New Orleans, the afternoon sun coming in strong through the kitchen window, waiting for my boyfriend to come home. I'm a nervous wreck because I'm about to tell him I'm pregnant and I have no idea how he's going to respond.

I hear the familiar click of the front door lock and a few seconds later Josh walks in. He's tired after a long day of lectures and studying, but his eyes are on me as he sets his backpack on the kitchen chair.

He slips behind me and pulls me in close. I smell his sweat and aftershave. I feel his body heat.

"Mmmm," he murmurs, his lips nuzzling my neck. "I missed you." It's what he always says when he gets home. He knows I like hearing it.

I smile and give his strong arms a quick squeeze.

Then I summon the courage — *do it now* — and turn myself around. I have to see his face. I have to know.

"I'm pregnant."

He blinks, then blinks again. I've surprised him.

As my words sink in, he flushes and whispers, "You're saying I'm gonna be a daddy?"

"Yes."

A grin lights up his face and he whoops with delight — a cry of pure joy — and he pulls me in close and says, over and over and over, "I love you so much, Callie. I love you so much. We're gonna have a family. I love you so much."

I never loved him more than I did in that moment. We were married at City Hall the next day.

And now, seven years later, I'm here and he's....

The tears come then, along with the sobs I've tried so hard to hold back. I surrender to my grief and cry and cry and cry, no longer able to fight the shock and pain rolling through me.

At some point a deputy brings me tissues and a cup of coffee and hurries away, clearly uncomfortable with my emotions. Dr. Franklin comes over and gives me a great big hug and I cry some more.

"I'm so terribly sorry for your loss, Callie. So terribly sorry."

When I stop crying, he takes a step back. "I can give you a sedative to help."

"No, thank you."

He's about to ask again when the sheriff and a deputy approach.

"They need you inside," the sheriff says to him.

"I'm here if you need me," Dr. Franklin says, then hurries toward the house.

"Miss Callie," the sheriff says. "If it's all right, I have a few more questions."

I swallow back a wave of emotion and wipe the tears from my cheeks, then do my best to focus on him. He looks nervous for some reason. Am I coming across as too emotional? "Of course."

"I'd like to hear about the note you found on the door last week."

My eyes widen with surprise. Oh, God, the weird note. It hasn't crossed my mind, not even once. How does he know about that?

Then I let out a gasp as I realize, with the force of a sledgehammer, what else I haven't told him about.

The attack on me. The two intruders.

How could I not have made the connection sooner?

Were my attackers the ones who killed Josh?

I take a deep breath, my mind rushing in a thousand directions, first and foremost into a deep dark pool of guilt. If I'd told someone about last week's attack on me, could I have stopped today's attack from happening? Would Josh still be alive?

Regret surges through me. How in the hell am I going to explain this? Where do I even begin?

The sheriff's gaze is steady. He's waiting patiently for me to answer. I need to get my head on straight.

"Yes," I finally say, my voice trembling. "The note on my door."

"What can you tell us about it, Miss Callie?"

I take another deep breath and decide I'll tell him about the note first, then the rest. "I came home from a walk and found a note on my door."

"When was this?"

"Last Tuesday afternoon."

"What was on the note?"

"It had a number on it — 5309."

"That's it?"

"That's it." I glance over at my front porch to where Beth is talking with two deputies. She must be the one who told him about the note.

"Did the number mean anything to you?"

I shake my head. "I thought maybe the note was for Beth, but it wasn't."

"You showed the note to Beth?"

"Yes, after she and Ava got home."

"So when you found the note, you were here by yourself?"

"That's right."

"And you didn't know what the number was?"

"I had no idea, but Beth thought it might be a passcode for one of those lock boxes that real estate agents use." I gesture toward the front door behind me. "Like, maybe the houses here on Sycamore are finally going on the market and someone left the code on my door by mistake?"

"We'll follow up on that. I understand you had dinner with Josh that evening."

"That's right. He came over."

"Did you tell him about the note?"

"No, I didn't."

"Why is that?"

I feel myself flush. As much as I'd prefer not to reveal this, I have no choice. "It came to me that the number might be a passcode to a phone, so I checked Josh's phone to see if it was his."

"Was it?"

"Yes."

"The number on the note — 5309 — was the passcode to Josh's phone?"

"That's right."

"What did Josh have to say about that?"

I swallow back my anxiety. "He was upstairs with Ava when I checked his phone."

The sheriff frowns. "You're saying he didn't know about the passcode and he didn't know you used the passcode to get into his phone."

"Right."

The sheriff's frown deepens. He doesn't like hearing this. His opinion of me just went down. "What did you see on his phone?"

"I wasn't on it long, but I saw texts between him and a woman named 'Tiff.'"

"As in Tiffany?"

"That was my assumption."

"What were the text messages about?"

"Well, it was clear that he and Tiffany had hooked up. He was telling her how much he was looking forward to seeing her again."

"What else did the messages say?"

"That was pretty much it."

He turns to a deputy. "Bring us Josh's phone."

We wait while the deputy goes to his vehicle and retrieves a phone in a plastic bag and hands it to the sheriff.

I watch the sheriff type in the 5309 passcode. It looks awkward typing through the plastic bag, but he manages it and starts scrolling through the messages.

"'Tiff,' you said?"

"That's right."

"Not seeing that."

He hands me the phone in the plastic bag and I scroll through. He's right. There's nothing from Tiff. All of the Tiff messages are gone.

I hand him back the phone. "He must have deleted the messages."

He frowns. "Just so I'm clear. You're saying that last Tuesday night, when Josh came here for dinner, you gained access to his phone and saw text messages from a woman named 'Tiff.' The messages suggested they were seeing each other."

"That's right."

"And now you're saying the messages were deleted."

"Well, they're not there now."

He doesn't like my answer. He hands the phone back to the deputy. "See what else is on it."

Then he turns back to me. "Let's stick with the events of last Tuesday night. You found out about Tiff from his phone. What did you do when you found out?"

"Nothing."

"Nothing?" His eyebrows go up. He's acting like he doesn't believe me.

"I didn't ask him about Tiff, if that's what you mean."

"Why not?"

"I didn't want him to know I'd been in his phone."

He tries to hide his frustration but doesn't succeed. "Was there anything else in the messages that might help us?"

"Wait, yes," I say, suddenly remembering. "Josh asked Tiff the name of the guy at the door, and Tiff said 'Big Ed.'"

The sheriff and the deputy exchange a glance. "Big Ed?"

"Yes."

"Is that a name you're familiar with?"

"At the time, no."

He frowns. "At the time?"

Oh, gosh. Explaining this is turning out to be a lot more complicated than I expected. "I figured it out later."

His frown deepens. "You figured out what later?"

I take a breath to calm myself, then tell them what I learned at the convenience store about the woman who raced out the door past me — how Alice told me her name is Tiffany and how her boyfriend works as a bouncer at Lola's.

"Did, uh…" — it takes him a second to remember the name — "Alice tell you the bouncer's name is Big Ed?"

"No. But I confirmed that when I went to Lola's."

He looks at me with astonishment. "You went to Lola's?"

"Saturday night."

"By yourself?"

"Yes."

He gestures to my leg. "How?"

"I drove."

"You can drive now?"

"Saturday was the first time since the accident and it hurt like hell, but yes."

He takes a deep breath. "Why did you go there?"

"To find out. I had to know."

"You had to know *what*?"

I glance over at Beth on my front porch. "I assume you know that, on Saturday at Marian's, Josh and Beth told us they're engaged?"

"Yes, Miss Beth told us."

"She told me that she and Josh started dating five months ago. The texts between Josh and Tiff were from *three* months ago."

He chews on that for a few seconds. "So you were wondering if...."

"I wanted to know if the Tiffany I saw at the convenience store was the Tiff on Josh's phone, and I wanted to know if Josh was seeing Beth and Tiff at the same time."

"What did you find out?"

"I was able to talk with Tiffany." As I remember the beauty of her dancing and the cruel things she said about Beth, I tense. "She confirmed that she and Josh had hooked up."

The sheriff lets out a sigh and glances over at Beth before turning back to me.

"And Big Ed?"

I flash suddenly to my attack — to the hulking shadow with the knife in my kitchen — and I must go pale or something because the sheriff leans forward and says, "Miss Callie, are you all right?"

"I'm sorry, Sheriff," I whisper, my stomach churning with dread. Telling him about Tiffany hasn't gone the way I'd hoped. Will telling him about the attack go any better?

But do I have a choice?

The situation couldn't be clearer. I was threatened with a knife in my kitchen. Josh was killed with a knife in my kitchen.

The attacks *have* to be related.

To help find Josh's killer, I have to tell the sheriff what happened.

"Yes, about Big Ed," I say, trying to keep my voice level. "I went there to see if he was the one who attacked me."

The sheriff frowns. "The one who attacked *you?*"

"Yes." I feel my face flush as the truth finally slips out. "Last week, a man with a knife attacked me in my kitchen."

CHAPTER 36

t all comes out then, the terror of that horrifying night tumbling from me in a torrent of words I couldn't stop even if I wanted to. The sheriff stares at me flabbergasted but eventually recovers and helps me through my account while the deputy furiously scribbles notes.

It feels good to be telling someone, to finally unload the burden of keeping everything bottled up inside. The sheriff is a good listener, letting me do most of the talking as I take him through all of it, from hearing the chair scraping downstairs to waking up the next morning on the kitchen floor. I don't hold back. I tell him about the big man lunging at me with the knife, me whacking the man with my cane, the man falling onto his own knife, the blood seeping onto the floor, and then the smaller attacker sneaking behind me and jabbing me with a hypodermic needle.

"Thank you for sharing all this with us." The sheriff's manner is sympathetic. "It sounds like you went through a terrible ordeal."

"It was horrible."

"You said one attacker was a large man and the other a smaller person, either a man or a woman."

"Yes."

"Any idea who they might be?"

"I had no idea at the time, but when Alice told me at the convenience store about the customer who injured himself...."

"You mean Big Ed."

"Yes."

"That's why you went to Lola's. To see if you recognized him."

"Yes, though also to find out if Josh cheated on Beth with Tiffany."

He sighs. "Miss Callie, why didn't you report the attack when it happened?"

I flush. This is the hardest question to answer because it's the same question my inner critic has been hammering away about nonstop.

Tears come. "I was afraid."

His eyebrows go up. "Of what?"

"I was afraid I wouldn't be believed." I touch my head. "I was worried people might think I imagined it."

"You mean, because of the injury to your head from the accident?"

"I was worried that, if people didn't believe me, they might be concerned about Ava staying here with me."

"People like Josh?"

"More like Marian. She's been after me to move into the mansion and there's no way I'm ever doing that."

He glances toward Marian, still over at the ambulance. "Why do you say that?"

"Because she's a raging bitch." I let out a big sigh. "As you know full well, Sheriff."

He doesn't nod, but he doesn't disagree with me either. "Getting back to Big Ed. Do you believe he's the man who attacked you?"

I hesitate. "I don't know. I'm not sure."

"Because your attacker wore a mask?"

"Big Ed's the right size, but…. I don't want you to think I'm one of those people who goes around accusing someone without evidence."

"What you're saying is, you can't say he is, and you can't say he isn't."

"Right."

He gazes at me for a long moment like he doesn't know what to make of me.

"Tell me," he finally says. "How did you feel about Josh and Beth getting engaged?"

"Married," I reply, correcting him.

"You know they got married?"

"Josh told me."

"When?"

"Saturday, while we were watching Ava on her favorite horse."

He consults his notes. "After lunch was over? After Josh drove Beth home and then returned to Marian's house?"

"Right."

"How did you feel about him and Beth being married?"

"I was upset. They hid their relationship from me. They lied to me."

"So you were angry."

"Not as angry as Marian. She was furious."

"But still, you were angry and upset with them."

"Josh brought Beth into my house under false pretenses. She was here with me and Ava for an entire month and I had no idea that she and Josh were together."

"That matters to you."

"Of course it matters." Irritation flashes through me. Surely the sheriff understands that. "It was a betrayal of trust."

"A betrayal of trust," he repeats, scribbling a note. "Yes, I see that."

My phone buzzes and I pull it out. *Gwen.* My heart quickens. "Sheriff, I have to answer this. It's Gwen, Ava's godmother."

I bring the phone to my ear. "Gwen."

"Callie," she says. "I just got your voicemail. What happened?"

"Josh is ... dead." I swallow back a surge of grief. "He's been murdered."

She gasps. "Oh, Callie."

The tears come again. "It's terrible, Gwen, it's just terrible."

"Oh, Callie, I am so sorry."

With extreme difficulty, I push back the wave of emotion. "I need your help."

"Of course. I'll come right away."

"I need your help with Ava. She's with a friend right now. Her name is Susan."

"Susan texted me. I have her number. I'll call her."

"Thank you."

"Callie, who are you with right now?"

"I'm with the sheriff."

"What are you doing with him right now?"

"I'm giving him my statement."

"Callie." I hear her take a deep breath. "What are you telling him?"

"Everything."

"You need to stop talking to him."

I blink, filled with sudden unease. "Why?"

"Because the sheriff is not your friend."

I feel a tingle of anxiety.

"His goal is to make an arrest."

"But that's not what—"

"No, Callie," she says, her words firm and deliberate. "He isn't after justice, no matter what he might have told you. His job is to collect enough evidence for the D.A. to indict. His goal is to make an arrest and close the case quickly."

What she's saying sounds so clinical. She hasn't heard the emotion in the sheriff's voice, the way he almost cried when he said Josh was a great kid and a fine man. "It's not like that."

"Yes, it's exactly like that. He might be targeting *you*. You need a lawyer. You're in legal jeopardy."

"We can talk about that when you get here."

"I'll be there in two hours. In the meantime, don't say anything else to the sheriff. I'm making calls. You need a good attorney."

"I've got to go. I'll see you soon."

"And Callie, I'm so sorry about Josh."

As I'm putting my phone back in my pocket, a deputy comes up and whispers in the sheriff's ear.

The sheriff frowns, then whispers something back. Then he says out loud, "Bring everything over here."

The deputy returns with a cardboard box full of plastic evidence bags.

"Did you find something, Sheriff?" I ask.

"We did. I'd like your reaction."

He reaches into the box and pulls out a plastic bag. The bag looks empty.

"I don't see anything."

"Come closer."

I lean forward and that's when I see that inside the bag are several long strands of brown hair, caked in blood.

"We found these hairs in Josh's hand."

I examine them closely. The hairs look like they could be *mine*.

Dr. Franklin walks out of my house and the sheriff notices. "Miss Callie, if you'll excuse me a moment." He walks over to Dr. Franklin and says something quietly to him, then walks him to a spot maybe eight feet away from me.

"What's the preliminary, Doc?" the sheriff says, loud enough for me to hear.

Dr. Franklin looks over at me like he's guilty of something. "Time of death around two p.m., give or take thirty minutes."

"Cause of death?"

"Sliced jugular. He bled out in seconds."

I shudder at his words. Part of me still can't believe we're talking about Josh.

"Any signs of a struggle?"

Dr. Franklin shakes his head. "No defensive wounds. The killer walked up behind him and sliced."

"What kind of knife?"

"Large and extremely sharp."

"What kind of strength was needed?"

"With a knife that sharp, not much."

"Thanks, Doc."

With another furtive glance toward me, Dr. Franklin hurries away and the sheriff returns to me. "Sorry about that, Miss Callie. Now where were we?"

"You were showing me a bag with hairs in it."

"That's right. Any thoughts about those hairs, Miss Callie?"

"Sorry, no."

"Any idea who those hairs might belong to?"

I shake my head. "No."

"I couldn't help but notice that the hairs look a lot like yours."

"I have no idea if they are or not."

His eyes narrow. "We're gonna run a test and get the answer real fast, I promise you."

"Good."

He reaches into the evidence box and pulls out the plastic bag with Josh's phone in it. "This is Josh's phone. When we went through it, we found texts from a number we didn't recognize. I'm wondering if you know the number."

"What's the number?"

"Let me show you the texts." He uses Josh's passcode to get into the phone, then taps to the messages and shows them to me.

848-555-7573

Hey, before you go to the memorial, can you swing by? I heard a strange sound in the garage.

JOSH

There in a few.

. . .

I frown. Who was Josh texting?

"Miss Callie," the sheriff says. "Can you tell me what you know about these messages?"

"I don't know anything about them. Who was he texting?"

"We're looking into that. The timing is interesting, isn't it?"

"What do you mean?"

"The first text was received on Josh's phone at one forty-five. He replied a minute later, at one forty-six."

"That's shortly before he died."

"That's right." He reaches down into the cardboard box and pulls out a different plastic bag. In it is another phone.

My stomach tenses. Gwen was right. The sheriff is leading up to something.

"Do you recognize this phone, Miss Callie?"

I shake my head. "No."

"We found it in the trash bin in your garage."

I blink. "In my garage?"

"Stuffed deep down in the bin, like someone was trying to hide it. Now, if I'm remembering right, you said Miss Beth drove you to the memorial service."

"Yes, that's right."

"She got here at about two?"

"Yes."

"When she got here, did she go inside?"

"No, I saw her pulling up and I went outside."

"She didn't go into the house? She was in her car the whole time?"

"Right."

The sheriff hands me the second phone, then picks up Josh's phone. "Let's see what happens when we dial the number of the person who at one forty-five asked Josh to come to your house."

He hits a button on Josh's phone.

A second later, the phone in my hand rings.

I stare at the phone, shock rocketing through me.

"What is this?" I gasp.

"You tell me, Miss Callie. You tell me."

The sheriff isn't acting sympathetic anymore. He's glaring at me with anger and contempt.

As the change in demeanor sinks in, a sense of disconnectedness washes over me. It's like I'm watching the scene from a distance and the sheriff and I aren't the ones talking. Right now I should be filled with grief or terror or anger or outrage or all of the above, but instead I'm numb, barely reacting as the sheriff wraps me in his net of suspicion.

"It's not my phone," I hear myself say.

The sheriff snorts.

"The killer must have planted it in my garage."

"That's not gonna fly, Miss Callie."

"I didn't do it."

"I'm gonna tell you what I think happened. It's possible Josh was murdered by someone who's not fully in her right mind as a consequence of a head injury she got when a reckless driver ran her down and left her for dead."

I gasp, shocked to my core.

"Maybe because of her head injury, the killer is bit more impulsive than she was before. Maybe by her own estimation, she's only ninety, ninety-five percent normal. Maybe she's even aware she's having trouble controlling how she behaves."

I can't believe what I'm hearing. I shoot a glance at Dr. Franklin and he quickly looks away. So much for doctor-patient confidentiality.

"Maybe the killer was angry and upset at her ex-husband." The sheriff's voice has an edge. "Not just because he cheated on her and divorced her, but because he hid his new relationship from her and hired his new fiancée to *spy* on her and his daughter."

Tears come and I don't even try to stop them.

"Maybe the killer considered what he did a 'betrayal of trust.'"

"You're twisting my words."

"Maybe the killer texted Josh and got him to come over here on some pretext, like hearing something moving around in the garage. And once he was here, maybe she stepped behind him and sliced his throat open before he even knew what was happening."

"No."

"Maybe the killer stuffed the knife and phone in the trash bin, then waited for Beth to arrive and drove off to the school."

"No."

"Maybe the killer did all this because her grasp of reality is a bit, I don't know, untethered. Maybe she even imagined someone attacked *her*. Maybe the attack she imagined sounds an awful lot like the attack that just occurred."

"I didn't imagine the attack on me."

"A knife attack. In your kitchen. A man down. Lying in a pool of his own blood."

I gasp. *No, it can't be.* I feel dizzy, faint. *He's wrong. He has to be wrong.*

"Maybe the killer doesn't even realize she did it. Maybe

her mental issues are more significant than she knows. Maybe her attorneys are gonna be able to make a really good argument for diminished capacity."

I can't believe what I'm hearing.

"But I'm getting ahead of myself. My job is to uphold law and order in Boudreaux Parish. Which means my duty today is sadly very clear."

The sheriff squares his shoulders and looks me in the eyes.

"Callie Crawford, you are under arrest for suspicion of murder."

CHAPTER 37

can't believe this is happening. The sheriff spins me around, yanks my arms behind me, and snaps handcuffs on. Almost theatrically, like he's putting on a show, he reads me my rights and pulls me by the arm to a deputy's car.

Everyone at the crime scene stops what they're doing and stares. On the front porch, Beth gapes at us, stunned. At the ambulance, Dr. Franklin looks away, clearly ashamed. Even Marian seems taken aback.

The sheriff opens the back door of the deputy's car and shoves me in, my hip crying out at the awkwardness of it. As I struggle to sit up in the seat, the handcuffs dig into my skin. Fear jolts me as I realize how vulnerable I am.

Maybe it's that awareness that jumpstarts me. "Bring my handbag and cane," I snap, glaring up at him. "I'll need them when I get out."

He blinks, surprised at my sudden spirit. "Miss Callie —"

"You're a fucking moron."

His mouth opens and his face goes red when he realizes that everyone heard me. "Young lady," he says with a weak attempt at a chuckle, "we're gonna have to have a talk about this attitude of yours."

"No, we won't. I'm not saying another word until I speak with my attorney."

"Miss Callie —"

"Fuck you."

He slams the car door shut and tells a deputy to book me. The deputy hurries into the car and we roar off.

Suddenly I'm in a moving cage, my hands trapped behind me, my hip protesting at every bump and swerve as the deputy races through the neighborhood, siren screaming. The back seat stinks of sweat and fear. The vinyl is moist and filthy.

Holy shit, I'm in trouble. The sheriff is, without question, a moron — but so am I. If I'd kept my trap shut like Gwen begged me to, if I hadn't told the sheriff about the attack on me, if I hadn't been so goddamned eager to be helpful, I wouldn't be handcuffed in a police car right now. I'd still be at the crime scene or maybe even on my way to Susan's house to be with Ava.

I'm such an idiot. When will I finally accept that, when it comes to the way things work down here, Gwen is always, always, *always* right? Why do I always, always, *always* push back and insist on trying my way first? *What is wrong with me?*

I need to accept, once and for all, that I'm an outsider in Louisiana. No more fairy tales about learning the lay of the land and blending in. As much as I want to understand this place, I don't. There are depths here I can't fathom —

rhythms, undercurrents, traditions, rules that aren't natural to me. You have to be from here — like Gwen, like Susan, like the alligators in the bayou, like the mosquitoes that feast on my flesh — to truly know it. You have to simmer in Louisiana like a slow-cooked stew before you can feel it in your bones.

I flash to Josh lying in a pool of his own blood on my kitchen floor and shudder. The favored son of Boudreaux, the sole heir to a grand and terrible legacy, is dead and gone. Marian's empire has been shattered.

I have to get out of Boudreaux, away from this horror show. I have to escape for my sake and Ava's.

My stomach clenches. *Ava.* How can I protect her when I'm in jail? How can I convince the sheriff I didn't do this?

And then it hits me — *I know how.* If only I'd realized it sooner.

"Deputy," I say urgently. "Deputy, there's something I forgot."

The deputy glances at me through his rear-view mirror. He's younger than me — early twenties, white freckled skin, earnest face. He's the one who arrived first on the scene and came out looking pale. "Ma'am, we'll be at the station shortly."

"I remembered something important."

"Ma'am —"

"Josh's truck wasn't in front of the house when Beth arrived to pick me up."

He's silent for a moment. "His truck wasn't there?"

"Which means Josh got to the house *after* Beth and I left."

"You're saying you couldn't have done it."

"That's right. Ask Beth — she can confirm the truck wasn't there."

"We'll do that when we get to the station."

I fall back into the seat. The deputy looks at me sympathetically.

"The sheriff's wrong about me," I say to him.

His expression becomes guarded. "We'll see."

At the station, the deputy brings me inside and removes my cuffs, then takes me to a female deputy who sits me down at a desk in the main room and types my arrest information into a computer.

"Can I call my friend Gwen?" I ask her. "She's going to get me a lawyer."

The deputy points to the phone on the desk.

I pick up the receiver and try to remember Gwen's number. Luckily, I get it right.

"Hello?" Gwen says.

"Gwen, it's me."

"Callie? Where are you calling from? Whose number is this?"

"The sheriff's station. I've been arrested. Suspicion of murder."

She inhales. "I'm on my way to Boudreaux now."

"I need a lawyer."

"I have calls out. You'll have one tomorrow."

"Thank you, Gwen."

"Don't say a word until you talk to your lawyer. Not a word, got it?"

"Got it."

"They treating you okay?"

"I think so. So far."

"We'll get you through this, Callie."

The deputy motions for me to set the receiver down. "Thanks, Gwen. I have to go."

"See you soon. Love you."

"Love you, too."

I set the phone down and the deputy walks me to a counter to fingerprint me, then stands me against a wall to take my photo. Then she leads me through a heavy metal door into a long, bare room with four jail cells in a row. The cells are all empty. I have the place to myself.

"We'll be ordering in dinner," she says as she locks me in. "Burger and fries okay?"

"Sure."

"Coke?"

"Diet, if that's okay."

And then she's gone. The door to the front room clanks shut and suddenly I'm alone. It's hot and silent in here. The cement walls are a dirty gray. The overhead fluorescent lighting is harsh. My cell has a metal toilet and a bunk bed with two threadbare mattresses. I can smell bleach and mold.

I eye the lower mattress with trepidation. It looks gross and sad, but tiredness is taking over and I need to sit. As I settle onto it, air escapes the mattress and I catch a whiff of urine.

God, I'm in such a mess. Fear grabs at me and before I know it, my heart's hammering away and I'm about to cry and that won't do, so I take a deep breath and then another and order myself to calm down. Eventually, my breathing evens out and my heart slows. I inch back on the mattress and lean against the cement wall and try my best to *think*.

The sheriff will have to see things my way once he understands that Josh's truck wasn't at the house when Beth picked me up.

I take another deep breath. Once the sheriff understands

that, he'll realize I couldn't have killed him and he'll see that what I told him about the attack on me is important.

Even as I think that, doubt flutters through me. I'm still having trouble with the sheriff's crazy idea that I *imagined* the attack on me. For him to suggest that is, well, outrageous.

Anger stirs and I admit it feels good. There's no way I imagined the two intruders — no way in hell. I may not be fully healed, but I'm getting closer every day. The sheriff's accusation is just another example of an older man in a position of power discounting the testimony of a younger, less powerful woman. He's a sexist asshole and a gaslighter to boot.

The door to the front room screeches open, startling me. It's him — the sexist gaslighter.

He's alone. He shuts the door behind him and walks up to my cell and stares at me through the bars.

I clear my throat. "I asked your deputy to tell you what I remembered."

"He told me."

"Did Beth confirm what I said?"

"She did."

Relief floods through me. I inch off the mattress and slowly stand up, taking care not to upset my hip.

"Can you let me out now?"

"Not so fast." There's a glint in his eye and I tense. What's he up to?

I step up to the bars. "I wasn't there. I didn't do it."

"Maybe your accomplice did."

I breathe in, taken aback. "My *what*?"

"You even told us his name." He looks so smug as he stares at me. "Big Ed."

I can't believe what I'm hearing. "*What?*"

"Not only that, you told us when and where you met him. Saturday night at Lola's."

"I told you why I went there."

"Maybe your real reason was to arrange a hit. Maybe you hired him to murder your ex-husband."

I gaze at him, speechless.

"See, we've had our eye on Big Ed for a while now. He's not what you'd call an upstanding member of society."

I find my voice. "Sheriff, what you're suggesting is crazy."

He chuckles. "Miss Callie, that's not a word I recommend you use, given your fragile state of mind."

Goddamn him. It takes everything I have to keep my voice level. "Sheriff, my recovery is coming along fine. I need you to let me out so I can be with my daughter."

He shakes his head. "We're gonna keep you overnight while we check out this lead you gave us."

"Sheriff, my daughter needs me."

"Your little girl is fine, Miss Callie. Your friends are with her. You arranged that yourself."

"Sheriff —"

"Look at it this way. If people really are out to get you, then this cell is the safest place you can be."

"Safe? You're saying this jail is *safe*?" Before I can stop myself, I say, "It wasn't safe the night you murdered John Bracken."

The sheriff's eyes narrow and my heart starts pounding. *Dear God, what have I done?*

A flush of anger — fear? — rises in his cheeks. "What did you just say?"

The worst possible thing, I almost admit. Antagonizing this man in his own house, baiting him with an accusation I can't prove — I really am a moron. He has all the power here. I have none.

"You heard me," I say, surprising myself. "And I gotta warn you, if a second prisoner dies in your custody, you won't be able to cover it up. Not again."

For several long seconds, he glares at me, his lips tight with anger.

"One death might be an accident," I continue, "but two? In a small place like this? That's a pattern."

He's beet-red now. There's no telling what he might do. Why am I poking the bear?

Finally, he lets out a long sigh. "You really are a piece of work, Miss Callie. Everyone was saying you aren't right in the head, but I was inclined to give you the benefit of the doubt."

He leans closer to the bars. "Now I know better."

"You know I didn't kill Josh. You need to let me out."

"We'll see about that." He turns to the door. "Get a good night's sleep, Miss Callie. You're gonna need it."

CHAPTER 38

won't linger on my miserable night in the Boudreaux Parish jail — the stink of mildew and fear and sweat, the air heavy and hot. At nine o'clock the overhead fluorescent light switches off and the room is plunged into darkness. Every couple of hours, the door to the front screeches open and a deputy steps in to check on me. Every time that happens my heart leaps into my throat and I wonder: Are they bringing in someone to beat me to death, the way they did with Bracken? Am I in the same cell the poor man was murdered in?

Somehow, despite not being able to banish my dark thoughts, I manage to doze and am awakened when the fluorescent lights flicker on. A deputy steps in and tells me he's ordering breakfast from the diner. I ask for a bacon-and-egg muffin and coffee. When he comes back twenty minutes later, the coffee is still hot and the sandwich is still warm and I tear into both, shocked at how ravenous I am.

An even bigger surprise comes a short while later when the door screeches open and Marian walks in.

I go still. What the hell is she doing here? A deputy follows her, but she waves him out. "No. This is private."

With a respectful nod, he retreats and shuts the door.

Leaving me alone with my former mother-in-law.

She's in the same blouse and slacks she had on yesterday, but her makeup's gone — she must have wiped it off — and the effect is shocking. Her skin is discolored and uneven, her eyes puffy and raw.

"Callie," she says, her voice barely a whisper.

Sympathy surges through me. As awful as losing Josh is for me, it must be even worse for her. I can't even begin to imagine the pain of losing a child. "Marian, I'm so sorry."

She doesn't say anything as she stares at me.

I blink back tears. "I want you to know I didn't do this."

She steps closer and I do likewise.

We gaze at each other through the jail cell bars, looking deep into each other's eyes.

"I would never hurt Josh," I whisper. "Even after everything we went through during the divorce, I loved him. I'll always love him."

No response. There's a blankness in her, like her soul is gone. The rage and grief from yesterday are absent, at least for the moment. She's been hollowed out. No, more than that — shattered.

With a jolt of urgency, I realize I have to make the most of this opportunity. If I don't convince her I'm innocent, there's no telling what the sheriff might do.

"Josh meant the world to me," I continue. "And to Ava. She loves her father. He loves her. I would *never* take that love from her."

Finally, she blinks. "Ava." I catch a flicker in her eyes. "Yes, Ava."

My heart quickens. If Marian and I are ever going to find common ground, it will be around doing what's best for Ava.

With a trembling voice, I continue. "Ava's with Gwen, her godmother, right now. She knows there's been a break-in, but she doesn't know about Josh. I need to tell her." Tears come to my eyes. "I don't know how I'm going to do that."

My words must strike a chord because she blinks and snaps back into herself — the blankness replaced by aware-ness, perhaps even purpose.

"I know you weren't the one who killed my son," she says.

I breathe in sharply, beyond grateful to hear her say that. "Thank you."

"Do you know who did?"

I shake my head. "I have a suspicion." As quickly as I can, I tell her about the attack on me and about Big Ed's injury. She takes in every word, listening raptly.

"Hoyt is a fool," she says when I'm done, then glances around the jail with distaste, as if surprised to find herself here. "Have you told him what you just told me?"

"Yes."

She frowns. "Ava needs you."

"Yes."

Her back straightens. "I'll see to it."

"Thank you."

"At some point, most likely tomorrow, I'll want to see her."

"Of course."

"Also, it's likely I'll need you. When I call, you'll come. No questions asked."

I hesitate — I'm agreeing to an open-ended deal with the devil — but what choice do I have?

"Sure."

She nods and without a flicker of hesitation or expression of interest in how I'm doing — typical Marian behavior, in other words — she turns and leaves.

I'm still wondering what she might need me for when a deputy steps in and unlocks my cell door. "The charges are dropped. You're free to go." In the main room, he gives me my handbag and my cane. With a mixture of relief and bewilderment, I walk out of the sheriff's station into the bright light of morning, grateful to once again be free.

It's early. No one else is around. I reach into my handbag and pull out my phone to call Susan and discover it has no juice, so I take a deep breath and start walking. Her house isn't too far and after the night I just had, I'm grateful for the chance to stretch my legs and unlock the tension in my hip.

Twenty minutes later, as I'm limping up the driveway to Susan's house, the door bursts open and Ava, Gwen, and Susan rush out and wrap me in hugs.

"I'm so glad to see you," I say as I kneel down and hold Ava tight in my arms. "All of you."

We go inside and I let them fuss over me. They give me a blueberry muffin. They make me a latte and watch me drink it.

Then Ava climbs onto my lap and says, in a little voice that rips at my heart, "Mommy, where is Daddy?"

I swallow back a rush of tears as I gaze at my beautiful daughter. She has Josh's eyes and cheekbones. Every time I look at her, I'll also see him.

I can't put this off any longer. With a tidal wave of grief looming over me, I take Ava into the living room and sit down with her on the sofa and tell her the worst thing you can ever tell a child. She shakes her head and says no over and over, and when she cries out for her daddy, my heart breaks into a million pieces because I can't stop her crying and I can't stop my sobbing and it's all just beyond awful. As she buries herself in my arms, the only thing that keeps me from collapsing completely is the knowledge that I will not rest until I find out who took Josh from us. If it's the last thing I ever do, his killer is going to pay.

I pick up Ava and carry her into Susan's guest room and lie down on the bed with her and we hold each other and cry and doze and wake up and cry some more.

At some point Gwen comes in and tells us we need something to eat and we say no, we're not hungry, but she insists and we follow her into the dining room. She sits us down and Susan serves us hot chicken noodle soup. Then Gwen takes Ava into her arms and retreats with her into the guest bedroom and Susan tells me I need to take a shower, so I do.

When I'm done washing the stink of jail off me, Susan takes me into her bedroom and gives me clothes that don't quite fit.

"I shouldn't," I say as she hands me blue jeans and a red blouse.

"You'll have to for now," she says. "I called and asked if I could get some of your outfits but they said no."

I frown. "They'll have to let me in. I need clothes. Ava needs clothes."

Her gaze is anxious. "Did they treat you all right in there?"

"I was the only one locked up."

"Thank God for that. I called Rory's friend — remember, the state investigator I mentioned?— and he had his boss the Attorney General call the sheriff."

"Thank you. When I saw Marian this morning, she said she was going to talk to the sheriff as well."

"Marian?" she says, tensing. "You saw her?"

"This morning. She looked awful. I can't even imagine what she's going through."

"Why was she there?"

I take a deep breath. "I think she was deciding for herself whether I did it or not."

"Did you convince her?"

"I'm here, so I guess so?"

"What did you tell her?"

"I told her I'd never take Ava's father away from her. I think that's what got through to her."

Susan sighs with relief. "Thank God."

A disturbing thought hits. "Has any of this made the news?"

"The local stations ran stories last night."

Anxiety surges through me at the prospect of cameras and reporters chasing after me. I take a deep breath to calm myself. I need to get ahead of this. I need a clear head. I need to figure out how to get me and Ava through this nightmare.

"Has Gwen found a lawyer?"

"A good one. She'll tell you about him. Maybe you won't need him?"

"I will if I get arrested again. If that happens, I want to be clear: Ava stays with Gwen."

"Of course."

"Not Marian."

"Hell, no." She reaches out and squeezes my hand. "Don't you worry. We're behind you all the way."

More tears come. "Susan, I'm so glad I met you."

"Same here." A cloud of worry passes through her eyes. "About Josh…."

"What about him?"

"Is there any chance my gun was involved in…?"

"No, no, no," I say quickly. "I had the gun with me. And Josh was killed with a knife, not a gun."

She blinks back tears. "I still can't believe we're talking about this. It doesn't seem real. Josh is the most alive person I've ever known."

"I can't believe it either." Another thought hits. "Have you talked with Beth?"

Susan shakes her head. "No. Why would I?"

She doesn't know, I realize. "Beth and Josh just got married."

She gasps. "They *what?*"

"I only just found out. They kept it a secret from everyone."

"Holy shit."

"I was stunned."

"You had no idea?"

"None."

She glances over to the kitchen counter where my phone is charging. "Maybe she called you?"

I hurry over and turn on my phone. My voicemail is full of messages, most from numbers I'm not familiar with.

But amid the clutter is a voicemail from Beth. I press the speaker button so we can both listen.

"Callie, it's Beth. I can't believe they arrested you. I told them Josh's truck wasn't there when I picked you up. They'll have to let you go, right? I...." She starts sobbing. "I'm sorry. I can't believe he's gone."

Tears fill my eyes as I'm listening. Her grief feels so real and so familiar.

"I feel terrible for her," I say to Susan.

"You should call her."

I glance toward the bedroom door. "I'll go outside."

"I'll make us coffee."

"Thank you." I walk out onto the front porch. The sun is bright and high in the sky, the air hot and still.

My thumb hovers over the phone. Last night in jail, in the lulls between waves of grief and fear, I was able to do some thinking about the questions I have no answers for, starting with:

Who killed Josh and why? Who benefited from his death? Did he have an enemy with an ax to grind? Was someone angry with him? Jealous of him?

Why was he killed at my house? It took careful planning to lure him there. Surely there would have been easier options?

Was he killed by the same intruders who attacked me? Again, I have to assume the answer is yes, given the location (my kitchen) and the weapon (a knife) used in both attacks.

Why didn't the attackers kill me last week when they had the chance? I was at their complete and total mercy after they jabbed that needle into me and knocked me out. Why am I still alive?

And finally, an idea that's only just occurred to me: What if the hit-and-run accident that put me in a coma wasn't an accident? What if I was run down deliberately?

A sigh escapes me. Everything that's happened seems so

senseless, but there's clearly an underlying pattern here — a plan — that I'm not seeing.

Keep your eyes open and stay alert, my inner voice says. *Find the answers you need. Your life, and Ava's, depend on you uncovering the truth.*

I look at my phone, take a deep breath, and call Beth's number.

She picks up on the first ring. "Callie, is that you?"

"It's me."

She sounds almost frantic. "Are you okay?"

"I'm okay."

"Are you still in jail?"

"No, they let me out. I'm at Susan's with Gwen and Ava."

"Thank God. I couldn't believe they arrested you."

"Well, I'm out now."

"I told them Josh's truck wasn't there when I picked you up."

"Thank you. I'm sure that helped." I take a deep breath. "How are you holding up?"

"Not good. Not at all." I hear her blow her nose. "I'm a mess."

"I'm so sorry for your loss."

"I can't believe this happened." There's a pause. "Have you told Ava?"

"Yes." Tears well up but I push them back. "A little while ago."

"I'm so sorry, Callie."

"Listen," I say quickly, hoping to push past another emotional upsurge. "There's something I need to tell you."

"What is it?"

"I met Tiffany."

There's a confused pause. "Tiffany? I don't know a Tiffany."

Tiffany must be a stage name, I realize. "I mean, I met your sister."

I hear her indrawn breath, followed by an explosive: *"What?"*

I blink, taken aback. "I met her. Your twin sister."

"Where?"

"Here in Boudreaux."

"She's *here?*"

"Working as a dancer at Lola's."

Beth gasps. "Callie, my sister has issues. She's not stable. She can get violent."

My heart leaps into my throat. "What do you mean by violent?"

"She has a kind of ... fixation on me. If someone gets close to me, she perceives that as a threat."

Oh my God. I'd been hoping to eliminate Tiffany as a suspect — her involvement seemed far-fetched — but what I'm hearing suggests the opposite. Dread grips me as I leap to the horrifying, inevitable question:

Did Tiffany kill Josh?

"Callie," Beth says, her voice almost a whisper. "Does she know that you know me?"

"Yes," I whisper.

"Does she know that I've been helping you?"

"I told her that we're friends."

"Does she know about me and Josh?"

"I don't know."

I hear her hold back a sob. "She did it. I know it. She killed him."

"You can't know that."

"I know my sister, Callie."

"But Beth, you can't —"

"Callie, you're in danger." Her voice is fierce with fear. "You, Ava, your friends — everyone you're close to. All of you are in terrible danger."

CHAPTER 39

The story that pours out of Beth is sad and horrible — an account of mental illness tearing a family apart. She and her sister were close as kids, she tells me, but as they entered their teenage years, her sister began experiencing mood swings — sullen and suspicious one day, exuberant and excited the next. She started doing drugs, skipping classes, picking angry fights with Beth for no reason, then crawling back and begging for forgiveness. Her parents tried to get her medical help but she resisted at every turn. At seventeen, she ran away from home and shacked up with an older man, cutting off all contact with her family.

"Every once in a while she'd show up," Beth tells me. "And she knew everything that was going on with me and I realized she'd been watching me, spying on me."

I feel awful listening to her. "That's so frightening."

"She'd say bad things about the people in my life — jealous things, things that made it clear she knew a lot about them."

"Oh, no."

"Two years ago, I was dating a guy — nothing serious, but he was a good guy — and all of a sudden he broke it off and I asked why and he told me someone had gutted a pig in his parents' kitchen and pinned a note to it that said, 'Beth is mine.'"

I breathe in with horror. "Oh, my God."

"There was blood everywhere, he said. His mom slipped in the blood and injured her back and ended up in the hospital."

"Beth, I'm so sorry."

"I'd always tried to defend my sister, always tried to find some way to explain her behavior, but that was the last straw."

"What did you do?"

"I reported her to the police, and then I confronted her and told her I never wanted to see her again." I can tell she's struggling with her emotions. "That's when she attacked me. I barely managed to get away."

"What happened?"

"She was arrested and convicted and sentenced to five years in prison."

"And you thought she was still there?"

"The prison is supposed to notify us of any change in her status."

The horror of what I'm hearing is almost overwhelming. "Beth, I'm so sorry. I had no idea."

"I'm sorry I didn't say anything sooner." Her voice is quieter now. "It's not something I talk about."

That's when a thought hits me like a sledgehammer — a realization so undeniably true and spot-on that I become nauseous as I stand there baking in the heat on Susan's porch:

Josh is dead because I kept quiet about the attack on me.

If I'd told Beth about the attack, she might have recognized the pattern and called the prison to make sure her sister was still locked up. If she'd learned her sister was out of jail, then she would have been able to warn us, and the authorities would have been able to investigate. Her sister might have been arrested and put back in jail.

And Josh might still be alive.

I break into a sob — and realize Beth's saying my name over and over.

"Callie, are you all right?"

"I'm sorry," I say, pushing back against the emotional surge. "Lost in my head again. Listen, there's something you should know about."

I tell her about the two intruders who attacked me.

"Oh, Callie, I'm so sorry," she says when I'm done. "I can't even imagine."

"It had to be your sister, right? Her and her boyfriend."

"It sounds like her. But wait, she has a boyfriend?"

"A guy named Big Ed who works as a bouncer at Lola's."

Beth is silent for a moment. "He'd have to be as crazy as she is."

"Maybe he is."

"Maybe." She takes a deep breath. "Regardless, my sister being here in Boudreaux changes everything. I need to tell the sheriff."

"You want me to help with that?"

"No, I'll do it. I have to be the one. She's my sister. If it turns out she's the one who did this…."

"Well, maybe she isn't," I say, even though I don't believe that. "Maybe they'll investigate and clear her."

"God, I hope so. I'll call you later. Is there anything I can help you with?"

"No, Susan and Gwen are here."

"Anything you need, you let me know."

"Thank you, Beth."

We hang up and I take a few moments to collect myself before heading back inside. Gwen's with Susan in the kitchen and she tells me that Ava is sleeping. Susan makes us lattes and we sit down at the dining table and in a low voice I tell them — finally — about the attack on me and what Beth just told me.

They listen, appalled.

When I finish, Gwen says, "I wish you'd told us sooner about the attack."

"I completely agree."

"It must have been beyond terrifying," Susan says. "No wonder you wanted my gun."

"I just felt better having it."

I can sense that Gwen wants to say more — a lot more — about my unfortunate habit of not asking for help when I need it, but she refrains and says instead, "I don't know Beth. Tell me about her."

"Well," I begin, "We're just getting to know each other. She's quiet, she's been really helpful, she's a bit on the shy side —"

Susan snorts.

"What?"

"She may be all that, but she's also really good at keeping secrets."

"Sure, but —"

"And not just about her psycho twin sister. I mean, secretly getting married to Josh?"

I blink back a rush of tears. "You're right."

Gwen clears her throat. "All we're saying is that we need to know more about her."

"Well," I say, feeling the need to defend her, "she definitely wasn't the person who killed Josh. She was with me when that happened."

"A point in her favor." Gwen glances at her watch. "The call with your lawyer is coming up. We should get ourselves ready."

"Ready how?"

"Well," she says, "the more prepared we are, the better he'll be able to help."

"Okay, but how?"

"For example, do we have any ideas about who killed Josh and why?"

Even though I was just asking myself the same thing, I tense up. It seems surreal to be discussing this.

Perhaps sensing my discomfort, Susan jumps in. "It had to be a mistake. I can't see anyone wanting Josh dead."

"Did he have any enemies?" Gwen asks. "Anyone he got on the wrong side of?"

I clear my throat. "Well, maybe Big Ed."

Gwen nods. "The bouncer at the strip club and maybe-boyfriend of Tiffany."

"If Big Ed found out about Tiffany and Josh," Susan says, "then maybe he went after Josh out of jealousy?"

"Maybe," Gwen says. "Of course, money's also a good motive. Who benefits from Josh's death?"

"Beth probably inherits whatever he has, but he really

doesn't have all that much. Marian controls the purse strings. She's always kept him on a pretty tight leash."

"He has no real money of his own?"

"His law income is good, but aside from that, not really. He always expected he'd inherit the family fortune."

"Now that he's gone, who inherits?"

Anxiety surges through me. "Ava, most likely."

"Marian told you that?"

"No, but that's what I expect. Marian will want the Dupre family fortune to go to her granddaughter."

Susan's frowning. "So with Josh, it doesn't seem like money is a strong motive."

Gwen nods in agreement. "Everything we just discussed, we need to tell your new lawyer."

Which we do a short while later, when we dial into a conference call with Jermaine Clement, Attorney at Law. Gwen has already told me about him — noted defense attorney, charismatic in court, effective at using the media to present his clients in a sympathetic light — and he comes across pretty much as she's described.

As succinctly as I can, I tell him about everything that's happened in the past week. He listens carefully, occasionally asking questions for clarification.

When I finish, he says, "You've been through a painful ordeal, Ms. Crawford." His voice is warm and rich, with a cadence that seems to imbue meaning in every word. "I commend you for your fortitude."

"I'm just trying to get me and my daughter through this. Can I ask you a question?"

"Please do."

"The sheriff dropped the charges. Do I still need a lawyer?"

"Well," he says, "that depends. If the authorities don't come after you again, if the members of the press treat you fairly, if your ex-husband's killer is identified quickly and prosecuted successfully, then you may decide you don't require legal counsel."

"I'm hearing a lot of 'ifs.'"

He sighs. "My concern is that Boudreaux isn't done with you. Your parish isn't known for its faithful adherence to due process."

"You think the sheriff might come after me again."

"It's possible he will do that, yes."

His words settle heavily in my stomach. He's right, of course. I'm pretty sure the only reason I'm not in jail right now is because Marian ordered the sheriff to let me out. And the only reason she did that was so that I could take care of Ava.

How long will that reason hold?

Not long — that's how long. At best, Marian views me as temporary childcare, useful only until she finds a way to push me out of Ava's life forever. With Josh gone, there'll be no one to stop her from coming after me.

"Mr. Clement, I'm afraid you're right. I'd like to officially hire you."

"Representing you will be an honor, Ms. Crawford." He tells me he'll send me a document to sign and gets me to agree to refer all legal and media inquiries to him. "I'm preparing a statement for the press, which I'll send to you to review. Our friends in the media will want something from you and it's in your interest to provide it to them."

"Okay."

"Most importantly: If the sheriff comes after you again, what do you tell him?"

"That I need my attorney."

"What else do you tell him?"

"That I need my attorney."

"Excellent." Though his tone is reassuring, his concern is clear. "Ms. Crawford, I sincerely hope you won't require my legal services, but it's best we prepare for that eventuality."

CHAPTER 40

There are moments in the aftermath of a loved one's death when the battering waves of grief recede temporarily and you find yourself aimless and adrift, uncertain of where you are and unwilling to find out. The world feels wrong but you can't bring yourself to care because it's all you can do to keep breathing.

Our afternoon at Susan's is like that. The sheriff doesn't bother us, probably because he's hunting for evidence to support his stupid theory that I hired Big Ed to murder Josh. Reporters keep buzzing my phone and I ignore them, but it's only a matter of time before they discover we're at Susan's and swarm us. Ava awakes from her nap and wants me and Gwen to play with her, so for a while we do that. Mr. Clement emails a press release for me to review and approve. Susan decides she's going to cook us an elaborate dinner and gets busy with that.

All of us are distracting ourselves, pretending what we're doing is good or helpful when what we're really doing is waiting for the next disaster to strike. We can't even fill our time with the usual decisions that go into burying a loved one. As Josh's ex-wife, I have zero say in planning his funeral, though I'd like the service to be appropriate for Ava. But who do I discuss that with? His devastated mother? His grieving new wife?

The answer comes after dinner. Gwen and I are cleaning up in the kitchen and Susan and Ava are in the guest bedroom putting new sheets on the bed when my phone buzzes.

I look at it — it's Marian. "I should get this." I dry my hands and pick up. "Hello, Marian."

"I need you to come to the house to discuss the plans for the funeral." As usual with her, there's very little chit-chat.

"Of course. When would you like me to come over?"

"Now."

"Now?" I look over at Gwen and we exchange surprised looks.

"Yes. We also need to discuss our other matter."

"Other matter?"

"Punishing Josh's killer." Up to this point she's sounded normal, but now I hear a tremble in her voice. Has she been drinking?

"Marian, who's there with you right now?"

"I sent them all home."

"Who did you send home?"

"All of them. Edmond, Ella, Hank. Useless, all of them."

I take a deep breath. She's alone at the mansion and really shouldn't be. "You're saying you know who did it?"

"Yes, I know."

"Who?"

"I need to tell you in person." Her voice drops to a whisper. "I need to tell you how I'm going to mete out punishment. Justice must be mine."

What she's saying seems unhinged — biblical even. There's no way she can know who killed her son, at least not with any certainty.

But what if she does know? What if she somehow found out? She has resources, after all. Given her emotional state, what is she about to do?

"Marian," I begin, still hoping to beg off, "it's getting late and I need to get Ava to sleep and…."

"Is Ava all right?"

"No." Now *my* voice is trembling — it must be contagious. "She's not."

I can almost hear Marian's brain snapping back into place. "You told her."

"Yes, this morning." A shuddering sigh escapes me. The memory of my daughter crying out for her daddy will haunt me until the day I die.

"I'm very sorry you had to do that," she says with more sympathy than I've ever heard from her. "I was the one who told Josh about his daddy's hunting accident. Ava needs to be strong now."

No, she doesn't, I almost reply. *She's six years old.* But there's no point in arguing — Marian never listens to me anyway.

"Is it okay if we plan to meet in the morning?" I say instead.

"No, Callie, I need you to come to the house immediately. Also, I need you to pick up Devlin and bring him here."

"Devlin?" I repeat, surprised again. "Why him?"

"He's helping plan the funeral. The two of you did a fine job with Rory Freeman's memorial."

"But, Marian —"

"He called and told me his car won't start. He needs a ride."

"It's been a really long day and I —"

"No," she says, cutting me short. "We have a funeral to plan. And I know who killed my son. I need you here now."

"Marian —"

"I mean it, Callie." Her voice rises and the trembling returns. "Your daughter's future is at stake and I won't listen to your excuses. When I say I need you here now, I mean it."

CHAPTER 41

And so, after an agonizing moment of indecision, I agree to her request — command, really — to drive over and see her.

A few minutes later, as I'm tucking Ava into bed, she gazes up at me and whispers, "Mommy, are you going out?"

She must have heard me and Gwen in the kitchen. "In a little while, yes, just for a bit."

Her eyes are anxious. "Why are you going out?"

I lie down on the bed close to her, face to face. "To check on your grandma and make sure she's all right, but that won't take long and I'll be back soon."

"Is Grandma okay?"

"She's very, very sad. I'm going to check on her and make sure she's able to get a full night's sleep. It's important for all of us to be rested."

"Can I see her?"

"You and I will go see her tomorrow."

Her gaze is so solemn. "Is she as sad as I am?"

Tears well up. "Yes, sweetie, she is. She loves your daddy so very, very much."

"I love him very much too, Mommy."

"I know you do, sweetie. We all do."

"He's not in the hospital."

"No, sweetie."

"He can't wake up like you."

I blink back more tears. "No, sweetie."

A few minutes later, to my immense relief, my daughter's eyes close and she falls asleep. As gently as I can, I ease off the bed, turn off the light, and shut the bedroom door.

In the living room, I confer with Gwen and Susan before heading out.

"You're sure you want to do this?" Susan asks.

"I'm not sure at all. But Marian sounded close to unhinged on the phone. I need to make sure she's all right."

Susan cocks an eyebrow. "Do you though?"

"She's Ava's only grandparent, so yes."

Gwen speaks up. "I still think I should go with you."

"I appreciate that, but I'd prefer for you and Susan to stay here with Ava."

"I know, but I —"

"If she wakes up, it's important for you to be here. Plus, it's only a matter of time before reporters figure out where we are and come knocking."

"Still, the idea of you being out there by yourself...."

"I'll be driving straight to Devlin's to pick him up and then I'll be at the mansion with him and Marian. I'll call right away if I need anything."

She gestures to my hip. "You sure you're okay driving?"

"I managed it the other night. I'll be fine."

Susan rises from her chair and hustles toward her bedroom. "Hang on a second."

Gwen's voice drops to a whisper, which is what it does when she's worried. "You sure about this, Callie? I've got a bad feeling about you going there."

Before I can answer, Susan is back and giving me her gun. "I want you to take this."

"No." The gun feels heavy and cold in my hand. "I couldn't."

"It'll make me feel better, knowing you have it with you."

"But I —"

"Callie, please."

I glance at Gwen, who shrugs. "You never know."

I try to hand it back. "What if you need it?"

"Honey," Susan says with a hint of amusement, "you think that's my only gun? Rory's got a rack of hunting rifles in the closet and believe you me, I know how to use 'em."

I know when I'm beat, so I slip the gun into my handbag. "Thank you."

Gwen hands me my cane. "Sure you don't want backup?"

"I want you here with Susan and Ava. Just in case."

She doesn't argue because she knows — we all know — that *just in case* means a lot more than *just in case Ava wakes up* or *just in case the media come calling*. It also means *just in case the killer comes here and tries to break in*. To prepare for that possibility, we've already gone through the entire house and locked every door and window.

I run through my checklist of essential items — phone, cane, Susan's gun, Susan's car keys. "Okay, I'm off."

"Call if you need anything," Susan says.

"Will do."

From the front door, the two of them watch me limp to Susan's car and carefully climb in. After shifting around in the seat to find the least painful position, I wave goodbye, back out of the driveway, and aim the car toward Devlin's.

His house is near the school, a short drive away. The road is dark and quiet. A big drop of rain splatters against the windshield, followed by another. The sky is pitch-black — no stars, no moon. Is a storm coming? My hip starts complaining as I make a right turn, so I shift my position again to ease my discomfort.

It's odd that Marian chose me and Devlin to help plan the funeral, but I can't let myself get hung up on that. The loss she's suffered is horrendous and life-changing. She isn't thinking clearly. Making sure she's okay is the right thing to do.

I reach Devlin's house and pull into the driveway. The windows are dark. I grab my phone and text him but he doesn't answer.

I'm getting ready to climb out of the car and knock on his front door when I decide to call Marian instead.

She picks up immediately. "Callie?"

"Hi, I'm at Devlin's but it doesn't look like he's here."

"He found another ride. We're waiting here for you."

Irritation surges through me but I tamp it down. Interactions like this are vintage Marian — thoughtless, impatient, zero regard for me. "I'll see you in a few."

As I'm pulling away from Devlin's house, my irritation increases. I need to stop letting Marian slip under my skin. I know how she is. I know *who* she is. For a few enjoyable seconds, I indulge in the fantasy of calling her out for her arrogance and telling her to go to hell.

But you'll never tell her to go to hell, my inner voice says. *She's your daughter's grandmother. For Ava's sake, you'll put up with her.*

At the main gate of the Dupre estate, I pull in next to the entry keypad, lower the car window and, with difficulty, reach out and type in the code that Josh had me memorize. The gate swings open and I drive in.

The winding road through the cypress grove feels different tonight — eerie, unsettling. The rain's coming steadily, accompanied by occasional gusts of wind.

The big house seems to be watching as I pull up. Marian's Caddy is parked out front next to a black pickup truck. Through the front parlor windows, I see light coming from inside.

I turn off the car and sit there for a few seconds, unwilling to move.

Stop dawdling, I finally tell myself. *The sooner you make sure she's okay, the sooner you can get back to Ava.*

With a sigh, I open the door and clamber out. The rain is really coming down now, so I grab my cane and handbag and limp as quickly as I can to the porch steps. A rumble of thunder comes as I knock on the front door.

I'm brushing rain off me when the door opens and Marian is there, gazing from the gloom like a pale wraith in a white silk blouse and slacks. She looks a whole lot better than she did this morning, her makeup and silver hair once again immaculate.

"Callie," she says, her voice calm and steady. "Come in."

I step inside. The hallway is dark, the house silent.

"Let's go into the study," she says.

I follow her through the darkened front parlor, her heels clicking on the wood floor. In the study, a desk lamp is lighting up the area right around the desk, leaving the rest of the room swathed in shadows.

She gestures to a chair in front of the desk. "Have a seat."

I set my handbag on the floor next to the chair and settle in. So far she seems to be acting normally, at least on the surface. "Where's Devlin?"

"In the kitchen." She walks to a window and gazes outside. "Making coffee. He'll join us shortly."

Her manner is calm, which is an encouraging sign. "Whatever planning you want me to help with, I'm happy to help."

"You know, that's the thing about you," she says, still looking outside. "Always ready to be of help."

I'm not sure what to make of that. Is she complimenting me — or complaining?

"Josh always gravitated toward people who like to *help*," she continues. "Help, help, help. He loved the *help* so much, he married them — two of them, in fact."

She whirls on me, eyes blazing with rage and grief, and I can't help but gasp.

"Marian," I begin.

"He told me about you."

"Josh?"

A bitter laugh escapes her. "My son? No, my son told me *nothing*."

I'm totally not following. "Who are you talking about?"

"I know what you asked him to do."

She's accusing me of something — but what? Even in the dim light, I can see she's trembling and nowhere near to being okay. "Who are you talking about?"

"Ed."

It takes me a second — then hits me with a jolt. "Big Ed?"

Another bitter laugh. "So you *do* know him."

I can't believe this. Is she serious? "We've barely spoken."

"That's a *lie.*"

"Like, two words at the door at Lola's."

"He *told* me what you asked him to do."

I stiffen with alarm. What does she mean? Am I in danger? Has she lured me here to — how did she phrase it? — "mete out punishment?"

What is she planning?

I have to calm her down. "Marian, I didn't ask him to do anything."

"You asked him to kill Josh."

I inhale sharply. "No."

"You tried to hire him to kill my son."

"Marian, no. I would never do that."

"I believed you this morning when you said you would never harm Josh."

"Because it's the truth."

"I believed you when you said you'd never take Ava's father from her."

"Because I never would."

"But Ava is *exactly* why you did it."

"Marian —"

"It's always been about her for you, hasn't it?" Her voice rises. "Never about Josh. Never about being a good wife for him. No, everything is always about *her.*"

"Marian —"

"And now that Josh is gone, everything here" — she waves her arms — "will be hers."

"Marian —"

"You knew that, didn't you? Just like you knew you had to act fast — before Beth got herself pregnant."

My heart is thudding with fear. She isn't thinking clearly. Her grief has pushed her off the deep end.

I need to get the hell out of here. I tighten my grip on my cane, immensely grateful that I have it with me.

I'm about to get up, readying myself for whatever she might do next, when I hear it —

No, feel it —

A whisper of movement, air flowing over my skin —

I turn and gasp —

There's a man in the study doorway!

CHAPTER 42

gasp, fear racing through me.

It's Big Ed!

He looks so huge looming behind me, so tall and wide, so imposing. There's a creepy grin on his face, his eyes gleaming with anticipation. "Evening, Callie."

He chuckles and I freeze in horror —

Because I *know* that chuckle.

I heard it a week ago — *when he attacked me in my kitchen.*

Before I even know what I'm doing, I'm standing up and raising my cane over my head and swinging it as hard as I can at him —

But this time he catches it in his hand and rips it from me — effortlessly — and laughs.

"Nice try."

I have one more chance. I reach for my handbag —

But he shoves me away and I crash to the floor.

Before I can stop him, he's grabbed my handbag.

"What do we got here?" he says, a pleased grin on his

oafish face, squeezing the bag with his meaty fingers. "Something good? Something *fun*?"

He pulls out Susan's gun. "Now how about that?"

"Give it to me," I hear Marian say.

Startled, I look over. She's gazing at Ed eagerly, her hand outstretched.

Dear God. She knew he was here. *She planned this.*

But why?

Why in the hell is she working with him? Doesn't she know what he did? How can she not realize that he *murdered her son?*

"Marian, what are you doing?"

"Shut up, Callie," she replies, her eyes still on Ed. "The gun, young man."

He walks over and hands it to her.

"Thank you." Marian points it at me. "Get off the floor, Callie."

With difficulty, I climb to my feet.

"In the chair."

I do as ordered. My hip is killing me but I don't care. "Marian, you don't know what he —"

"Shut up."

"He killed him. He killed Josh!"

She laughs. "I won't be falling for your lies again."

"Told you she'd say that," Ed says. He's at the window now, my cane in his hand, watching me like a guard dog.

"Yes, Ed," she says, almost purring, "you certainly did."

I have to get through to her — but how? "Marian, the attack on me last week — it was *him*. I recognize his laugh."

"Ah, your so-called attack. Ludicrous, of course."

"It *happened*."

"Did it?" She smiles like a cat toying with its prey. "Why didn't you report it?"

"I was afraid no one would believe me."

"Why would they? It's laughable."

Her gun hand is steady, her expression avid and self-righteous. She truly believes I hired someone to kill Josh and she's ready to *mete out punishment.*

I have to convince her I'm innocent — but how? "How can you trust him? The sheriff told me that Ed's a bad guy — not exactly an upstanding member of society."

She shrugs. "No one's perfect."

"He killed Josh."

"No, he didn't."

"How can you know that?"

Impatience flashes through her eyes. "Of your many bad traits, the one I like least is your habit of challenging my competence."

"That's *not* what I'm doing."

"You don't think I checked his alibi?"

"I can't wait to hear the bullshit he cooked up for you."

"He was with his girlfriend yesterday afternoon."

I can't help it — I laugh. "Who told you that — his *girlfriend*?"

She flushes. "The manager of the motel confirmed they were there."

"How can he know?"

"The walls are thin."

"Meaning what?"

"Do I need to spell it out?"

"Given what's at stake, yes!"

"He heard them *fucking*."

I snort. "Well, the motel manager lied. Maybe they paid

him off. Maybe they have something on him. Maybe they played a porn video real loud."

Marian laughs. "Is that the best you can come up with? A conspiracy or a porn tape?"

"You can't do what you're thinking of doing, Marian. Please."

With deliberate slowness, she flicks off the safety on the gun. "I've wanted you gone from the moment I found out about you. Eight long years I've put up with you."

"Marian, you're not a killer."

She smiles. "You have no idea who I am. That's always been your problem. You've never understood certain basic truths. You don't belong here. Josh was never yours. All you've ever done is get in the way."

"Marian, please. You have to do what's best for Ava."

Marian blinks at the mention of her granddaughter but her gun hand remains steady. "I'm doing what's best for Ava's future. She'll miss you in the short term. But I'll be there for her. She'll grow up to be a strong, capable woman. I promise you that."

My God, she actually believes what she's saying. She's about to pull the trigger and murder me.

Then I realize what she hasn't said — and I grab desperately at my last chance.

"You haven't met Ed's girlfriend, have you? You don't know that she's Beth's twin sister."

Marian's about to scoff but pauses as my words sink in. "Twin sister?"

"Her name is Tiffany, or least that's her stage name."

Marian's frowning. "Beth has a twin?"

"She's a dancer at Lola's. Beth told me she's dangerous. Violent. Mentally unstable."

Marian breathes in sharply. "What did you say her name is?"

"Tiffany."

Then I see it: Panic flaring in her eyes. She bolts upright from the chair and turns and grabs a Briarton yearbook from the bookshelf.

In an instant, I know it's the 2008 yearbook — the same edition that's missing everywhere else.

"It can't be," she whispers as she sits back down, flipping frantically through the pages.

Abruptly she stops, her eyes frozen on the open page. "No," she whispers. "No!"

She grabs the gun and swings it toward Big Ed —

But he's already behind her —

His hand slashing across her throat —

I catch a flash of metal —

A knife!

Her mouth opens, her eyes wide with shock —

And then blood starts gushing from her neck, pulsing out of her in huge spurts.

She sits back down in her chair, staring at me as her life flows out of her, her mouth open, surprise flickering through her eyes —

Until, just like that, the light in her eyes goes out —

And she's *dead*.

CHAPTER 43

arian's dead.

Dead, dead, dead. My stomach heaves. I can smell her blood. I'm about to throw up.

I can't breathe — yet I can't turn away, unable to stop myself from absorbing every awful detail.

The gash goes deep — her head is barely attached. From the neck down, she's drenched in blood, her silk blouse and slacks soaked red.

But from the neck up, she's as polished and immaculate as ever, her makeup still perfect, not a single silver hair out of place.

"Now ain't that a shame," I hear behind me.

I gasp and whirl around and find myself staring at —

Tiffany!

"Awww," she says, amusement in her voice. "I wanted to have some fun with her first."

She looks just like she did the other night — flashy and trashy. From beneath her thick curly hair, she's gazing at me with knowing, aggressive eyes. She's dressed in jean shorts and a dark tank top.

"Sorry," Ed says. "Had to act fast. She figured it out."

Tiffany shrugs, clearly not bothered. "Oh, well. It is what it is."

I can only gape at the two of them, my heart hammering away. How can they be so casual about what they just did? How can they be like this right after they *murdered a human being*?

Tiffany gives me a big smile. "Hey, girl," she says cheerfully. "How you holding up?"

Maybe I'm insane or stuck in a bad dream, a hallucination, a bizarre mind trip. Maybe my head's playing games with me. Please let that be what's going on. Please let me *not* be in the middle of this horrifying nightmare.

"Tiffany," I say, struggling for words. "Why are you doing this?"

She laughs, clearly delighted. "Don't feel too bad, Callie. You'll catch up soon enough. It *is* an awful lot to take in."

Ed shows her my gun. "Get a load of what she brought with her."

Tiffany lets out a low whistle and walks around the desk. "Now this is a surprise." She takes the gun from him and hefts it in her hand. "Where'd you get this, Callie?"

"I bought it last week," I lie, the words flowing without conscious thought.

"Hmm," she says. "You mean after your appointment with Dr. Franklin?"

How does she know about that? "That's right."

She's looking at me intently. "You really are full of surprises."

"I am?"

"Any sign of him yet?" she says to Ed.

He looks out the window and shakes his head. "Not yet."

"You check the phone?"

"Give me a sec." Ed wipes his bloody knife on Marian's back and returns it to a sheath on his belt, then picks up Marian's phone from the desk and aims it at Marian's dead face. "Gotta love this face I.D. shit." He scrolls through for a moment. "No, nothing yet."

"Should be soon," Tiffany says, then turns to me. "Callie, give me your phone."

Trembling, I reach into my pocket and push it across the desk.

"What's the passcode?"

I tell her — I have no choice — and she types it in.

"What are you doing?" I ask.

"Texting your friend Gwen."

Alarm shoots through me. How does she know about Gwen? "What for?"

"Oh, don't you worry. Long as she stays at Susan's, she'll be just fine." She finishes typing, then shows me the text.

CALLIE

Hey, Marian's a mess. She shouldn't be left alone. I'm going to stay here tonight. I'll call if I need anything. Text if you need me. See you in the morning.

"This sounds like you, right?"

It does sound like me. "Sure."

She arches an eyebrow. "Listen, I'm trying to keep your friends away from here and out of danger."

And keep them from alerting the authorities, I don't add. "It sounds fine."

"Anything I should add?"

"I'd ask about Ava — make sure she's okay."

She smiles. "Good catch from Supermom Callie."

"Is that how you see me? Supermom?"

"Super Obsessive Mom is more like it." She finishes typing and sends the text.

For a few seconds, the three of us are silent. They're waiting for someone — but who? Devlin, perhaps? Is he in the kitchen like Marian said, or was that a lie? Is he involved in whatever the hell is going on?

I almost ask but realize: What if Tiffany and Ed don't know Devlin's here? What if he's hiding somewhere in the mansion?

What if he's calling for help?

My hopeful thoughts are interrupted by the ping of my phone.

"Ah, good," Tiffany says. "Your friend Gwen."

She pushes the phone across the desk and lets me read:

> GWEN
>
> All good here. Ava's asleep. Want me to come over and keep you company?

Tiffany takes the phone, types a response, and shows it to me.

． ． ．

CALLIE

> Thanks, but I'm good. Marian's resting. I'm gonna get some sleep. Please do the same. Tomorrow will be a long day. I'll text if I need anything. See you in the morning.

"This sound okay?" she asks.

"Sure."

"You sure you're sure?"

"Yes."

She sends the text and gives me a smile. "That wasn't so hard, was it?"

I need to keep them talking. The more they communicate with me, the longer they'll keep me alive. My gaze lands on the yearbook on the desk. "Can I ask about that?"

Tiffany glances at Ed. "You're curious, aren't you?"

"I am."

"You wanna know what the big deal is."

"I do." I gesture toward it. "May I?"

The gun in her hand is steady. "No sudden moves."

I stand up, reach across the desk, and pick up the open yearbook. Amazingly, there isn't a drop of blood on it.

As I suspected, it's a 2008 yearbook, the same edition missing from the headmaster's office and the town library.

What did Marian discover?

The yearbook is open to a page of photos of sixth-graders — some kids smiling, some not. I scan the page quickly and nothing jumps out, so I take a deep breath and look at each photo more carefully.

Finally, at the bottom of the page, I see a name I recognize: Reece Bracken.

Bracken. My heart rate quickens. Reece must be the son of John Bracken, the handyman murdered in jail.

The photo shows a sullen kid with a doughy face and dead eyes. I look up at Big Ed, my stomach clenching as I see the man he grew up to be.

"Hi, Reece," I say, my heart thudding heavily.

Reece chuckles.

Then I glance down at the photo next to his and suddenly I can't breathe.

Tiffany Bracken?

Holy shit. Yes, it's definitely her — a much-younger version of the stripper she grew up to become.

I keep my eyes on the page, thinking furiously. Reece and Tiffany aren't a couple — they're *brother and sister*.

But wait — I'm still missing something.

What about *Beth?* There's no photo of her on this page. If Tiffany and Reece were enrolled at Briarton, why wasn't her twin sister enrolled as well?

Maybe Beth's photo is on the next page? I flip to the next page but find nothing.

I freeze. No, it can't be.

Yes, my inner voice says, *it has to be.*

Trembling, I look up at Tiffany.

Holding my gaze, Tiffany removes her wig and in a flash her manner changes. She becomes smaller somehow, meeker. There's shyness in her eyes as she says, in Beth's voice, "Callie, I'm here to help. Anything you need, you just let me know."

"You're Beth," I whisper, the horror of it rushing through me.

"There is no Beth," Tiffany whispers back, still in Beth's voice.

Tears come. I can barely breathe. "It's been you all along."

And then, just as quickly as she appeared, Beth vanishes and Tiffany lets out a long, delighted cackle, joined by her brother's guffaw.

The effect is shocking and powerful and awful. I never would have believed it if I hadn't just witnessed it.

"Gotta admit, Callie," she says gleefully, "fooling you has been so much *fun!*"

CHAPTER 44

od, she's sick. What she's celebrating is *frightening*. She and her psycho brother killed Marian and they don't give a damn.

And don't forget Josh. Tears come. *They killed Josh.*

I feel like screaming. Why did they do that? What in the hell are they up to?

Yes, *up to.* They have a plan. I'm trapped in a scheme of some sort — but what?

"Who are you waiting for?" I manage to ask, my mouth dry.

Tiffany exchanges an amused glance with Reece. "Let's see if you can figure it out."

It could be Devlin they're waiting for, I realize. Clearly he's involved — why else would Marian ask me to pick him up and bring him here? Why else would Marian tell me he was in the kitchen making coffee?

But is he actually here? If he is, then why hasn't Tiffany

mentioned him? I have to hope he's hiding somewhere and calling for help.

"If you're gonna make me guess," I say, trying to keep my voice level, "I'd say you're waiting for the sheriff."

"Good job, Callie."

"I'm guessing Marian had something for him to do, so she gave him a call and told him to come here, the same way she did with me. He's basically her servant."

"That he is," Tiffany says.

"If it's the sheriff you're expecting, then I have to wonder if you're in cahoots with him, too."

"Cahoots," she repeats, pleased. "I like that word."

"Of course, if you're working with him, then your plan is flawed."

The words are out of my mouth before I have time to think about them — and that's a problem. I have no idea what the flaw in their plan might be because I don't have a clue what their plan is.

But Tiffany's eyebrows go up. "Flawed?"

"The sheriff's deputies will know he's coming here."

She chuckles. "Why do you think that?"

"He'll check in with the station when he gets here."

She shakes her head. "He isn't on duty. Marian called his private number, not the station."

"Why did she do that?"

She smirks. "She told him she needs his help with the coverup."

"Coverup?" I flash to Marian aiming the gun at me. "You mean, she was gonna have him help her get away with killing me?"

She grins. "Bingo."

"Which means...."

"He ain't telling anyone he's coming here. His deputies think he's at home, fast asleep. They have no idea he's headed here."

Dread grips on me. Whatever their plan is, they've thought it through.

"Covering up is his thing," Reece says. "Like he did with you."

"With me?" It takes me a few seconds. "You mean my accident?"

Tiffany laughs and so does Reece.

"What did he cover up about my accident?"

"I can't believe you still don't get it," Tiffany says.

"Get what?"

"Your accident wasn't an accident. She did it deliberately."

"Who? *Marian?*" They laugh as I glance at her corpse. "No way."

"It was a surprise to us, too," Tiffany says. "That afternoon, when she rolled up here with her car dented in, we didn't know what to think."

I blink rapidly, my mind racing. There's a lot to unpack in what she just said. "You were here at Marian's house on the afternoon of my accident?"

She points outside. "See that big tree at the end of the gravel? Nice place for surveillance."

Dear God. "So how do you know she....?"

She laughs again. "Reece, show her the video."

Reece chuckles as he leans across the desk and holds his phone in front of me. A video starts playing. It looks like it was shot from up in the tree. Thick leaves obscure most of the view.

I hear a door car slam shut, followed by the sound of

another car pulling up.

Then two voices, a man and a woman.

Marian walks into view beneath the tree. "Over here. It's cooler in the shade."

The sheriff joins her. "Sweet Jesus, Marian, what have you done?"

"I saw an opportunity and took it."

"Jesus."

"No one else was around. No one saw me."

"You check to make sure she's dead?"

"Of course not. But she has to be. She hit the tree hard."

"Jesus."

"I need the car repaired. Quickly and discreetly."

"Marian, when is this gonna stop?"

"It stops now, Hoyt. It's finally over. Word of honor. She was the last loose end."

"Jesus."

They leave the shade under the tree and their voices become indistinct.

Reece steps back. "Told ya."

Tears rush up and I blink them back furiously. "They were talking about me."

"Sure were," Tiffany says.

"Marian ran me down."

"She sure did."

"With her fancy silver Caddy."

They laugh at that.

"She tried to kill me."

"Yep."

"And she and the sheriff covered it up."

"Yep."

I can't believe it, even though I just saw the evidence.

Even though it's all right there. The confession and the coverup. The murderer and her accomplice.

The last loose end.

That's all I was to Marian.

A cold fury rises up inside me.

Fuck her. I will myself to stay calm. *Fuck all of them.*

CHAPTER 45

Maybe it's the shock of being confronted with Marian's confession or maybe it's seeing how much sick fun Tiffany and Reece are having at my expense or maybe I've finally reached my limit for being fucked with.

Whatever it is, something in me snaps. The hesitation and uncertainty I've been caught up in burn away and I see my purpose again. I'm done being messed with. For my daughter's sake and mine, I'm going to find a way through this nightmare. I'm going to fight back and get away from these psychos. I'm going to *survive*.

Which means I have to keep them talking.

I take a deep breath. "Why did you put the note on my door?"

Tiffany smiles. "To fuck with you."

It's all I can do not to explode. The anger inside me needs to stay hidden.

"I was curious," Tiffany continues. "What would you do? Tell Josh? Do nothing? Forget about it?"

It hits me again: *They killed Josh.* Anger rushes through me, heightened by my aching grief. Part of me wants nothing more than to collapse into myself, but I can't. If I don't stay in the here and now, if I don't keep myself together, I'm dead.

Keep them talking.

"Why did you want to fuck with me?"

"You've been a puzzle. Day in, day out, all you seem to care about is getting better and taking care of Ava."

"Well, that's right," I say, trying to sound reasonable.

She snorts. "You know how *boring* that is, watching you limp around, always so serious? The human equivalent of paint drying. I figured — why not have a little fun?"

God, she's sick. There's so much anger in her. But at least I have her talking.

"So you put the note on the door. Why a note?"

"You tell me."

It takes me a second. "You were watching me."

"Bingo."

"From outside? No, wait, from the empty house next door."

"See? Figuring stuff out isn't all that hard when you set your mind to it."

"But it was about more than you fucking with me, wasn't it?" I say, trying to sound encouraging. "I mean, the plan you came up with is, well, complex. Even not knowing everything about it, I can sense that. You put a lot of thought into this."

She almost objects but doesn't. Maybe she likes the praise. Maybe she likes being recognized as a mastermind.

"Tiffany, come on, tell me I'm right about that."

"I'll give you that. Messing with you was helpful."

"How so?"

"You're the wild card. The unknown element. Reece and me, we know Boudreaux top to bottom, every single fucking inch of this shithole. But you? You're a stranger."

"I don't see how being a stranger matters."

"We needed to understand how you were gonna react."

"React to…?"

"Everything. And I gotta say, you kept us on our toes."

We're turning into a mutual admiration society. "Like how?"

"Like not dying after Marian ran you down. The way the doctors tell it, it's a miracle you pulled through."

"Sure, but I'm guessing you're also thinking about what happened in my kitchen last week when I fought back."

Reece speaks up. "Got me pretty good, I'll give you that."

I notice an odd respect in his voice. Can I use that?

"But if you wanted me dead last week," I continue, "I'd already be dead. You want me for something else." I glance at Tiffany. "I assume you were the one with the hypodermic needle?"

She shrugs. "Of course."

"Why attack me?"

"It was part of the plan."

"You *planned* to knock me out? Why?"

"The plan was for Beth" — for just a second, she assumes her helpful, friendly Beth persona — "to find you unconscious on the kitchen floor the next morning."

"Which would accomplish what?"

"Beth would call an ambulance and when you woke up and told the cops and doctors your crazy story about being attacked in your kitchen by two intruders, everyone would think you imagined it."

"But you injected me with a drug. They would have found the needle mark."

"The needle mark was supposed to be in your arm. And the needle and drug were gonna be found in your medicine cabinet."

I can only stare. "Your plan was to plant evidence of me taking drugs so that no one would believe the home invasion happened."

"Right."

"*Why?*"

"Because Josh kept defending you."

Grief stirs anew. "Josh?"

"After you came out of your coma, he was the only one who believed you could take care of Ava on your own. Marian was hell-bent on moving you into the mansion, but Josh told her no."

Tears come to my eyes. "Josh kept Marian away?"

"And we all know how hard that is."

"*Was,*" Reece says.

Tiffany laughs. "Fuck, I'm so glad that bitch is dead."

I need to keep her on track. "So you two attacked me because you wanted everyone to doubt my competence and sanity, so that Ava and I would be forced to move in with Marian."

"Right. The same reason why you didn't tell anyone about the attack."

My instinct is to argue the point, but I can't do that because she's right.

"Come on, admit it," she says eagerly, "our plan was pretty awesome. Reece and me get to gaslight the shit outta you and plant evidence about you doing drugs — how cool is that? And with you saying crazy shit about attackers coming after you in the middle of the night, there's no way Josh could've stopped Marian from swooping in."

"But…." It takes a few seconds to get the words out because I'm still trying to absorb it all. "If your goal was to make people think I'm crazy, then I get you gaslighting me with the attack. But I'm still not clear about the note with Josh's phone passcode. How did that help you?"

Tiffany's look is sympathetic. "That was a nice-to-have. I know you can figure it out. Come on, give it a go."

Okay, this coaching vibe is downright weird. "You were hoping I'd figure out the note was a passcode."

"Right."

"And you were hoping I'd sneak into Josh's phone."

"Right. Go on."

"Because … you wanted Josh to find out I was snooping on his phone."

"See? You're catching up just fine."

I swallow back a surge of emotion. "Because if he found out I was snooping on his phone, then he'd be upset with me. He'd question my judgment. He'd wonder if my head injury had affected my ability to make good decisions."

She grins. "Couldn't have said it better myself."

"But why did you want me and Ava living here at the mansion?"

She shakes her head. "Come on, Callie. After everything you just learned, you know why."

And then, with a chill, I do. "If Marian had me here, it'd be easier for her to kill me."

"Bingo."

"Here at the mansion, she could have come up with a way to get rid of me. A push down the stairs, for example."

She smiles. "The possibilities are endless."

"Bottom line, she wanted me dead."

"Yep."

I glare at her and sit forward. "And now so do *you*."

CHAPTER 46

Tiffany's eyes widen. "Whoa." Unconsciously, she glances at the gun in her hand as if to reassure herself it's still there. "Feisty all of a sudden. Where's *that* energy coming from?"

I'm in no mood to answer. "Why do you want me dead?"

Until this moment she's been enjoying herself. But I've just made her wary, which was a mistake. "None of this is about you, Callie."

I take a deep breath. "I think I get that."

"You're just in the way."

She says it so casually — it's chilling to hear. "In the way of what?"

"In the way of what's about to happen."

I want to press for more details but I can tell she isn't ready to tell me.

At the window, Reece is still looking outside. Yes, the two of them are definitely waiting for someone — the sheriff, most likely.

And I realize: *They don't want to get rid of me yet.* They still need me. But for what?

"Come on," I say. "Tell me more. Clearly you put a lot of thought into this plan of yours."

Tiffany looks at me, considering.

"Tell me how it started."

"Revenge," she answers after a moment. "That's how it started."

"Revenge for what happened to your father, John Bracken."

Her gaze sharpens. "You mentioned him at lunch on Saturday. How much do you know?"

"Only a bit. John Bracken, handyman at Briarton. Arrested for arson. Died in Boudreaux Parish jail. That's the official version of events."

"What else do you know?"

"I know Marian started the fire at the school. I know your father tried to put out the fire before it spread. I know the headmaster accused your father of setting the fire. I know the sheriff arrested him and charged him with arson. I know he was murdered in jail by another prisoner."

Tiffany's on full alert. "How do you know all this?"

"Research. Online and at the town library."

"You can't know all that."

"Well, I do."

She leans forward. "Who'd you talk to?"

Too late, I realize she's worried about loose ends — people who might know more than they should. Susan's the one who told me about Bracken — I have to keep them away from her. Have I said too much?

"The library has old issues of the *Herald* in microfiche. An article about your father's arrest is in there."

"The *Herald* wouldn't have printed anything about Marian starting the fire."

"Right. That part I figured out. I mean, why else would Marian be at the school that night?"

I'm hoping my lie is good enough to convince them. I'm hoping Tiffany hasn't read the *Herald* article or that if she has, she doesn't remember that the article doesn't mention Marian at all.

"Why were you researching Daddy?"

"I was researching how the school handles memorial services — you know, to help plan the service for the teacher who died. That's when I found a reference to your father."

Her frown tells me she's unconvinced. "You said the same thing at lunch. But it sounded like a lie then and it sounds like one now."

I touch my head. "I don't like admitting this, but the truth is, I'm still not completely healed up here. I realized I was maybe getting a bit obsessive about helping with the memorial service. I ended up doing way too much research."

It helps that what I'm saying aligns with Tiffany's sense of me. She glances at Reece and he shrugs.

Before she can dig deeper, I try to return the focus to them. "So you came back to Boudreaux for revenge against Marian."

"For what she did to Daddy," she says.

"Was it always the plan to kill her?"

"Of course. But then...."

"Then you found out she tried to kill me and realized you could blackmail her?"

"Bingo."

"Pay up or...?"

"Well, that was the plan, at least at first. Pay up or we

send the video to every newspaper and TV station in Louisiana."

"How much were you planning to ask for?"

"A hundred grand."

That's a lot of money, though not for Marian. "She has way more than that."

"Oh, we know. That was just gonna be the first payment."

"But you never actually approached her about the blackmail."

The excitement is returning to Tiffany's eyes — she's enjoying telling me. "We realized we could go much bigger."

She's itching to reveal more. I need to keep her talking. "It sounds like a complicated plan. It must have been tough keeping all the pieces moving forward."

She shrugs. "Success is built on a foundation of preparation."

The words sound like a slogan, like something a teacher or a coach once told her. "I'm not sure what you mean."

"Meaning," she says, "when you're going up against Marian Dupre, you do your homework."

"One thing I didn't know until tonight," I say, glancing at Reece, "is that John Bracken had children. I'm so sorry for the loss of your father. I lost my parents during my senior year of high school."

Reece speaks up. "Senior year?"

"That's right."

"Too old to go into care?"

"Mom died a week after my eighteenth birthday."

He grunts. "You dodged a bullet."

I keep my eyes on him. "After your dad died, what

happened? Was it just you and Tiffany? Where was your mom?"

He shakes his head. "Mom passed when we were six. Overdose."

Dear God. "So where did you two end up?"

"Different homes. They split us up."

"I'm so sorry. I can't even imagine."

"Sure you can," Tiffany says, breaking in, an edge to her voice. "Imagine hell and crank up the volume."

"How did you two find each other again?"

She ignores me and glances at her watch. "Still nothing?"

"Nothing," he replies, checking Marian's phone and then the window.

They're getting impatient. I need to keep them talking. "What happened when you turned eighteen? Clearly you found each other."

"Took a while, but yes," Tiffany says.

"What did you do then?"

She sighs. "Well, we could have done all this sooner except my genius brother got pulled over with a kilo of coke and spent five years in prison. As for me, you saw what I've been up to."

A stripper and a drug dealer — what a family. "And now you're here in Boudreaux for your revenge."

She waves the gun. "Plus all of this."

What is she talking about? "I don't get what you mean."

"I know you don't."

"Explain it to me."

"Soon."

"Are you waiting for the sheriff to call or something?"

Before she can reply, Marian's phone pings.

"That him?" Tiffany asks.

"I'll buzz him in," he says.

Tiffany gestures toward the study door with the gun. "Okay, get up."

I can't help but glance at my cane in Reece's hand.

Tiffany notices. "Sorry, Callie. You're way too handy with that. You're just gonna have to limp around."

I gesture to Marian's phone. "Was that the sheriff at the front gate? Did you just buzz him through?"

"Go to the front door. When the sheriff knocks, I want you to open the door and let him in."

I stare at her. "You want me to *what*?"

"Exactly what I said. No funny business or I'll kill you. If you warn him, or try to shoo him away, or do anything other than open the door and let him in, you're dead. Got that?"

Through the windows, I catch headlights approaching the house.

"Now get moving."

CHAPTER 47

don't have a choice, not with Tiffany waving the gun at me and Reece staring at me with my cane in his meaty grip.

I get to my feet. Moving carefully to avoid aggravating my hip, I limp out of the study and through the darkened parlor to the front door. Tiffany's a few steps behind, close enough to shoot me but too far for me to lunge at her.

In the entry hallway, I peer through the windows as the sheriff's car pulls up. The rain is really coming down now. Lightning crackles across the night sky. Thunder rumbles.

When the sheriff climbs out, still in uniform, I'm struck again by how ordinary he looks. After checking his gun, he hurries up to the front porch.

"Let him in when he knocks," Tiffany whispers. "And remember — no funny business."

The knocks are sharp and echo in the silence. My heart starts hammering. I have no idea what's coming next and that terrifies me.

With a tremble, I take hold of the handle and open the door.

The sheriff's eyes widen. "Miss Callie."

He's surprised to see me — why? Because he was expecting Marian? Because he came here to help Marian cover up a crime and expected me to already be dead?

He looks past me into the darkened house. "I'm here to see Marian."

"She's in the study," I hear myself say.

I open the door wide. As he steps past me, a rush of fear and uncertainty and *guilt* rush through me. Does my going along with what Tiffany told me to do mean I'm weak? Am I complicit in what's coming next?

It means you're a survivor, my inner voice says. *You're going to do whatever it takes to get through this.*

The sheriff's hand is on his holster. "Why are the lights off?" he asks, his voice tinged with suspicion.

"It's how they were when I got here."

"You said she's in the study?"

"Right."

"Lead the way."

He doesn't trust me. He's keeping an eye on me. He senses something's off.

I start limping through the front parlor.

"Where's your cane?" he asks.

"It's —"

That's when I catch movement in the shadows and I turn and gasp as —

Reece emerges from the darkness and with astonishing speed cracks my cane down *hard* on the sheriff's head.

The sheriff grunts and staggers.

Reece whacks him again —

And the sheriff collapses onto the carpet.

I stand there, stunned and horrified, listening to my own ragged breathing. It happened so fast. How can he move like that?

Tiffany joins us from where she'd been hiding in the entry hallway, gun in hand. "He still alive?"

Reece yanks the gun from the sheriff's holster and stuffs it into his jeans, then presses two fingers against the sheriff's neck.

"Oh, yeah."

"Good. Let's get him in there."

Reece grabs the sheriff under the arms and drags him into the study.

I'm still frozen in place, still trying to take in what just happened, when Tiffany clears her throat. "Good job, Callie."

"You don't have to do this," I say, desperate to dissuade her from whatever's coming next. "There has to be a better way to get your revenge."

"Nah, this is the only way. In Boudreaux, violence is the only language that matters." She gestures with the gun. "Get moving."

"What are you going to do?"

"You're about to find out."

I limp into the study and she points to the same chair I was in before. Trembling, I settle in.

Just a few feet away, on the carpet in front of Marian's desk, the sheriff is unconscious, lying face down as Reece cuffs his hands behind his back.

On the carpet next to the sheriff, momentarily unattended and just a quick dash away, is my cane. My pulse quickens. If I can somehow grab it while Reece is distracted —

"Stay put, Callie," Tiffany says from behind me. "Don't even think about it."

I ease back. "I wasn't —"

"Oh, yes, you were."

I glance across the desk and shudder. Marian's corpse is still staring at me, surprise frozen forever on her pale dead face. The smell of her blood and — yes, her excrement — hangs thick in the air.

"Why are we back in here?" I ask, nauseous. "It stinks in here."

"We'll be outta here soon, promise," Tiffany says.

Reece has finished with the handcuffs. "He's coming to."

Indeed, the sheriff is starting to groan. His legs move and a few seconds later his eyes open.

I can just make out his face in the shadows. Gradually he realizes where he is. He twists his arms, testing his handcuffs.

Tiffany steps between us and kneels on the carpet next to him, her face close to his. "Hello, Sheriff Denton," she says softly, using her Beth voice.

The sheriff blinks with confusion as he stares at her. "Miss Beth?"

"That's right, Sheriff."

"What are you doing here?"

"Something terrible has happened," she continues, her voice still soft.

"I need your help. My hands are cuffed." His voice is thicker than normal, but he's thinking clearly enough. "Get the key from my belt."

"Let me help you sit up." She helps him roll over onto his back and then sit up.

That's when he sees me in the chair next to him.

"Miss Callie?" he says, squinting, as if not trusting his eyes. "Is that you?"

I swallow back a rush of fear. "We're in trouble, Sheriff."

He frowns and almost says something but no words come out. It's like he's trying to figure out why I'm sitting in the chair and why Beth's here and why he's handcuffed, but nothing's making sense.

Tiffany says, her voice still warm and helpful, "Sheriff, let's get you off the floor and into a chair."

With her help, he struggles to his feet and settles into a chair in front of the desk.

And that's when he looks across the desk and sees Marian. His eyes widen and then — when he realizes she's dead — he cries out in horror.

"Lord Almighty, what the fuck is going on?"

Tiffany leans closer and says, still in her Beth voice, "Whatever do you mean, Sheriff?"

He tries to stand but she pushes him down, then pulls out her gun and aims it at him.

He stares at her in astonishment and she lets out a delighted cackle.

"Are you upset about Miss Marian, Sheriff?"

He gapes at her, stunned.

"I don't understand," he finally says. "Miss Beth, what have you done?"

She laughs again. "You hear that, Reece? You hear what he just called me?"

From a darkened corner of the room, Reece steps

forward, a gigantic grin on his oafish face. "Should we tell him?"

"Might have to," she says with a pout. "Though I was hoping he'd have figured it out by now."

Eyes frantic with confusion, the sheriff's gaze goes from Tiffany and Reece over to Marian's corpse, then finally lands on me. "Miss Callie," he whispers, "what is this?"

"Revenge," I whisper back.

He frowns. "For what?"

Without warning, Tiffany smacks the side of his head with her gun. "For what, you said? You telling me you don't know?"

Blood starts flowing from his scalp as he eyes her fearfully.

Reece steps closer. "He might not remember us, Sis, but I bet he remembers Dad."

The sheriff goes still as he stares at the two of them. Then he breathes in sharply. "No."

Tiffany leans closer. "No, what?"

"It can't be."

"What can't be?"

The sheriff's shaking his head. "You two kids got it wrong. What happened to your father was a terrible tragedy."

Without warning, Reece smashes my cane into the sheriff's face.

The sheriff cries out as his nose explodes in blood. "You got it wrong!" he screams.

"Nah," Tiffany says as the sheriff gasps for breath. "See, we got hold of Daddy's autopsy. Not the piece-of-shit autopsy you had old Doc Franklin do for you. No, the one the state pathologist did when they launched their investigation of you."

Blood is pouring out of the sheriff's nose. He looks around wildly. "You don't want to do this."

"The state report is quite a read. What did it tell us, Reece?"

"It told us Dad was beaten to death."

The sheriff's shaking his head. "You two weren't there. You don't understand."

"I think we do," Tiffany says. "Thanks to that autopsy report. Told us a lot, didn't it?"

"Sure did."

The sheriff shakes his head. "Reece, Tiffany, this is just a terrible misunderstanding. What happened to your father was a tragedy and nothing more. The state investigated and closed their case."

"Thanks to your boss," Tiffany says, gesturing toward Marian.

The sheriff looks over at Marian and shudders. "She's not —"

Tiffany laughs. "Don't you get it yet? That bitch can't hear you anymore, she can't blackmail you anymore, she can't control you anymore. We took care of her for you. You should be *thanking* us."

He looks at her like she's crazy, which she probably is. "Tiffany, what happened to your father was terrible and should never have occurred and I continue to feel remorse for the procedural gaps that allowed it to happen."

Tiffany stares at him a long moment. Up till now, she's been content to toy with him. But now she looks offended.

"Reece, what else did that autopsy tell us?"

"It told us our dad had deep bruising and cuts around his wrists, inflicted pre- and post-mortem."

"Gosh, that's a lot of big words. What do those big words mean?"

"It means Dad was handcuffed when he died."

Tiffany shakes her head. "Who in the world had the power to put Daddy in that cell without taking off his cuffs?"

"The sheriff who arrested him, that's who."

She leans closer to the sheriff and he shrinks away. "I see."

The sheriff's shaking his head desperately. "We didn't do that. The other prisoner had the cuffs. He snuck 'em into the cell. He's the one who put 'em on your dad."

Without warning, Tiffany slaps him — *hard*.

"You threw him in the cell with his cuffs still on, right?"

"No, I didn't."

Slap!

"It wasn't me!" he gasps.

Slap!

"Tell me the truth or I'll have Reece take over."

The sheriff glances fearfully at Reece. "All right, all right, that's what happened. But he wasn't supposed to die."

"Is that so?" Tiffany says, her hand poised to strike again.

"The plan was to rough him up. Scare him. Get him to leave Boudreaux."

"To stop him from talking."

The sheriff looks again at Marian's corpse — he can't help it. "It wasn't supposed to go the way it did."

A silence falls in the room and Tiffany and Reece exchange a long look, like they're checking with each other to see if they've heard what they've been hoping to hear.

Tiffany returns her attention to the sheriff.

"What did Daddy know, Sheriff? What did he know that Marian didn't want him to know?"

"I don't know."

Tiffany raises her hand again and the sheriff says, "I don't know the specifics, I swear. All I know is, the night of the fire at the school, your dad overheard or saw something. To this day, I don't know what."

Tiffany leans closer. "Devlin Chatterton knows, doesn't he?"

The sheriff nods miserably. "Him and Marian. It's their secret."

My heart rate quickens — *Devlin*. Why did Marian ask me to pick him up on my way here? Why did she tell me he was here? Is he here somewhere, hiding in the mansion? Has he called for help?

Sweat and blood are dripping from the sheriff's face. His lower lip is trembling. He looks defeated and exhausted and terrified in that chair, his hands cuffed behind him. The stench of Marian's excrement has taken over the room, putrid and overpowering.

Tiffany leans in real close, as if memorizing every detail of the sheriff's face. Barely a step away, Reece is looming over both of them, his hand gripping my cane. The two of them have been planning this moment for a long time. The lengths they've gone to — taking on fake identifies, spying on Marian, spying on me — is frightening.

I believe them about returning to Boudreaux for revenge. Their hatred for Marian and the sheriff is crystal-clear. But they're after a lot more than that. They've been careful, patient, deliberate. A whole lot more is coming and I don't know what it is.

"You know, Reece," Tiffany says, "I think the sheriff is finally telling us the truth."

"You do?"

"I think he's told us everything he can."

"You sure? There's still some stuff we don't know."

"There is?"

Reece steps closer to the sheriff, looming over him. "The autopsy tells us what happened to Dad, but it doesn't tell us in what order."

"Like, what do you mean?" she says, taking a step back, her eyes alive with anticipation.

"I mean, did the killer bash in Dad's head first?" He swings the cane into the side of the sheriff's face and the sheriff screams.

"Or did he break Dad's arm first?" He slams the cane hard into the sheriff's arm and I hear a horrifying *crack*.

Groaning, the sheriff falls from the chair.

"And what about all those kicks to Dad's abdomen?" Reece says as he starts kicking the sheriff in the stomach.

The sheriff screams and groans as Reece keeps kicking.

"The internal organs that got ruptured — what order did that happen in?"

Oh my God. I can't breathe. I want to scream, I want to run, I want to shrink to nothing, but I can't. This is beyond horrible. What I'm seeing can't be happening.

I'm about to bolt when all of a sudden Tiffany's hands are on my shoulders and she's pushing me back into my seat. "Just a little longer, Callie."

"You know," Reece says as he lands a brutal kick on the sheriff's ribs, "it's possible we'll never know the order it all happened."

"Don't forget the jaw," Tiffany says.

"Thanks, Sis." With a horrifying crunch, he slams his boot down hard on the sheriff's face.

The sheriff shudders and gurgles and finally, mercifully, his body goes slack.

Tiffany and Reece look at each other and start laughing with delight. I turn to the side and throw up. I retch and heave as my vomit splatters on the carpet next to the sheriff's brutalized body.

Oh my God.

Oh my God.

Oh my God.

CHAPTER 48

'm sitting there in shock, nauseous and overcome with horror, when Tiffany turns to me. "Oh, come on, Callie. After everything that man did to you?"

My God, she's a monster. There's no humanity in her, not an ounce. All I see is rage and calculation. I have to get away.

"He was a human being," I whisper.

"Barely," she snorts.

"What you did to him is...."

"What he deserved." She points at Marian's corpse and laughs. "Her, too. They both got what was coming."

She's not sane, at least not completely. Reveling in violent death like this is sick. The part of her that's human is missing or broken.

Reece glances at his watch. "Time to get moving."

"Right," Tiffany says, then looks around. "What do we need to do before we...?"

Reece grabs the 2008 yearbook from the desk. "Any blood on you?"

Tiffany looks herself up and down. "I'm good, I think?"

"Adjust the books on the shelf so the missing yearbook isn't obvious."

She scoots behind the desk and, using a handkerchief, carefully rearranges the yearbooks.

"Can't have folks wondering about the missing year-book, can we?" she says cheerfully.

Reece is scanning the room. "Got everything you came here with?"

Tiffany checks her pockets and looks around the room. "Check. You?"

"Check."

"Okay." She steps past me, leans down to the sheriff, wipes his bloody face with the handkerchief, then turns to me. "Hands out."

My eyes widen. "What?"

"Hands out, Callie."

I watch in horror as she rubs the bloody handkerchief over my hands and arms, and then my blouse and jeans. She then stuffs the bloody handkerchief into my front jeans pocket.

"There," she says, stepping back. "That wasn't so hard. Now, I want you to rub your shoes over the body."

"*What?*"

"You heard me."

"I'm not doing that."

She pulls out her gun. "Now, Callie."

I glance at Reece, who's right behind her, staring at me impassively. I don't have a choice. Revulsion surges through me. I get to my feet, step forward, and brush my sneakers against the sheriff's uniform.

"More," Tiffany says. "I want him all over you."

I nearly throw up again, but I press harder and smear more of his blood over my sneakers.

"Good," Tiffany says. "Now get going."

Shakily, I walk out of the study and across the front parlor, Tiffany a few steps behind.

When we reach the entry hall, Tiffany says, "Outside."

I open the door and limp onto the front porch and breathe in the humid air, relieved to be away from the stench of shit and blood. The rain is still coming down but the lightning and thunder are gone, at least for the moment.

"Get out your car key," Tiffany says.

Fear jolts me. Are we going somewhere? Trembling, I reach into my jeans pocket and pull it out.

"Good girl."

Reece joins us on the porch, a backpack over his shoulder and my cane in his left hand. He shuts the door carefully, using a handkerchief to grip the handle.

"Final check," he says to his sister. "All good?" When she nods, he hurries through the rain to his pickup truck.

Tiffany waves the gun at me. "We're gonna get a bit wet, Callie. Off we go."

"Where are we going?"

"To your car." I limp down the porch steps and head across the gravel to Susan's car.

"Open the trunk," Tiffany says.

I do as I'm told. As the trunk door swings up, the thought comes: Maybe there's something in the trunk I can use. A weapon. A tire iron or a —

"Now, now, Callie. Back away."

I go still. "I wasn't —"

She laughs. "Oh, yes, you were. Back up. Now."

I retreat a few steps. From the back of his truck, Reece is pulling out a rolled-up carpet. He drops the carpet to the ground with a thud, then kneels down and unrolls it.

I breathe in sharply. There's a *person* in the rug — wrapped inside. A man. He moves and groans. *He's alive.*

"Get up," Reece says.

When the man sits up, I see — it's Devlin!

"Please," Devlin says. "Please don't do this."

"I said get up," Reece says.

The headmaster struggles to his feet, glancing around wildly. "What are we doing at Marian's?" He sees me and Tiffany and gawks. "Callie, is that you?"

"Over here, Headmaster Chatterton," Tiffany calls out, waving the gun so he can see it.

He peers at her through the gloom as he steps closer. "Do I know you?"

"You do," Tiffany says. "Or at least you did."

At his truck, Reece is rolling the rug back up. Even with one arm in a sling, he's making it look easy.

"Need any help?" Tiffany calls out.

"All good," Reece grunts as he tosses it in the truck.

Devlin's staring at me. "Callie, what's going on?"

"They're going to kill us."

He gawps. "What?"

Reece joins us at the car. "Hey, Dev," he says.

Devlin turns toward him just as —

Reece whacks him in the face with my cane.

Devlin cries out and falls to the ground. "Stop! Please!"

Reece shoots me a big grin. "Gotta say, Callie, this cane of yours is pretty damn awesome."

Devlin is gasping for breath, his face a bloody mess. "Please don't do this."

"Now, now, Headmaster," Tiffany says, pointing to the car. "Get in the trunk."

Devlin gazes at her, aghast. "What?"

"Climb in."

"But —"

"Now!"

He struggles to his feet. "Please, I —"

"Get a move on."

"Why are you doing this?"

"You'll find out soon enough."

He looks at me but all I can do is shake my head. He starts sobbing as he climbs into the trunk.

Tiffany shuts the door with her elbow, then turns to me with a satisfied smile.

"Excellent. Time for a ride, Callie!"

CHAPTER 49

stare at Tiffany and Reece, my heart hammering away, too scared to move.

"Here's the thing, Callie," Tiffany says. "I'm gonna be driving your car and you're going with Reece in the truck."

My eyes dart to the truck and then to Reece.

"What we're hoping is you won't get any funny ideas on the drive over."

I shake my head. "No."

"If you'd rather, we can roll *you* up in the rug."

I inhale sharply. "No, that won't be necessary."

Reece reaches into his backpack and hands Tiffany a pair of gloves and what looks like a hair net.

Tiffany arranges the hairnet over her head, then slips the gloves on.

"Give me your car key," she says.

I quickly hand the key over.

Tiffany and Reece exchange a look and then Reece says to

me, "Let's go."

I limp over to the truck and climb into the passenger seat.

As Reece slides in next to me, I'm struck again by how big, how powerful, how menacing he is. Even with an arm in a sling, there's no way I could overpower him.

Your moment will come, my inner voice says. *You'll know when.*

I can smell his sweat and — yes — the coppery scent of blood. It must be all over him.

He's not carrying my cane, I realize. Where is it? Did he toss it in the back?

And the sheriff's gun — where is it now? Did he put it in the backpack? Is that in the back of the truck as well?

And his knife — where's his knife? My eyes go to his belt. With a pang of disappointment, I see the knife sheath on his left side, away from me.

He settles in. "Put your seat belt on."

I do as I'm told while he watches.

"No funny business," he says.

"I promise."

He starts the engine and backs out. I swallow back a rush of fear. The more I can get him talking, the more I can learn about what's coming next.

"Where are we going, Reece?"

He grunts. "The school."

"Why are we going there?"

He grunts again. "Part of the plan."

"Tell me about the plan."

"You'll see soon enough."

He pulls away from the house and heads toward the main gate of the estate, Tiffany a short distance behind.

"I know you're trying to implicate me in all this," I say,

hoping to keep my tone level, "but the blood on my shoes won't convince anyone."

He grunts. "You think that's all we got?"

"I don't see much else so far."

"Why do you think we had you drive to Devlin's?"

It takes me a second, but then my stomach sinks. "When I got to Devlin's house and found out he wasn't there, you knew I'd call Marian."

"Right."

"So when the cops check my phone records, they'll see I called Marian and they'll look at the cell records and see I was at Devlin's when I called."

"Right."

I flash to Devlin climbing into the trunk of the car. "And when they examine the car trunk, they'll find Devlin's blood in there."

"Right."

"The evidence will suggest I went to Devlin's and forced him into the car trunk."

"Right."

This plan of theirs — they've thought out every detail.

"And when the cops find the sheriff's blood on my shoes and my hands and arms, they'll have evidence that I killed the sheriff."

"Right."

"And I suppose they're also going to find evidence I killed Marian."

He shoots me a glance. "Right."

The main gate is ahead now. There must be a motion sensor because as we approach, the gate opens. We pause at the road, looking both ways for traffic. The road is quiet, the rain still falling steadily. He turns toward the school.

"Why are we going to Briarton?"

He grunts. "You ask a lot of questions."

"I'm being cooperative. I just want to understand."

He gazes at me for a long second. "It's too bad, really."

"What's too bad?"

"You got me pretty good the other night."

He doesn't seem angry about that. It's almost like he respects me for taking him by surprise.

"I was scared. I was acting out of instinct."

He chuckles. "When you showed up at Lola's, I thought you had us."

"Wait, what?"

"You know, figured it out."

"I wish I had."

He falls silent. I glance in the side mirror at Tiffany's headlights behind us.

The school's up ahead, but to my surprise he drives past it.

"I thought we were going to the school."

"We are."

He signals a turn and eases off the road into a thicket of bushes and trees.

"Leave your seat belt on," he says, then shuts off the engine and hops out.

A few seconds later, Tiffany pulls in behind us, turns off the car, and steps out.

"Okay," Reece says to me. "Unbuckle and get out."

At first I can barely see a thing in the murky darkness, but as my eyes adjust, I start making things out. I climb down from the truck and watch Reece grab his backpack and my cane from the back.

"Get behind the wheel," Reece says, pointing to the car.

I walk over to the car, open the door, and slide in.

"Grip the wheel," he says.

I do as he says, my stomach clenching as I realize I've just transferred the sheriff's blood from my hands to the steering wheel.

"Good," Reece says. "Now get out and go around and get in the front passenger seat."

I do as I'm told, the two of them watching me like a hawk.

Tiffany slides into the driver's seat. With gloves on and her hair in a net, she looks like she's dressed for a factory job.

She gives me a friendly smile, which is creepy as fuck. "How you doin', Callie?"

When I don't answer, she laughs.

"She cause you any trouble?" she says to her brother.

"Nah," Reece replies. He opens a back door and lays a plastic sheet — the kind you use when you're painting a room — over the entire back seat. Then, very carefully, he sets his backpack and my cane on the plastic sheet and climbs in. It's a tight fit — he's big — but he manages.

I swallow, terrified by the care he's taking.

Tiffany laughs. "I know you're full of questions, Callie. But don't you worry, you're gonna find out everything. This next part's gonna be so much *fun!*"

CHAPTER 50

can't help but shudder. God, she's sick. Is there any humanity in her at all? Within Reece I sensed a tiny tinge of regret about my imminent death. Is there any way I can turn his reluctance — assuming I can even call it that — to my advantage?

The drive to Briarton doesn't take long. We turn into the school grounds, the huge lawn passing by in a blur.

Tiffany stops in front of the administration building but keeps the engine running, the car headlights aimed at the front steps. Aside from the area illuminated by the headlights, everything around us is dark. No one's here but us. The patter of raindrops on the windshield would be comforting if I weren't trapped with two murderous sociopaths.

Reece gets out, retrieves the backpack and my cane, carefully pulls the plastic sheet out of the back seat, then folds up the plastic sheet and stuffs it in the backpack. Tiffany turns to me and says brightly, "Your turn, Callie."

I unbuckle my belt, open the door, and climb out, my hip aching. The rain is warm on my face. The humid air carries the earthy aroma of the nearby bayou.

A thought comes: Am I hyper-aware of the air and rain and the smell of the bayou because I know my end is near? Am I breathing it all in and appreciating it because it's my last chance?

Reece is in the shadows a few feet away, my cane in his hand, his backpack on the ground next to him.

Tiffany gets out of the car and unlocks the trunk. The door pops up and Devlin peers out fearfully.

"Out," she tells him.

"Why are we here?" he asks as he clambers out.

"Move into the light," she says. "We're gonna have a talk."

"Please don't hurt me." He walks into the light and stands there, exposed and terrified.

She takes off the gloves, removes her hair net, and hands them to her brother, who puts them in the backpack. She does it slowly, knowing that Devlin and I are watching and waiting for her next move.

Finally she returns her attention to him. "You know why you're here?"

He starts crying. "I'm sorry."

"On your knees."

Trembling, he lowers himself to the ground. "Please don't hurt me."

Tiffany steps forward and slaps his face — *hard*. He cries out.

"All of this is because of you."

"I'm not a bad person."

She *whaps* him again. God, she's angry. No way this ends well. Nausea fills me.

"Tell us what you did."

"Please. I didn't mean —"

Another *whap*.

"Please."

Whap!

"Please don't…."

Whap!

Tiffany snorts. "I can do this all night. Or maybe I should let my brother take a turn?"

Devlin's eyes dart to Reece. "No!"

"Tell us why Daddy had to die."

"I had no idea that was —"

Whap!

"Stop, please!" He takes a deep breath. "Your father overheard me and Marian talking about a … private matter."

"So to keep him quiet, Marian had you accuse him of starting the fire."

He starts crying. "I'm so sorry."

"And based on your accusation, the sheriff arrested him."

"I'm sorry."

"And then the sheriff had him killed."

"I didn't know he was going to do that, I swear."

Tiffany raises her hand. "And?"

"I told everyone I fired your dad."

"And what else did you do?"

"I expelled the two of you."

"That's right," she says. "Not only did you send Daddy to his death, you condemned me and Reece to years of hell."

He's trembling. "I'm so sorry."

"Are you?" Even though she's hearing what she wants to hear, she's becoming even angrier. "What are you sorry for?"

"All of it."

"You're sorry for the beatings?"

"I'm sorry."

"You sorry about my first foster dad *raping* me?"

He flinches. "I'm sorry."

"Or how the system ripped me and Reece apart, then kicked us to the curb the second we turned eighteen? Are you sorry for the years he spent in prison and the years I spent on the stripper pole, getting pawed over by gross disgusting men like you?"

"I'm so sorry," he says over and over between sobs.

Tiffany takes a deep breath and steps back. She and Reece look at each other, checking in to make sure they're satisfied by what they're hearing so far.

"Keep going," she says. "Time to share the rest of it."

He gazes up at her. "The rest?"

"Yeah. Spill."

"I'm not sure what you want me to say."

"Go ahead and tell us what Daddy overheard you talking about."

He licks his lips, as if relieved to be sharing that. "In the old storage building here at the school, I found a box of papers, including a land lease agreement."

"And?"

"The agreement was between Jeremiah Dupre and a man named Henri Fortineau."

"And?"

"I researched the Fortineau family and found out they settled in Louisiana years before Jeremiah Dupre."

"And?"

"Jeremiah didn't buy the land he used for the Dupre plantation. He leased it from the Fortineaus."

"And?"

"The lease was for ninety-nine years."

"Which means?"

"Since 1933, the Dupre family hasn't had rights to their land. They're squatters. Their fortune is built on a lie."

Tiffany shoots me a triumphant look, as if hoping to impress me. "And Marian knew."

"Her husband told her. He called it the family's darkest secret."

"And she told you this because…."

"The only time she shares anything is when she's rattled. She was furious that day. She hates surprises. She thought she'd destroyed all the records from that period."

I can't believe what I'm hearing, yet at the same time I know in my heart it's true. Marian's wealth and power are built on a foundation of lies and fraud.

Tiffany isn't done with him. "And what about you?"

"Me?" he repeats, stammering.

"Tell us your deep dark secret."

"I don't have any—"

Whap!

"I made a copy of the lease!" he cries out.

"There you go. Now why'd you do that?"

"I wanted to be headmaster."

"You blackmailed Marian."

He starts sobbing.

"And what did she have on you?"

His eyes widen. "Nothing."

She slaps him again.

"Nothing, I swear!"

Whap!

"Please, stop!"

Whap!

"She thought she had something but she didn't. The accusations were false!"

"Accusations of…?"

He's shaking his head. "Complete lies."

Whap!

"Stop, please!" He's breathing heavily. "At my previous school, I was accused of going easy on certain students."

"Going easy?"

"Grades."

"You took *bribes* to give students good grades."

"Prominent families were involved. I had no choice."

She snorts. "So you're greedy *and* weak."

Maybe because her snort sounds like a sneer, defiance flashes in his eyes. "At least I'm not trash like you."

Whap!

"I'm sorry! I didn't mean it."

"Yes, you did." She takes a deep breath and a step back. "Reece, I'm getting tired of listening to this pile of garbage."

Reece steps into the light behind Devlin and I tense up, terrified of what's coming next.

"You got what you needed, Sis?"

"Almost." She bends down to stare at Devlin, face to face. "Out of everyone, I blame you the most."

He's trembling now, completely terrified. "I'm sorry."

"You knew us, but you kicked us out of here. You abandoned us." Her voice becomes husky. "You banished us to hell."

"I'm so sorry."

"Marian Dupre and Sheriff Denton — they didn't know

us. But you did. You were our teacher. We thought you cared about us."

"Tiffany, I'm so sorry."

"For a minute there, me and Reece actually thought you were gonna help us."

"I'm sorry."

"You're only sorry you got called out."

"No." He's shaking now, eyes wide with terror.

Tiffany stands up and wipes tears from her eyes.

"Okay," she says to her brother. "I'm good."

"You sure?"

"I'm sure."

"Last chance."

"I'm good."

Without hesitation, he leans down and savagely jams his knife deep into Devlin's stomach.

Devlin screams, a horrid guttural cry, as Reece carves a huge gash through his midsection.

Reece yanks his knife out and steps back, the blade flashing in the light.

Still conscious, Devlin looks down at himself in shock as his intestines spill out of him.

"You die as you lived," Tiffany pronounces. "A gutless coward."

Then the two of them laugh as Devlin collapses to the ground and dies.

CHAPTER 51

O*h, God. They did it. They killed him.*

I can barely breathe. I'm in a nightmare and there's no escape. I've just watched these maniacs slaughter three people.

And now the only person left to kill is — *me*.

They're reveling in their revenge, laughing up a storm, practically dancing around the corpse. I take a step back and they don't notice. Can I sneak away? I inch into the shadows a bit more, then more. I'm about to make a dash for it when Reece says —

"Don't even think about it, Callie."

I freeze. Tiffany looks over and laughs. "You don't give up, do you?"

"Why did you drag me into this? I've done nothing to you."

She lets out a big sigh. "True enough." She glances at Reece. "Except last week in your kitchen."

Emotion surges through me. "I was defending myself."

"Which we appreciate. No hard feelings. Right, Reece?"

"Right."

I can only stare at them. How can they sound so normal, so gracious, so reasonable, mere seconds after gutting a man?

Because they're following a plan and the plan's not done, my inner voice says. *Keep them talking.*

"I get why you've kept me alive." My voice sounds more confident than I have any right to expect. "I'm your patsy."

"Patsy," she repeats with a laugh. "You are *full* of fun words."

"Fall guy — fall gal, I suppose. Stooge. Victim. You're gonna pin all this on me."

"Well, that's true enough and we're sorry about that. I mean, aside from being incredibly *boring*, we got nothing against you."

The cheerful cruelty of her words brings tears to my eyes. After all of the horrors I've just witnessed, after the carnage and torture and bloodshed, why do I give a damn what she thinks of me? Does she not understand how important it is for me to get better so I can be there for my daughter?

I have to get away. With Josh gone, I'm all Ava has left. I have to survive.

When your moment comes, don't hesitate.

Reece wipes his knife on Devlin's shirt and returns it to the sheath. Then he walks over to the car and shuts it off and we're plunged into darkness.

I know they're watching me and waiting for me to run, but I force myself to stay still as my eyes adjust.

"We're going for a walk," Reece announces, presumably for my benefit.

"Please, for my own sanity, I need to know the rest of your plan."

"Plenty of time for that."

"Where are we going?"

He ignores me and says to his sister, "You got everything from the car?"

In the dimness — my eyes are still adjusting — I can make out Tiffany nodding.

Reece walks to his backpack on the ground and pulls out something. I squint, trying to make out what it is.

As he steps closer, I see that it's a plastic bag with a bloody handkerchief in it. When he opens the bag, I smell fresh blood. With a gulp of revulsion, I realize the blood is Marian's.

"Meant to do this earlier," he says. "Hands out."

Nauseated, I do as told. He smears the handkerchief over my hands and forearms, Marian's blood sticking to my skin.

"Now go to the car and get in and grab the steering wheel."

I walk over to the car and get behind the wheel and grip it.

"Now get out and shut the door."

Again I do as told, the two of them watching my every move.

He walks over to Devlin's corpse, dips the handkerchief into Devlin's fresh blood, then walks back to me.

"You know the drill," he says.

I hold my hands out, my stomach churning as he smears Devlin's blood over my hands and arms.

He takes a step back and looks me over, admiring his handiwork. "Go to the trunk and press down on it, like you're shutting it."

Sick to my stomach, I do as instructed.

And in that moment, trembling with fear and disgust, my mind leaps ahead and I see how this will play out.

When the cops investigate what happened tonight, the evidence they collect will point to *me* as the perpetrator of these awful crimes. The cops will find me covered in the blood of all three victims. Phone records will show that I called Marian from near Devlin's house. Devlin's blood will be found on and inside the car trunk, pointing to me attacking him at his house and driving to Marian's with him in the car trunk. The blood on the steering wheel will show that, after killing Marian and the sheriff in the study, I drove to the school and killed Devlin.

As for Reece and Tiffany — will there be any evidence they were even here? Back at Marian's, Tiffany used a handkerchief when she rearranged the yearbooks on the shelf in the study, and Reece did the same when he shut the front door. Did I actually see them touch anything in the mansion?

And as for the drive to the school.… Tiffany wore gloves and put her hair in a net. Reece covered the back seat of the car with a plastic sheet before he got in. It's possible that no trace of either of them will be found.

I hear my name being called and I blink.

"Callie, Callie," Tiffany's saying. "Earth to Callie."

My brain's done it again — fled the present without me realizing it.

"I know why you didn't tie me up," I announce.

Tiffany's eyes widen. "Oh, do you now?"

"You don't want the investigators to find marks on my body," I say, trembling as I talk about myself as a future corpse. "You don't want them thinking I was tied up or handcuffed or knocked out or anything like that."

Reece grunts. "You got us on that, Callie."

"Don't be getting any bright ideas," Tiffany adds. "What you're talking about is Plan A, but we got Plan B and C and neither of them needs you alive."

"I have no interest in being tied up."

"Good. Just keep doing what we say."

I take a deep breath. Not being tied up hasn't meant much so far. I'm outnumbered and they have all the weapons. Tiffany has Susan's gun and Reece actually has three weapons: his knife, the sheriff's gun, and my cane.

Wait for your moment. Be ready.

Tiffany and Reece exchange a look. "We got everything?" he asks.

She turns to me. "Okay, Callie," she says brightly. "Time for a walk."

"Where to?"

Her tone is cheerful. "We're gonna mosey on down to the bayou."

CHAPTER 52

Tiffany's upbeat tone is horrifying. We aren't "moseying" — we're on a death march. How could I have missed who she really is? How did I not see through "Beth's" quiet, helpful exterior? I allowed a monster into my home and not once did I catch a glimpse of her true nature.

"I believed you," I say bitterly as I turn toward the path that leads across the campus to the bayou. "I let you into my house. I let you take care of my daughter."

"You sure did," Tiffany says cheerfully.

"I trusted you."

"You shouldn't have, but boy am I glad you did," she says with a laugh. "Never trust me, Callie. That's the lesson here."

With my heart pounding so loudly I can hear it, I limp past the administration building down the path that leads to the bayou. The rain is coming heavily now. I'm soaked to the skin, my jeans heavy with water. Lightning slashes the night sky and thunder rumbles.

Tiffany and Reece are a few steps behind. We've all gone silent. Something terrible is about to happen and no one wants to discuss it.

A thought comes: How did Tiffany manage to fool Josh? They were together for months and far more intimate.

"I have to know," I say over my shoulder. "How did you trick Josh into marrying you?"

Tiffany laughs. "Oh, Callie. That was actually the funnest part of all of this."

She still wants to talk. I need to encourage her. "Tell me how you did it."

"Well, Josh wasn't part of the plan, at least not at first."

"The original revenge plan, you mean?"

"Right. The original plan was just about getting back at the people who hurt us and Daddy."

"When did the plan become bigger?"

"Only after Josh and I hooked up. I didn't even know who he was at first."

"I assume you met him at Lola's?"

"He put a twenty in my g-string." She laughs. "My God, the body on that boy. And the sex."

Anger surges through me but I push it back. "How did it go from being something casual to something more?"

"Actually, that happened because of you."

Huh? I stop in my tracks and turn around. What she's saying makes no sense. I need to see her face. "What do you mean?"

"Every time we hooked up, he kept talking about you. Callie this, Callie that." Though she's still smiling, her tone now has an edge. "I was getting ready to cut him loose when I found out who he was."

"And that changed things."

She laughs. "Hell yeah. It was like *boom*, the universe laid it all out on a silver platter."

"You'll need to unpack that. I don't understand what's on that silver platter of yours."

She sighs. "Reece, am I not making sense?"

"You're making sense, Sis."

"You're not making sense to me," I insist. "How does any of this relate to *me*?"

Tiffany sighs again. "Let's start with the basics. You and I look like each other, right? Not close enough to be sisters, but similar."

"Sure," I say cautiously.

"When I saw that, I realized Josh had a type."

I'm starting to follow. "And so then…."

"I found out how you dress and how you act, and when I found out you used to be a waitress I got myself a job at the diner and changed my hair and started acting like you and…."

"And what?"

"Well, I turned into a version of *you*."

I must look as perplexed as I feel because she bursts out laughing. "You catching on now?"

"But…." I try to collect my thoughts. "Didn't Josh realize you were putting on an act?"

"Oh, sure," she says with another laugh, "but not the way you think. See, I got him believing that 'Tiffany the dancer' was the act — you know, acting tough because I had to be strong to survive in a rough world blah blah blah. He thought 'Beth the waitress' was the real me."

"He bought it?"

"Of course."

"But pulling off something like that is…."

"Difficult? Challenging?" She nods emphatically. "Hell yeah. Being nice all the time? Being *you*? It's *exhausting*."

"And he believed you?"

"Callie," she says, "he *wanted* to believe."

"But…."

"Especially when you were in the hospital in a coma. He was afraid he was gonna lose you forever. That's when he really started getting into the idea of me being the new you."

Tears come and I brush them away. Poor Josh. What she's saying is so heartbreaking.

"And then, when you didn't die and he saw you were gonna need help, I volunteered. I couldn't miss the opportunity to study you up close."

"Because by then the plan had changed. The new plan was for you to…."

"Marry him."

"But not because you loved him."

She shrugs. "I mean, I didn't mind him, but no."

"You married him for the money."

"Bingo."

"But…." I can see there's a logic to her plan, but it isn't straightforward. "Josh didn't have much money of his own."

"Well, the original part of the plan was gonna take care of that."

It takes me a second to get it. "Because taking your revenge on Marian was still on. Once she was dead, Josh would inherit everything."

"Right."

"So the new plan was to get your revenge and become Josh's wife and live a life of luxury?"

"Not quite." She's smiling at me, clearly enjoying herself, waiting for me to catch up.

"Since you didn't love him and found it exhausting to act nice all the time, you planned to divorce him?"

"For a while that was the new plan."

"Get rid of his mother and then divorce him and get a nice big settlement."

"Right."

I try not to show how angry I'm becoming. "Why didn't you stick to that? Why did you have to kill him?"

Tiffany's eyes narrow. "Touched a nerve, have we?"

I take a deep breath. "I just want to understand. I don't get why he had to die."

"Well," she says with a glance at Reece, as if weighing whether to share more.

Reece shakes his head. "Don't."

"Why not?" she says right away.

"It's better she not know."

"Because…?"

He gestures. "It's dark."

She snorts. "She can barely walk."

"It ain't necessary to tell her."

"Who cares about *necessary*?"

He gestures again toward the swamp. "I don't want problems."

It's the first disagreement I've witnessed between them. Tiffany is clearly aching to share more of her diabolical plan and Reece doesn't want her saying something because he doesn't want me misbehaving or running off.

But all of a sudden my body goes rigid because I realize: They killed Josh *before* they killed Marian.

Before he inherited the family fortune.

And then I realize —

With Marian dead, the Dupre family fortune passes to —

Ava.

I breathe in sharply and my heart starts thumping. I feel faint as the unspoken part of their plan slams into me.

Their ultimate target isn't Marian or Josh. It's *Ava.*

I nearly start crying. The scale, the scope, the audacity of what they're planning is *shocking.* Do these maniacs actually believe they have a shot in hell at winning custody of my daughter and using her to gain control of Marian's estate?

The words leave my mouth before I can stop them. "What makes you think you will *ever* get your hands on Ava?"

Reece frowns — he doesn't like me asking this — and Tiffany chuckles but doesn't respond.

"Ava has a godmother," I say, trying hard to keep my voice sounding calm. "If anything happens to me, Ava goes with her."

"Right, your friend Gwen," Tiffany says. "But you know, it's a dangerous world out there."

Reece isn't pleased. "Quiet, Tiff."

"I mean, muggings happen all the time. Car accidents. Suicides. Burglaries gone bad. In this day and age, is anyone truly safe?"

Dear God. When they're done with me, they're going after *Gwen?*

Adrenaline rushes through me. I need to escape. I have to. It's not just about me. It's about my best friend. It's about *my daughter.*

Reece is glaring at his sister. "Shut up, Tiff."

"She said she wants to know."

"It ain't right."

"'*It ain't right?*'" she repeats. "Really? We've been over this."

"What's the point of rubbing it in?"

They're getting angry with each other. Maybe Reece feels bad about what his psycho sister is planning or maybe he's worried I'll run off and he doesn't want to have to chase me through the swamp or — *oh my God is this the chance I've been waiting for?*

I take a step back and they don't notice.

I'm about to take another step when Tiffany whirls toward me. "You said you want to know everything, right, Callie?"

"Right," I manage to stammer.

She shoots a triumphant glance at her brother. "And by everything, you mean you're okay with knowing *everything*, right?"

I feel nauseous. "Right."

Reece gives up. "Fine. But if she bolts, you're chasing her."

"Fine." Pleased to have won their skirmish, she turns back to me. "Now, where were we?"

"Please don't bring Gwen into this," I whisper.

"I tell you what, Callie. I'll make this promise because I like you. If your friend doesn't get in the way, she'll be all right."

"She's a good person. She doesn't have to be involved in this."

"Oh, I agree. Though I'm a bit skeptical about her stepping aside. That's not who she is. She's big on standing firm

— I saw that at the hospital when she camped out by your bed three nights in a row. No, your friend's a fighter."

"You can't actually believe that getting rid of Gwen" — God, I can't believe I just said that — "will make it possible for you to gain custody of Ava."

She chuckles. "You need to think about how things are gonna look when this is all over."

Fear stabs through me. "What do you mean?"

"Everyone's gonna believe poor Callie went crazy and killed a bunch of people on account of her head being messed up."

"No one will believe that," I whisper, even as I realize that *of course they will.*

"I mean, all that physical evidence, they won't be able to ignore that."

"They'll see through it."

She chuckles. "Plus, Doc Franklin weighing in on how unstable you were."

I blink with surprise. "How can you say —"

And then I see it. *She already has him.* She's blackmailing him or sleeping with him or God knows what. He's going to do exactly what she wants.

Tiffany's watching me closely. "What did you just figure out?"

"Does Doc Franklin realize you're going to get rid of him as soon as he stops being useful to you?"

She laughs. "Now *that's* the Callie I like."

"He's part of your revenge tour."

"Of course. He helped cover up what happened to Daddy."

"So Doc Franklin will tell everyone I was mentally

unstable and the physical evidence will indicate I killed everyone and…."

"I'll tell them about all the weird stuff you did at home."

I flush. "What weird stuff?"

She laughs. "Oh, you know, like claiming intruders broke in and attacked you. Like not bothering to tell anyone about your supposed attack until *after* your ex-husband got murdered in your kitchen. Like getting your hands on a gun and taking it everywhere with you, including multiple times to your daughter's school. Like barricading yourself and your daughter in her bedroom every night because you were so scared."

I shake my head, wanting to argue, but how can I? "You're twisting everything around."

"Shit, Callie, every single thing I just said, you actually did. I'll barely have to make anything up."

"None of that means I'm crazy."

"It sure as hell *sounds* like you are."

For a long second, we just stare at each other. She's so twisted. And so relentless. She's been planning this for months, playing me and everyone else for fools.

"Funny thing is," she says with a smug smile, "it's gonna be quiet, helpful 'Beth' who closes the book on crazy Callie."

"Fuck you."

She laughs. "Reece, let's make that her nickname. Crazy Callie. It has a nice ring."

He doesn't respond because he's watching me like a hawk, waiting for me to do something.

I have to dissuade them — cut through their confidence, get them to reassess what they're planning. "There's no way a court will ever give you custody of Ava."

Tiffany shakes her head. "Once your bestie's out of the

picture, who's gonna step up? Your parents are dead. Your aunt and uncle — they're old and not in the best of health and halfway across the country."

Oh my God, she's really researched me. "But no court would ever consider you a responsible —"

"Oh, but it won't be 'Tiffany' petitioning the court. It'll be 'Beth,' the grieving widow of the girl's murdered father, the quiet young woman who hopes to be a nurse someday, the helpful woman who's already formed such a strong bond with the poor girl."

"But —"

"And don't forget where we are. The folks who take on the running of Boudreaux Parish will be rooting for me to gain custody. They'll want someone young and inexperienced looking out for Ava and her fortune, someone in over her head, someone they think they can influence...."

She's right about that. With Josh and Marian gone, with me and Gwen gone, Tiffany will have a clear path to gaining custody of Ava.

And with custody comes control of her inheritance.

"You're going to adopt Ava," I whisper.

"Of course."

I can barely get the words to leave my mouth. "And then you're going to kill her."

My heart is pounding and blood is rushing everywhere and oh my God I can barely stop myself from lunging at her.

Tiffany glances at Reece, as if realizing her brother maybe had a point about not telling me the full plan.

"When she dies," I whisper, my voice trembling, "as her legal mother, you'll inherit everything."

She takes a step away from me. "That's how it works."

"She's just a child."

"A pretty good kid, I'll give you that."

"Please don't hurt her."

"How about this. I promise it'll be quick."

"No!"

"A horse-riding accident, probably."

I gasp.

"She sure does love horses. What's her favorite, Midnight Star?"

An image — a memory — rushes through me, a memory of Ava gazing up at me with her trusting hazel eyes, her thick frizzy hair catching the light of the afternoon sun as we play in her bedroom. And then —

Before I even realize what I'm doing —

I'm running!

CHAPTER 53

'm off the walking trail and tearing through the brush and pushing past trees in a blind panic, with a single desperate thought pulsing through me:

Escape!

I have to get away — I have to save my daughter!

I can barely see where I'm going and branches are scraping me and my hip is killing me but I can't stop no I can't stop I have to keep running and stay alive.

The ground is uneven and I stumble and nearly trip and branches are tugging at my shirt and tearing my skin and I can't catch my breath but I can't stop moving —

They're shouting for me to stop and Reece is yelling, "You said you'd go after her!" and Tiffany is screaming, "What the fuck are you waiting for?" and my heart surges because every precious second means more distance between me and them.

I push blindly past a bush and my foot catches on a tree root and —

Bam — I fall hard.

Pain shoots through my shoulder and arm. I'm in a ditch or a channel and half-submerged in water and my mouth is full of dirt. I push myself up, gasping for breath, my hands sinking into mud and I want to scream but don't because —

Flashlights are bearing down on me.

I raise my head and see them crashing through the brush toward me —

Heart thundering, I lower myself and slide deeper into the muck. The skin of my arms is gleaming like a beacon and as quietly as I can I smear handfuls of mud over my arms and my face and —

I take a deep breath and go still, praying they can't see me —

"Goddamn it, Tiff," Reece says from maybe ten yards away, a hulking shadow in the gloom, his light sweeping across the swamp.

"She can't be far," Tiffany replies and I nearly gasp because she's somewhere right behind me, her light perilously close.

"I told you to keep your mouth shut about the kid."

"Sorry, but you know me. Never been good at that." Despite the problems I'm causing them by running away, she still sounds cheerful. "Don't worry. We'll find her."

I can see her now. She's barely ten feet from me and holding her gun. If she turns my way, it's over.

"Eyes on the ground," Reece snaps.

She sighs dramatically. "So serious." But her flashlight sweeps become more methodical, her swinging ever closer. I hunch lower — just as lightning strikes a nearby tree and a deafening clap of thunder vibrates through the swamp.

Tiffany's flashlight beam wavers. "Damn, that was close."

"Anything?" Reece asks.

"Not yet."

"Why's your gun out? Put it away."

"I don't want her jumping me."

"She ain't gonna jump you."

"That's rich, coming from you. She's sneaky."

"She doesn't have a weapon."

"The entire swamp is a weapon."

"I don't want you shooting her by accident."

"I won't do that."

"Just put it away."

They've been walking past me as they bicker. Through the gloom, I see Tiffany stuff the gun into the back of her jeans.

"Turn off your light," Reece says.

"No way."

"You'll see more."

"I ain't turning off my light."

"She can see us a mile away."

"But —"

"Tiff, turn off your light."

With a frustrated sigh, she snaps off her light.

And my heart starts hammering away because when Reece turns off his, the swamp goes utterly dark and I can't see a thing.

But then, as my eyes adjust to the gloom, I realize he's right. Even through the rain, I can make out the outline of him about thirty yards away. He's standing still, taking in everything. Anything that moves, anything that makes a sound, he's gonna sense it.

The instant I leave this mudhole, I'll be exposed.

The two of them start whispering to each other. It's like they know I'm nearby and don't want me listening in.

Then I watch, my heart in my throat, as they break apart and vanish into the gloom.

My heart is thudding away in my ears. Whatever slim advantage I might have had knowing where they are has just disappeared.

I'm alone. With no weapons. Hunted by two vicious killers.

Something brushes my foot and I nearly cry out. Is it a water moccasin? A fish? A bug?

A gator?

I can't stay in the water.

Somehow, I force myself to stay still. I take a deep breath, then another, trying to calm myself.

Don't make a sound, I order myself.

Move slowly.

I need a plan.

Assuming I didn't get turned around in the darkness, I know the direction of the walking trail. If I can find the trail, then I can follow it through the park until I find help.

Very slowly, I raise myself onto my hands and knees and crawl out of the water. The ditch isn't deep, but it's muddy and slippery. My hands and knees keep getting sucked down into the muck.

Being covered in mud has an upside: It'll be harder for them to see me in the darkness.

Still on my hands and knees, I inch forward, listening for sounds of movement. But all I hear is the rain hitting leaves.

Another bolt of lightning strikes nearby and I freeze as the thunder rumbles through me.

Still no sign of either of them.

I keep crawling, scurrying from bush to bush, pausing at each hiding place to listen for danger.

I'm barely getting anywhere on all fours. I'm going to have to stand up. I'm going to have to walk.

Heart thudding, I rise to my feet —

And gasp as —

A hand grips my hair from behind!

CHAPTER 54

Pain tears through my scalp as I try to escape but Reece tightens his grip and says, "No, no, Callie. Stay still."

"Fuck you," I say but oh my God he's so strong. His hand on my head is like steel. I grab his wrist and kick out at him but he slams my head to the ground and I collapse onto my hands and knees.

"Okay, Callie," he says, his grip on my hair fearfully strong. "I'm going to let you go and you're not gonna run, got it?"

"Yes," I manage to say between ragged breaths.

And then the hand is gone and he's gazing down on me like a mountain.

"Get up," he says. "We're almost there."

Fearfully, I struggle to my feet. He doesn't seem angry. It's like my brief run through the swamp was no big deal to him.

"Where are we going?"

"You'll see."

He points and I start limping. Eventually we hit a walking trail and he points again and we continue on.

"Where's Tiffany?" I ask.

"Somewhere near."

"Shouldn't you call her?"

"Nah. We don't need her for this."

"You mean you don't want her riling me up again with her big mouth?"

He grunts. "That's one way of putting it."

We round a bend and suddenly I know where we are.

Dead ahead of us is the creepy old oak tree.

In the darkness it's even more frightening. As we step underneath its vast canopy, a flash of lightning illuminates the dark branches above.

"See the yellow crime scene tape?" he says, pointing to the far side of the clearing. "Head there."

Oh my God — he's taking me to the same spot where Rory Freeman was found dead.

"Please don't do this," I whisper.

"I tell you what. You do one thing for me, I promise I'll protect her."

"Her?"

"Your daughter."

Fear stabs me — along with crazy irrational *hope*. "What do you mean?"

"I won't let Tiff kill her."

Tears come. "How can you promise that?"

"I'll get Tiff to change the plan."

"But how?"

"We'll get the money a different way."

We're almost at the crime scene tape. I turn to face him,

my heart thudding. Is this how I spend my final seconds? Bargaining with a killer?

"How can I believe you?"

"You got spirit," he says with an intensity that takes me aback.

"Spirit?"

"Fight. I respect that."

Oddly enough, I believe him. Yes, he's a killer who viciously slaughters people left and right, but he has a code of sorts. *If you fight back when I kill you, I'll respect you afterward.*

"You can't control your sister."

"She'll listen to me."

"You can't trust her. She'll get rid of you, too."

"No, she won't."

"Tell me something. When you got out of prison, who found who? Did she find you, or was it the other way around?"

His silence is my answer.

"If you hadn't done the hard work of tracking her down, would she have bothered?"

"It's not like that."

"She doesn't care about you. You're just a useful tool. She only cares about herself."

"You're wrong."

"She's a full-on psychopath."

"Stop talking like that."

"But you're different." I don't believe that for a second — he's a violent monster who gets off on killing people — but I keep talking. "I can see the hurt and the anger but also the spark of humanity deep inside you."

"She's —"

"She's broken, Reece. There's no fixing her. She can't be trusted. She'll betray you."

"Stop saying that."

"The cops know I didn't kill Josh. Tiffany will tell them you were my accomplice."

"Stop."

"She'll throw you under the bus. Probably kill you before they can arrest you. I mean, she can't have you talking."

"Stop!"

"Reece, you know I'm right."

"Why are you going on about this?"

"Because I have to save my daughter."

He shakes his head. "I told you I'll protect her."

"I don't believe you."

"You don't think I can deliver."

"To use your sister's favorite word — bingo."

"I got proof," he says suddenly.

"Proof?"

"Yeah, your friend."

I frown, totally not following. "What do you mean?"

"Mrs. Freeman."

"Susan?" A sick sensation forms in the pit of my stomach. "What does she have to do with this?"

"She was married to Mr. Freeman."

Horror rushes through me as I realize why he brought me to this spot. "Rory didn't kill himself."

"That's right."

"You killed him." I point to the crime scene tape. "Right here."

"Yep."

"*Why?*"

"He was our teacher at Briarton. He recognized me at Lola's."

"You killed him because he *recognized* you?"

His tone is defensive. "I had no choice."

"Of course you had a choice!"

"He would've ruined everything."

"So he wasn't one of your targets? He wasn't on your revenge list?"

"He was always good to me and Tiff."

I can't keep the anger from my voice. "He was a good man and you killed him anyway."

"Had to."

"You brought him here and staged his suicide."

"I made the same promise to him I'm making to you."

My heart's thudding in my chest. "You mean...."

"I told him we'd leave his wife alone."

I'm nauseous again. "As long as he helped you make his death look like a suicide."

"Right."

"You had him put the gun in his own mouth and then you had him press the trigger."

"Right."

"You're a monster."

His eyes flash. "His wife's still alive, right? There's the proof."

"And he actually went along with it?"

"Yeah, he did."

I blink with horror as he pulls the gun from his belt and holds it in front of me.

"Sit down next to the tree."

Trembling, I walk to the tree and lower myself to the ground.

"Now lean back against the tree."

Oh my God, is this it? "Please don't, Reece."

"Lean back against the trunk."

I inch back until I feel the tree pressing against me.

Reece drops to his knees in front of me, then pulls a handkerchief out of his pocket and wipes the gun down.

"He did one last thing for me, Callie. He did it because he loved his wife."

"He did it to protect her?"

He presses the gun against my cheek. The metal is wet and cool. His touch is gentle, even tender. "I kept my promise to him, Callie. I'll keep my promise to you."

He's close enough now that I can smell his sweat.

And that's when I realize — *he isn't holding my cane.*

When he pulled out the handkerchief to wipe down the gun —

He set down my cane.

I need to glance down. I need to see where it is.

But I can't let him see me looking.

Blinking furiously, I slowly bring my hand to the gun.

He holds his breath as I touch the handle. My fingers brush his.

"I want to be able to trust you," I whisper.

"You can trust me," he whispers back.

"My daughter means everything to me."

"I'll keep her safe. I promise."

I rub my cheek against the gun, almost like I'm caressing it. "You promise?"

His voice is husky. "I promise."

I close my hand over his. "How do you want me to hold it?"

As he focuses in on my hand, I risk a glance downward.

My cane's right next to him on the ground.

I slump lower and stifle a sob, like I'm losing my resistance. "You have to promise me, Reece."

"I promise you, Callie."

"You can't let your sister kill Ava."

He's carefully arranging my hand over the gun, getting me to hold it the way he wants.

I slide lower, reaching for the cane with my other hand.

"You swear to God?" I whisper.

"I swear."

My fingertips touch the cane.

"You're almost there, Callie," he whispers, staring deep into my eyes, coaxing my fingers over the trigger. "Now I want you to open your mouth."

Just a few seconds more. "Reece, please," I beg, even as my hand closes over the cane.

"You can do this," he whispers. "You can do it for her."

"Fuck you," I whisper.

"What?"

"Fuck you!" I scream.

I try to wrest the gun away from him —

Which of course he stops right away —

But I also slip beneath him and take hold of my cane with both hands —

And as he turns toward me in surprise —

I jab the end of the cane into his neck —

And hear a *crunch.*

He makes a wheezing sound and starts clutching his throat.

And with a fury like nothing I've ever known —

I *smash* the cane into his head.

He grunts and goes down, collapsing onto his back.

A huge wheeze comes out of him — he's able to breathe again.

Before he can recover, I scramble over him and raise the cane over my head and —

Stab it down into his face —

Right into his eye!

CHAPTER 55

The crack of his cheekbone breaking, the squishy resistance of his eyeball and brain as my cane drives deep into his skull, the wheeze he involuntarily utters, the way his entire body jerks and twitches and then collapses into an awful stillness —

It's the stuff of nightmares. Violence beyond imagination. I hear a shocked cry and realize it's coming from me. I've just killed a man. He's dead. What have I done?

With a gasp, I see I'm still gripping the cane and I let it go and to my horror the cane stays upright, stuck in his head like a daffodil in a flowerpot.

And then I'm retching but nothing's coming up and I'm gasping for breath, heart thudding, head spinning, struggling not to faint.

Through my nausea, I hear Tiffany's voice and snap back to attention.

"Reece," she's yelling. "Where are you?"

Fear jolts me. She's close. She has a gun. I'm still in terrible danger.

I have to get away!

She calls out again. As I struggle to my feet, I realize —

I need a weapon.

Reece has a gun and a knife on him.

I'm about to drop to the ground and get them when —

Tiffany appears in the gloom across the clearing, gun in hand.

No time! Desperately, I yank my cane from Reece's skull with a horrifying *squelch*.

Tiffany sees me. "Callie, stop!"

And then I'm running, cane in hand —

She fires —

A bullet whizzes past me —

And I hear her yelling, "Reece, get up! Reece!"

Seconds later, I'm still running when I hear her scream of rage. "You're dead, Callie! You're dead!"

I'm still pushing through the brush, stumbling over the uneven terrain.

Until suddenly I'm at the water's edge, the bayou extending in front of me, and I stop so abruptly that I almost fall in.

She's coming for me. No way I can outrun her.

I look around wildly. I need a plan.

I need to *hide*.

But where? I rush to a bush that looks big enough and crouch down just as Tiffany bursts through the gloom.

She stops short at the bayou's edge, just like I did.

"Callie!" she screams. "You can't escape!"

I hunch lower, hoping she'll move away from me.

But she doesn't.

Her breathing is heavy as she comes toward me.

Hunched behind the bush, heart hammering and mind racing, I grip my cane like a baseball bat and prepare to swing.

She stops on the other side of the bush, clearly on high alert. She must know I'm nearby.

"I've got a gun, Callie," she says into the darkness. "You can't get away. Come out now and I promise I won't shoot you."

I remain completely silent, frozen in place behind the bush.

"Better yet," she continues, "how about this? Come out now and I promise I won't go after Ava."

Rage blazes through me and I nearly charge her but — just barely — I hold myself back.

"Ava is just Plan A," she adds, her voice shockingly calm. "I'll do Plan B instead — sue the estate and get a settlement as Josh's grieving widow."

She's actually saying all this in a *let's-be-reasonable* tone. God, I hate her.

I hear a soft sucking sound as she pulls a foot out of the mud. She's moving again. A few more seconds and she'll have me.

Don't be a sitting duck.

She has a gun and a knife. She has the advantage.

But I have my cane.

I can take her.

I have no choice. *I have to move.*

My daughter's life depends on *me*.

Furious tears blur my vision.

I inch forward and risk peeking around the bush —

Right into the barrel of Tiffany's gun!

I duck desperately as she fires, the gun shockingly loud —

Then I race around the bush.

As she whirls around —

I tackle her!

She grunts as we hit the ground hard and —

Oh my God she's like a rabid raccoon, scratching at my face and hitting me with the gun and screaming and trying to get away —

I swing my cane wildly and try to knock the gun out of her hand —

And get rewarded when I hear a sharp *thunk* of wood on metal and the gun goes flying.

I try to whack her head with my cane but the angle's wrong and suddenly she's on top of me and her hands are closing around my neck and I can't breathe —

Oh my God I can't breathe —

My fingers grip the smooth mahogany of the cane —

I swing it up —

And *whack* her!

Her grip loosens and I scramble away and —

We're facing each other on all fours in the muck, snarling at each other like feral dogs.

I struggle to my feet, gripping the cane like a baseball bat, as she whips out her knife. She lunges and I dart back and then we're circling each other, each of us trying to catch our breath.

"Damn, girl," she says, wiping blood from her mouth. "Didn't know you had it in you."

"Fuck you." I say between gasps.

"Offer still stands." I can't believe what I'm hearing — she's still trying to come across as *reasonable*. How in the hell is she keeping her composure when all I can do is snarl and gasp and swear?

She points at the cane. "Put that down and I promise I won't go after Ava."

"Fuck you."

She lunges again, then pulls back. "You can't win."

"I beat Reece. I'll beat you."

She lets out an amused chuckle. "You definitely got the best of him — twice. I think he had a soft spot for you. But me? No way."

"You don't even care that he's dead."

Another chuckle. My God, her brother just died and she's in a *good mood*. "Of course I do. He was kin."

"All you care about is how useful he was to you."

"Well," she says with a shrug, "he ain't useful now."

Her composure — I can't get past it. Then I realize: She's been here before. She's done this before. She knows she can win.

And then I see what's really going on:

She still doesn't want to stab me. She's still hoping to frame me. She's still hoping to make my death look like suicide.

I take a swing at her and she leaps back, surprised.

"I'll use this if I have to," she says, waving the knife in front of her.

"No you won't."

"Yes I will."

"Your *plan* says otherwise."

She laughs. "Callie, Callie, Callie. We went over this. That's just Plan A. You wanna know what Plan B is?"

"No."

"Sure you do," she says.

"Fuck you."

"Plan B is all about poor Beth. Crazy Callie took her hostage and dragged her to the bayou."

"Won't work." We're near the water's edge now, testing our reflexes, looking for weaknesses.

"Luckily for poor Beth, she'll get her hands on Callie's knife and end up using it to defend herself."

"No one will believe you."

"Of course they will. The evidence will tell the same story. I mean, you just killed Reece. His blood and brains are all over you."

She's so confident. I have to shake her up, rattle her.

"How can you live with yourself?" I spit out, going for guilt. "I trusted you."

She chuckles. "You shouldn't have trusted me, Callie. Never trust me."

"You're a monster."

"No, I'm just someone who deserves something good in her life for a change."

"No matter how many people you have to kill to get it."

She shrugs. "It's the way of the world."

"Not my world."

She laughs. "You're a fool."

I grip my cane. "Life is nothing without the people we love."

She snorts.

"Of course, you'll never know that because no one will ever love you."

"You think I care?"

Of course she doesn't care. She's been alone since she was a child. She doesn't know anything else.

I lick my lips and taste blood. "I hate you for taking Josh and Rory from us. I hate you because you're greedy and broken and disgusting. You're a vile, sad, pathetic horror show."

Her lips tighten — something I said just got under her skin.

"You're damaged goods. There's no fixing you."

"Shut up."

Finally, a hint of anger. Is that how I can do this — attack her by going after her ego? "You have nothing to offer. All you are is rage and grievance."

"I'm more than that and you know it."

I laugh. "I suppose you think you're *smart?* You're nothing special. You only fooled us because you got lucky."

"Shut up."

"You're pretty pedestrian, actually."

"Shut up."

"I mean, I guess you're kind of pretty. But in an ordinary, boring way."

I'm rewarded with a snarl.

"And your so-called acting skills? Staying quiet and not saying anything mean?" I laugh. "How hard is that?"

"I know what you're doing," she says. "You're trying to get me mad."

"Gosh, really? That's so brilliant of you."

"Shut up."

"Getting you mad is the easiest thing in the world. Look at you now."

"Shut up."

"A few words from boring old me and you're a total mess."

"Am not."

"Boo hoo hoo," I sneer, using my meanest tone. "Poor Tiffany."

She lunges and I dart back with a flush of hope.

"Not only are you pathetic and ordinary, you're completely incompetent. You can't do anything right."

"Yes I can. I came up with a great plan."

I laugh again. "Your plan was shitty and you got lucky."

"Shut up."

"You screwed up everything. You let me run away. You lost your gun. You managed to get your hands around my neck — and what happened? I'm still here!"

"Shut up!"

"Reece was the one who knew what to do. He was the one running the show. He had to step up because you're so clueless and in over your head."

"Shut up!"

"You know what, Tiff? When we're done here, everybody's gonna know how pathetic and useless you are because I'm gonna tell them. They're gonna laugh at you and why shouldn't they? You're sad and lame and useless."

"I'm gonna kill you!" she snarls.

She's so close to snapping. Then I remember how she described Beth back at the strip club. "You're a small, tedious, unimportant person. A fucking loser. A total waste of space."

With a cry of rage, Tiffany rushes me and —

I step away from her flashing knife and swing my cane and —

Hit her on the head —

And she goes down!

As she struggles to get to her feet —

I whack her again.

And *finally* she stays down.

As lightning flashes above me, I raise my cane to the sky and scream, surrendering to the primal rush — of rage and grief, of triumph and exhaustion — that rips through me.

CHAPTER 56

sit next to Tiffany at the bayou's edge for a long time, grateful to be alive. Gazing up into the black sky, I let the warm rain gently rinse the muck and blood from my face, breathing in the rich air and squeezing the thick mud between my fingers as lightning flashes and thunder rumbles through me.

Finally, after the storm moves off and the night turns quiet, I tune into the soft hum of this wild place and discover that it's beautiful. The bayou is at peace with what happened here tonight. More importantly, it's at peace with me.

Every now and then, Tiffany lets out a moan and I give her another whack. I've given her several as the night's progressed and it's possible I've been a tad excessive — her breathing is getting labored. Left untreated, I suppose it's possible she might die, though I doubt she'd let it come to that. This determined woman lying next to me, this remorseless monster, has led a hard life. Her will is strong. If anyone knows how to suffer and survive, it's her.

Soon enough, I'll alert the world to her evil deeds — bring in the sheriff's deputies, the crime scene investigators, the medical folks who deal with tragedy and death every day. I'll explain what happened, my new lawyer at my side, and then I'll go to my daughter and hold her close and never let her go.

I've been giving the future some thought. The matriarch who ran Boudreaux is gone. Everything she owned is now Ava's. The mansion and estate. The Briarton school. The town newspaper. Half the land in the parish. A law firm eager to do her bidding.

As Ava's guardian, control of all that will fall to me, which means a lot of work is ahead of me. Change is a-coming to Boudreaux. The parish is overdue for a house-cleaning — a thorough dismantling of the systemic power structure, as Gwen might put it. Basically, I'm gonna tear this fucking place apart. By the time I'm done, Boudreaux won't have a legacy left to defend.

But first things first. Before limping out of the swamp, I have a couple of final tasks to complete.

I reach over and slip Tiffany's shoes from her feet, then set the shoes on the ground next to my beloved cane. I'm going to hide the shoes in a bush and later, after things settle down, I'll take the shoes to the creepy old oak tree and nail them to the trunk — pointing downward, of course. It's important I do everything possible to ensure that Tiffany ends up where she belongs.

The bayou waters are deceptively still. A bird chirps nearby. From the east comes the faint light of the approaching dawn.

It's time to get moving. I clamber to my feet, my hip protesting with the effort. Then I reach down, grab Tiffany by her bare ankles, and drag her across the muddy ground to the water's edge, toward the glowing eyes that await.

She lets out a moan — she's waking up again — and this time I'm glad.

"This is on you," I say as I pull her knee-deep into the murky waters, hoping she's conscious enough to understand. "This is for Josh. This is for Rory. This is for everyone you've ever hurt. This is for everyone you'll never hurt."

Her eyes flicker open. She's heard me.

"Look what you're making me do. Look who you're making me be."

Then I let go of her ankles and wade to shore.

And stand there and watch and wait.

It doesn't take long. Metallic eyes close in around her and powerful jaws snap down. By the time she cries out for help, it's too late. The waters churn as her flesh is consumed and her soul consigned to the darkness she so richly deserves.

Eventually, finally, the bayou goes still. I take a deep breath and welcome the day's first light. I exhale slowly and breathe in again.

The old me is dead.

Long live the new Callie. An outsider no longer. Bound forever to this moment and place. Awakened irrevocably to the fierce beast within.

About the new me, I know one thing.

When it comes to protecting those I love, I won't be stopped.

When it comes to protecting those I love, I can and will do anything.

Anything.

THE END

GET A FREE BOOK

A DINNER TO DIE FOR BY MICHAEL RYDER

When a beautiful socialite begs him to prove she *didn't* murder her rich old husband, private investigator Daniel Hannity reluctantly takes the case — and finds himself immersed in a deadly family drama.

Get this mystery for FREE when you sign up for Michael Ryder's email newsletter.

The author solemnly swears he will *not* email you a nonstop barrage of desperate, frantic, promotional missives when you sign up for his newsletter. Instead, he'll email you only when his next book is available (which won't be often because he's a very slow writer) or when something totally awesome happens (like scoring a movie/TV deal, because wouldn't that be amazing).

Sign up now at
AuthorMichaelRyder.com/Newsletter

BOOKS BY MICHAEL RYDER

Never Trust Me

The very book you're reading right now. :-)

Shock and Awe

Special Exploits secret agent Jack Ford and microbiologist Lucy Kimball must overcome their mutual loathing to outplay a lethal adversary whose bloody ambition knows no bounds....

A Dinner to Die For

Private investigator Daniel Hannity has his hands full when a beautiful socialite begs him to prove she *didn't* murder her rich old husband....

Crinkles and Other Stories

A collection of short fiction, including stories published originally in *Compelling Science Fiction, Penumbra, Fiction River*.

Learn more at **AuthorMichaelRyder.com**.

ABOUT THE AUTHOR

Michael Ryder's novels include *Never Trust Me* (a psychological thriller) and *Shock and Awe* (a spy thriller). His short stories have been published in *Compelling Science Fiction*, *Penumbra*, and *Fiction River*. After working as a journalist in Tokyo, New York, and Hong Kong, he moved to San Francisco and dove into technology and banking. Now a full-time purveyor of fiction, he's found most days in neighborhood cafes, typing madly into his trusty laptop.

Sign up for his newsletter and read his blog at
AuthorMichaelRyder.com.

Thank you for being a reader.

facebook.com / AuthorMichaelRyder

www.ingramcontent.com/pod-product-compliance
Lightning Source LLC
Chambersburg PA
CBHW031003190726
48285CB00004BB/1445